LUCID

C.G. Matteini was the recipient of a Literary Titan
gold award for *The Peace Quaternity*, a collection
of two poems and two historical fiction short stories.
He published a book of poems, entitled *Us*, and an
illustrated children's book, entitled *Cloud Jumping*.
His writing on sustainability can be found in the CPA
Journal, and his short story "Tooths"
was published in the *Mug of Woe*,
edited by Jenn Dlugos and Kyle Cranston.

C.G.'s blog (on writing and what inspires his writing),
poems (about light and dark),
and other writing can be found on his website
www.cgmatteini.com.

SINE I

LUCID

C. G. MATTEINI

ISBN: 979-8-9886642-3-9 (paperback)
ISBN: 979-8-9886642-4-6 (e-book)

Any references to historical events, real people,
or real places are used fictitiously. Names, characters,
and places are products of the author's imagination.

Cover design by Laura Duffy
Book design by Karen Minster

PRINTED IN THE UNITED STATES OF AMERICA
FIRST PRINTING, 2018

www.cgmatteini.com

Friends, family and co-workers (also my friends),

I spent significantly less time with all of you because I was writing this. I wanted to hang out more. Without this, I would have lost my heart and head and been no good to any of you. But I've always needed you too, even if it hasn't always been obvious.

Mom and dad,

Sorry it took me becoming a parent to fully appreciate you, but I guess that's the cycle. Now I understand what you did and continue to do for me. Thank you.

This book is dedicated to my wife,

who didn't complain once, not once,

when I would have a thousand times.

•

I can never write the rare times we fight

It's all for you and the ones you grew

Frightened by my unrefined visibility

I reach through the fog and can't feel you next to me

I start to lose control, fall to my knees, ready to die

Then your face begins to form,
    as a bird dives through a hole in the sky

My tear-stained eye

GIDEON

(Long Ago)

The planetarium was dark but for two candles. One, on a desk at the edge of the round room, cast a dim halo over a drift of parchment littered with star charts and equations. The other burned strong on a ledge fastened to the side of a large telescope.

Gideon stood on a wooden ladder at the base of his instrument and adjusted a set of dials. His eyes darted from the dials to the eyepiece, back and forth. Inside, the ancient lights collected in his curved lenses. Above the world they glistened like crystal dust.

One hung in relative isolation, as though in its own small pool of black space. It shone larger and weaker than all the others. Gideon stared at it through the opening in the dome and allowed himself to hope.

Twenty turns in wait for the orbits of Qol and this dark star to converge again. Twenty turns building and refining his telescope. All that time growing more obsessed with reaching this moment, for he was certain that it was no star at all but another planet revolving around Nurin.

Some in Teles believed him. Those strong in the faith warned him and reminded any who gave him an audience that the Mind dreamt only of Qol. Most were unmoved. Even if he was right, it would be nothing but a cold, lifeless rock.

This fact plagued him through the long nights. The idea that they wouldn't care even if he finally reached his goal—that terrified him.

They will care, he told himself as he stroked the curved body of the telescope. *They will care, and they will write songs of me.*

Gideon looked into the eyepiece. Within was a dull nimbus. It grew bigger and brighter as he turned a dial, and he began to fear the worst, that it was just a star after all.

Mind, I'll end it now if I'm wrong.

The light began to fade. A gray sphere grew larger in the lens, then consumed it.

Gideon pulled back. It was done. He was right. He held another world inside his telescope. He raised his arms to the sky. The stars showered him with light, and he bathed in glory and vindication. He laughed in the face of that old haunting thought, that this discovery could possibly fail to capture their minds and cement his name.

But what he saw next, as he drew closer, was inconsistent with his theories. First a patch of atmosphere. Then a jagged line bisecting the surface of the planet. Closer still.

An ocean!

Three hollowed mountains along the coast.

Surely volcanic.

Around the middle one, a semicircle of six dark squares, evenly spaced.

No.

He went limp and fell from the ladder.

PART ONE

WILL

1

Will Lark drove south on 101 from Sonoma to San Francisco on a cool evening in March. The sky was clear and blue north of the city, out of the fog's reach. The sun hung above the rolling green hills of Marin as they flew by in the windows of his faded green hatchback.

He rolled up the windows, muting the wind and the traffic, and hit play. New rock emerged from the void, first the beat, then the bass, then an echoing voice wrapped in soft distortion. He got lost in it for a while, lost in the overgrown jungle of his thoughts and feelings. He turned it down and called Elle.

"William," she said. "How far are you? Doors open at seven-thirty."

"Almost to the bridge, love."

"Good boy. I'm just finishing a couple of things."

"I have some thoughts."

"Can they wait? I'll be home in an hour."

"They certainly cannot. It's the universe, for crying out loud." He chuckled, but he wasn't kidding.

She sighed. "The universe. Two minutes. I want to get out of here."

He dove in. "So I've been thinking a lot about consciousness these days. You know, what it is, what it's made of, that kind of stuff. Is it part of us, part of our physics, from conception? Is it something we tune into at a certain point in utero? Has it been there all along? You know what I mean?"

"Probably? I'd have to think about it. Transhuman psychology?"

"Trans*personal*."

"Let's pick this up later."

"Eh," he groaned. It was how these conversations always went. He was sure she didn't get it, but he never explained it well, and he was always picking the wrong times. "Fine."

"See you in an hour."

"Elle?"

"What's up?"

"I've got some real doubt."

"Don't doubt it. It's a good job."

He paused, felt. "It doesn't feel right. I'm going against my mind."

"That's from a song."

"It's the truth. Everything I've learned about myself contradicts this decision."

"We'll make the best of it. You know that."

Sometimes he didn't. "You and this place for the concrete jungle. And the winters again."

"I'll be there in less than a year, and we'll learn to love it."

Sometimes he wasn't sure.

"I've gotta go," she said. "We'll talk later, promise."

He tossed his phone onto the passenger seat, cranked the radio, and breathed. Change was coming, and he had his doubts, sure, but he was still here and still living. And he wasn't going to get this view many more times, so he dropped the drama and soaked it in as he slipped into the tunnel north of the city: the road curved; the far mouth opened slowly like the eye of a camera; the south red tower sprung from the left wall and slid right into the center; and the near north tower followed, looming over the highway as he emerged into magic hour glow. Beyond, radiant in slanted light, was the bay and a city built on hills.

———

They lived at 1449 Washington Street, a blue, three-story apartment building with a red door facing north on the steep western slope of Nob Hill, one of San Francisco's original seven. Will stood on the roof drinking a beer. He squinted at the sun, which hung between the towers of the Golden Gate. Pastel buildings rolled away in waves beneath him. The park was golden green in the distance. The bay and ocean shined.

He reflected. Three years had been an era. California was a myth when he and Elle started out across the country, and they drove right into it, fearless. They came looking for something, and they didn't know what, but it didn't matter. They knew they would find it, and so they did, their own versions. They found it in the mountains and the ocean and their crew of fellow soul-searching, party-going misfits. They heard it at the Fillmore and the Warfield and the Boom Boom Room in the music that defined their era and fueled their individuality.

Connections, he thought.

They'd grown like neurons, linking the crew to each other, to the city, and to the surrounding green and blue beauty.

I could swear it's physical.

This feeling was the proof Will had been searching for his entire life, proof that he belonged in this world. It was a bridge over the chasm inside him, the vacuum of his orphan identity. And she'd helped him build it, one bolt and cable at a time.

And I'm leaving. But I've got my reasons, sure.

He tried to let it slide.

Chapters close and people move. You might as well deal.

He wrote a few thoughts down in the little blue spiral notebook that he carried in his back pocket. Then he opened his wallet, took out two concert tickets, and held them up for the city to see. He downed the rest of his beer, cracked another, and watched the red sun sink into the Pacific beneath the bridge.

He climbed down the fire escape ladder onto the landing outside of their apartment on the top floor. Their building was flush with 1447 except for a column of space housing a wooden staircase and a narrow, fenced-over gap at ground level. He was about to walk inside when he saw someone pass under 1449 into the laundry room and storage spaces. He'd been meaning to tell their neighbors that he was leaving and that Elle was moving out, so he started down.

He looked around. "Hello?" But there was no one there. He took the short passage to the half-submerged door that led to Washington Street. He opened it and looked up the hill, down it. No neighbors. Nobody. A trolly clanged past. Maybe whoever he'd seen had run to catch it. He walked back up.

Raider, black mutt of boundless energy, bottomless, iron stomach, and unknown origin or breed—some lab, some shepherd probably—waited in the kitchen, pawing his bowl and wagging his tail. Will hugged him, kissed him, fed him, grabbed another beer, and danced into the living room. He'd left the stereo on, and it was now blasting another inspired medium of the new rock. He brought his head to the speakers and sang for the cheap seats. Raider ran to the front door, which meant that someone was coming up the stairs. He didn't bark, which meant it was Elle. Will opened the door, and Raider took off down the hall.

"Who's that?" she called from the stairwell. "Is that my baby? Hello, baby!" Raider came running back, and Elle was fast on his heels. They had places to be, and she was never late for a party. Her freckled cheeks were rosy from her hustle. Her thick brown bun bobbed. She beamed her gray-green eyes at Will and kissed him on the cheek without stopping. "Hello, William."

He watched her go, indulging in the view, wondering why in God's name he was leaving. She disappeared into their bedroom, popped out seconds later wrapped in a towel (that milky skin, those subtle curves, *Jesus*), and turned a sharp corner into the bathroom. He smiled and thanked his lucky stars. She could shower and dress quicker than most men. But what she gained in time she did not give up in beauty, for she was a natural.

They drove over Pacific Heights and down Fillmore Street. The bars and restaurants were alive with pulsing music, flashing flatscreens, and a buzzing, happy horde of human beings fired up over not having to work for two and a half days.

Elle put her chin up on the steering wheel. "This place is awesome."

"It really is," Will replied and slipped into heavy thoughts.

Goddamn, it's getting harder not to slip.

But this time he was not alone, and every pang in his heart was a pang in hers.

"We did it right, didn't we?" she said.

He exhaled. It was the exact question he needed to answer. "Yeah, we did."

Three years was an era.

They parked a block from 2000 Post, a labyrinthian five-story apartment complex home to two of the crewmembers. It was once the site of Winterland, a hallowed dive of a music hall infamous for being too hot and having terrible sound. It was a beloved venue despite these qualities, maybe more so because of them, and the Grateful Dead had played there over fifty times. Now all that remained of the counterculture was an eleven-by-sixteen black-and-white in the lobby, a freeze frame from one of those heady nights. But Will, Elle, and theirs did their part to keep the spirit alive before making their own history at another historic SF concert hall a few blocks away.

They performed their preshow ritual with the fervor and passion of their youth. They indulged in drink, smoke, loud music, loud conversation, laughter. Work? What work? Fuck work. Worries? About what? Quarter-life crisis? What's that? They were present, living, together. The city was *on*, and there were tour buses parked outside the Fillmore. Life was a beer and a high five and music and a dozen bright smiles.

It was a spirited walk to the show. Will felt untouchable. And he decided it was time. As much as he loved this place and these people, he was ready for the next step, ready to transition from incessantly asking questions about life (their time in SF had been, among other things, a three-year booze, smoke, and nature-induced brainstorm) to answering some for himself and harnessing the potential they'd discovered. It didn't matter where he was or what job he had. It didn't have to be perfect. There was no set path. He would be strong and in tune no matter what. Hell, maybe he'd even start looking into his parents again after he got settled, but no expectations.

Will felt *good*. He felt resolved. But it didn't last—it never did these days. Because every time he reflected on his decision, his mind started pushing back. Like he was going against it. Elle passed through a bleary puddle of light spilling from a streetlamp, and his stomach flipped.

Jesus Christ. Hold it together, man.

Fear gripped him. Fear of loss. Fear of that bridge collapsing and him falling into the void.

She'll be there in less than a year. Visits every month in the meantime.

It hit him like a hammer to the chest: the crux.

Love is a risk.

The more love you give someone, the more you receive, the more pain you'll feel when you're parted.

And it never doesn't happen.

She squeezed his shoulder. Her voice was an island in a sea of noise: "What are you thinking *right now?*"

They were buried in the heart of the crowd beneath the glowing billboard of the Fillmore. The heart throbbed, rumbled, cackled. He took her hand. "Nothing," he said.

"Not nothing."

"I'm ready. Let's go."

She touched her nose to his. Her eyes were twin gray-green galaxies surrounding black holes. "I know this transition is bringing up old shit. That's fine. We'll work through it. Life is good—you know that. Growing up is hard, but I love you, and it's Friday night, so deal with yourself, okay?"

"Exactly. I know."

She led him into the venue and up the red-carpeted staircase. The great wall grew from the top step as they ascended, floor-to-ceiling framed photos of epic performances and afterparties starting sometime in the sixties. The bucket of red apples sat reliably on its table. Will grabbed one, took a juicy bite, and strolled the gallery, feeling as he always did amongst these legends, hopeful and grateful and jealous. He stopped and stared at a young Miles Davis, trumpet to his lips, sunglasses on in a dark room backstage somewhere. There was some secret beneath those shades, Will was sure of it, and he wished he'd been born to do something instead of having to figure it out.

A heart-sparking whistle from beyond the double doors. A special bird. The shadow crowd, three thousand strong on a mission of joy, crackled with electricity and squirmed with delicious anticipation in the low, pre-show blue light. Elle, a singular silhouette at the edge, bounced and whistled and waved him in.

They went upstairs at set break, bought beers, and took a seat along the balcony rail. They talked about the set and kissed. She told him that she loved him, and he told her the same, but then he got quiet. He didn't doubt what they had, not really. Love was never the issue. It was life, and he felt it pulling them apart even as they sat there. "All these decisions," he said.

"It's life," she said.

He smirked. It was like she could read his thoughts sometimes.

She reached into her pocket. "I have something for you," she said.

"Oh."

"It's a moving-on-to-the-next-chapter present. Weird story, actually. I was in the Haight looking for something to get you. I walked around for a while, didn't see anything I loved, and I'm about to leave when this street vendor calls out to me. He's got a booth with a bunch of hemp jewelry, crystals, that kind of stuff. I say no thanks, and he says, 'Boy traveler?'"

Will frowned. "Huh."

"Yeah. So, I go over to him. He's got these tiny black eyes, and his face is cracked, like *really* dry skin, scaley almost. He's wearing a Giants hat, bald underneath, I think. He grabs my hand." Elle took Will's hand. "He opens it up and gives me this." She placed in his palm a small, rectangular, dark green stone tied to a black string. "He looks me in the eyes and says, 'Karma stone, boy traveler.' Then he closes my hand." She closed Will's hand around the stone. "Pushed his cart away after that. Didn't even ask for money." She paused. "Karma means things come around. You're headed back before me, but I'll be there soon."

Will rolled the stone over in his hand and traced its edges with his fingertips. It felt strangely familiar, not as though he'd seen it before, but as though he'd anticipated having it. "Thank you," he said.

"You're welcome. Two weeks left. Let's make 'em count."

He put the string over his head and dropped the stone into his T-shirt. They drank a toast to karma, then went downstairs for the second set.

2

Lying in bed, I watch the images flow through the living darkness that may be the back of my eyelids or the recesses of my mind. Shapes and faces emerge, shift, fizzle out, and reemerge as something new. But one image lingers: two large screws, which I know are mine, slowly coming unscrewed.

L shakes me awake. She holds a finger to her lips and flashes her eyes at the bedroom door. I grab my pocketknife off my bedside table and creep into the living room. There's no one there. I check the bathroom and the kitchen. Nothing. When I get back to our room, she's sound asleep. Raider hasn't stirred.

The next scene I know is a dream. I'm fighting my way through a mob, beating and killing with my hands, trying to get L to safety. We run into an abandoned building, down a narrow, dark hall, through a door, down another hall. We make it outside, and I feel release. I could have lost her, but it's over.

Except it's never over in my dreams.

We're living in a ghetto of cardboard boxes. The soldiers patrolling the border are drunker than usual, and I think we can slip past them. But the second it crosses my mind, more come and start building a wall. We live there for a long time. The struggle brings us closer. One day the soldiers set us free, just the two of us, but they never say why, and they're grinning as we leave.

We're standing on a mountain road overlooking a wooded valley. There's a boy with us, eleven years old or so, very sad. A bee buzzes around our heads. We all know that it's fatally venomous, but the boy keeps trying to get it to sting him. I see his face close up. He's frightened and defeated. He's seen the darkness and wants to give up. It feels merciless to stop him, and I wonder at the cruelty of our world that a boy should want to die.

The dream intensifies, purifies, deepens. The boy's hand fills my field of vision. The bee lands on his finger, walks around, settles, stings.

Staring up at the ceiling, Will replayed the dreams in his mind from start to finish, then wrote them down in his little blue spiral notebook. The bee dream in particular carried weight. He felt terrible for the boy.

He got out of bed and shuffled half-asleep into the living room—and froze. A black bumblebee clung to the screen outside the room's lone window. He tiptoed up to it.

"Strange of you to be here, bee."

He looked down at the decks and small courtyards inside the city block. He saw himself standing down there, staring up at something. He felt heavy, like something was trying to drag him down.

Elle stepped out of the bedroom. She looked rattled.

"You okay?" he asked.

"I think so," she said. "Nightmare."

"Tell me."

"It's messed up, and it's about you."

"It's fine," he said, though nothing about that moment felt fine. She noticed the bee. "All black."

He swallowed. "Yeah."

"We were in this dingy motel room. You'd slit your wrists and were bleeding out. I begged you to let me help, but you were belligerent."

"Man."

"Uh-huh. There was blood everywhere, on the bed, the walls. I tried to call for help, but you grabbed the phone and threw it against the wall. You blocked the door and screamed at me. You calmed down eventually but only so you could try and convince me to kill myself too."

Will said he was sorry. She said don't worry about it. He asked if she remembered waking him up in the middle of the night and motioning toward the door, but she was sure that didn't happen.

He took a scalding hot shower. He tried to burn it all off, the dreams, the bee. It didn't work. Something else was stuck in his mind now, something he remembered from a documentary that one of his professors at CHS, the Center for Holistic Studies, had shown in class one time. A transpersonal psychologist had said in an interview that every morning he asked the universe to show him some sign that day, some "coincidence," something to prove that he was connected to the universe and interacting with it. Apparently, it worked for this guy all the time. Will thought he would give it a try, but he'd start tomorrow. The universe had shown him enough for one day.

The beach at Crissy Field was empty, owing to a light, cold drizzle. It was good hangover weather, and Raider had the entire beach to himself to chase his tennis ball. The clouds made a fluffy gray blanket. A wet, salty breeze blew in off the translucent blue-green bay. Will listened to the waves. He gazed out at Alcatraz and Angel Island. He'd been to the prison a few times but hadn't stepped foot on the Angel in his three years. He imagined himself there now wandering the tree-lined paths, circling the hill on his way to the top, and looking out at the city.

He awoke from this daydream to find Elle and Raider a hundred yards down the beach. She threw the ball into the bay, Ray went crashing through the waves after it, and Will shed a happy tear. His girl and his dog in his city. The bridge in the background, the mountains of Marin.

But then, a shadow in the water. Will's heart rate kicked up. He started running. "Whoa, whoa," he yelled.

Elle looked at him, then out at the bay. "What?"

Raider snatched the ball and turned back to shore. A shark closed.

"Come on, Raider!" Will cried. "Let's go, buddy!"

"Will, you're freaking me out," Elle said.

"*Come on, Raider!*" Will skidded to a halt as a man in a wet suit stood up in the water. Raider walked out, tail wagging, tennis ball in his mouth and his tongue hanging out. "Holy shit," Will said. He put his hands behind his head and walked it off.

"What?" Elle shouted.

"Nothing, nothing. I'm sorry. I just—shit, I thought I saw a shark swimming after Ray."

Elle pointed to the swimmer, now walking up the beach and pretending not to hear them. "Him?"

"Yeah, him."

She punched Will hard in the shoulder. "You dick. You almost gave me a fucking heart attack." She leashed Ray and stormed off toward the parking lot.

Will rubbed his shoulder, looked at the swimmer, looked out at Angel Island. "Yeah," he said to himself. "Let's get out of here."

They were halfway home when Elle got a text from one of the crewmembers. They were headed out for some hair of the dog.

"You down?" she asked.

He shrugged. "Of course."

They stopped at 1449 to drop off Ray. Elle circled the block while Will walked him up. He whimpered and sniffed at the door as Will fumbled with his keys.

"Easy, man," Will said and opened the door.

Ray went rabid and took off into the kitchen. Will turned the corner in time to see an orange cat slip out of the window. A second later, a cat food commercial starring Garfield came on the TV, which apparently Will had left on. Will scratched a cheek and left.

Standing outside with his back against the red door, he watched a huge bald dude in a Canadian tuxedo roll down Washington on a bike way too small for him and with a white rubber snake wrapped around the handlebars. Elle pulled up, Will sat down in the passenger seat of the hatchback, and a DJ announced the song, "Here I Go Again" by Whitesnake. Will slapped the off button, chewed a fingernail, tapped a foot, and thought about that transpersonal psychologist from the documentary.

He went straight to the bar and downed half a vodka tonic before joining Elle and the crew at a picnic table in a back corner. They looked beat up from the night before, but they had beers in their hands, and they were starting to perk up.

Pitchers were ordered, delivered, and promptly emptied. Everyone raved about the show from last night and told stories (the jams, the drinks, the laughs, the minds blown) from past Fillmore shows and shows from the Warfield, the Elbo Room, the Independent, the Great American Music Hall, others. They played a few games of pool. Everything was in its right place.

Except Will couldn't quite get comfortable. He chalked it up to being more hungover than he originally thought, which was a solvable problem or at least should have been. He downed four drinks before the clock struck one and when that didn't work stepped outside for a couple hits of grass. Hits taken, he snapped his Zippo shut, turned to walk back inside, and noticed a poster on the wall advertising a show at the Boom Boom Room on St. Paddy's Day. There was no band name, just the time, the place, and two hands poised over a keyboard, ready to strike or cast a spell. Someone had drawn lightning bolts in neon highlighter from the fingers to the keys. Staring down at his own hands, Will wondered, he wasn't quite sure why, whether there was some physical truth to the image.

He walked straight past the crew to the bathroom, which was tiny and dim and reeked of piss. The red walls were covered in tags, poems, cartoons, solicitations, and phone numbers, all in black marker. The lone urinal was occupied, so Will took the lone stall, where it hit him, finally and all at once, the booze and smoke. He closed his eyes, tried to relax, tried to understand why he couldn't, and realized the obvious truth. It was the stress of leaving. It snuck up on him at times. It drove him to anxiety before he knew what was happening. But he told himself it was normal and nothing to worry about.

Then he opened his eyes and saw, at eye level on the right wall, in black marker, a snake wrapped around the body of a cat. They were both staring at him.

He suddenly doubted whether stress could account for dreams about suicide, bees that showed up on windows the next morning, phantom sharks, karma stones, and serial cat and snake sightings. He left the bathroom without zipping and made a beeline for the bar.

3

Getting obliterated worked. Will was in too much pain Sunday morning to feel any emotional disquiet. He spent the day napping on and off, eating cold pizza, and watching shitty TV. The image from the bathroom surfaced occasionally, but he saw it through a very foggy mind's eye.

Monday came, and he was back on stable ground, more or less. The change was shaking him up, yes, fine, but he wasn't going to let it prevent him from enjoying what time he had left. He hadn't quit his job waiting tables a month before departure (and borrowed a few bucks from George to do so) to sit around moping and freaking out. He went for a hard run with Raider, did three sets of pull-ups and sit-ups back at the apartment, then took a long, hot shower.

Towel around his waist, he sat on the futon and pulled his camera case out of the trunk that served as their coffee table. Inside the case, scribbled on a piece of mini looseleaf torn from one of his little blue books, was a list of filming locations within the city and outside of it in all directions. He'd formed a plan to memorialize his time in the Bay Area by traveling back to each of his favorite spots and capturing them on video. He was going to build himself a library that he could dip into back east whenever he needed it, whenever he felt his connection to the west side wavering.

He ran a finger down the list and stopped on Stinson Beach, a perfect place to start. It offered classic NorCal scenery and plenty of room for Ray to let loose. He grabbed a new little blue book from the trunk and tossed the latest one inside, its last pages filled with the bee dream.

They cruised up Lombard's main drag, Ray propped up on the center console, Will filming the Monday morning commute through the windshield and front windows of the hatchback. He shot the cars, the drivers, the storefronts, the pedestrians, the traffic lights. He shot the Palace of Fine Arts and the towers of the Golden Gate rising from the Presidio. Crossing over the bridge, he stuck his camera out of the window and shot the shimmering Pacific through the flickering red cables to the soundtrack of the rushing wind.

They picked up Route 1 at Tam Junction Center beneath Mount Tamalpais and headed northwest up the winding mountain road. Ascending, Will captured streaming trunks and valleys through gaps in the timber. Descending, he captured rolling green hills and the ocean again as they snaked their way down into the sleepy seaside village of Stinson.

The beach was empty on a Monday morning. Raider ran off and dug a hole. Will took panoramas of the crescent shoreline, the sighing sea, the hills, the endless blue sky. He took close-ups of rocks and dead crabs, weathered sticks, ripples in the sand. He filled his camera with every broad perspective and every fine detail so he would never forget, so he could always look back and see exactly how it was. Underlying it all was the slow rhythm of the waves. Engulfed in the scene, Will walked out into the water.

Waves slide slowly up the beach, then recede, fracturing into a billion tiny ripples. I close my eyes, listen and feel. Cold water laps my legs. Warm wind caresses my face and body. Energy flows behind my lids, a matrix of pixels where images form and fizzle, form and fizzle. I breathe deep. I think I understand for the first time how the word psyche can

*mean mind, breath, and spirit at the same time. And for a timeless
split second of intuition, I know what the Buddha and the Dead meant
when they said this is all just a dream.*

Will took a seat on the sand and wrote those words down in his fresh
little blue book. He then dropped it into his bag and pulled out another
book, a thick paperback that had been assigned, just before he dropped
out of CHS, by the same professor who'd shown that documentary.
According to the back cover it summarized the findings of two Nobel
Prize-winning scientists, one a quantum physicist and the other a neu-
rosurgeon and psychologist, who had independently come to the conclusion that reality and perception had holographic properties. Will
cracked the binding.

He didn't get very far.

In the epigraph the physicist assured readers that the world of appear-
ances was real, the world as humans perceived it on a daily basis. But,
he said, if one examined the world using a holographic system, if one
penetrated that surface experience, one discovered a more elemental
reality, the quantum-mystical properties of which helped explain things
that had hitherto been inexplicable scientifically, things like paranormal phenomena and synchronicity.

The instant Will finished reading this, a bee landed on the book,
walked across it, then buzzed off. Heart thumping, he slammed the
book shut, shoved it into his bag, and bade farewell to Stinson Beach
with a forced smile.

The corner store was dead, and Will was grateful for that as he speed-
walked back to the coolers. Only the cashier would see him buy a six-
pack before noon on a Monday. But his hopes were dashed: another
customer reflected in the glass doors. He turned. There was no one
there. He slapped himself in the face, paid, and left.

Two cold ones and some psychedelic rock blasted at thought-obliterating volume eased him down a few notches, and he decided not to let this bullshit anxiety get in the way of his filming. He pulled off 101 just north of the Golden Gate and took the steep switchback road up to the Marin Headlands.

He walked the clifftop trail with one eye on the foldout viewing screen of his camera and the other on the smashing surf far below. He shot the north tower, which had never seemed to him so red, so towering, and so close. He shot the city, which had never seemed such a massive, complex, and alluring maze, jutting out on its peninsula and framed by the curvy, green Santa Cruz Mountains. The bay was a big blue lagoon. Sailboats circled the Angel as though in ritual worship.

He reached the crumbling battlement foundation at the top of Headlands and only then noticed the wall of fog advancing on the coast. Freight ships raced for the bridge.

They'll never make it, he thought. *They'll all be consumed.*

A hawk crossed his screen, one second thirty feet above the cliffs and the next a thousand feet over the ocean and heading straight for the fog.

Turn away, Will pleaded.

Someone moved in his periphery, down by a patch of trees. He watched. Waited. Nothing.

"Raider," he said. "Let's go."

He felt for his knife in his pocket and started down.

He cranked the stereo, tapped his left foot, drummed the steering wheel, turned the music off, rolled the windows down, rolled them up, turned the music on, turned it off, punched the steering wheel. "This is bullshit, man. Pull yourself together." He managed to slow his heart rate as he hit the toll, but it picked back up again as he crossed over the bridge and was swallowed by the fog.

He raced through the city, parked illegally on Washington, and ran up the hill with Raider to 1449. Inside he turned the stereo on, turned it off, slammed a fist on the kitchen counter.

"You're *not* being followed, you *freak.*"

And just like that he felt better. It helped just giving voice to that ridiculous idea. He was queasy about leaving, but this was getting out of hand. What he needed was to talk it over with himself and pick apart what was really bothering him. Then the symptoms would fade. What he needed was some time on the roof.

But the fog. He'd almost forgotten about it. This wasn't your routine San Fran mist, rolling in late afternoon with every intention of lifting before sundown. It was slate gray and thick as soup. It had swallowed the city from the Sunset District along the coast to lower Pacific Heights and was now creeping up the streets of Nob Hill.

Shadows swam in the fog sea. The sky rumbled. A pigeon took flight from a puddle on the roof, lifted, and turned south in a long, smooth arc. It passed behind a door protruding from the roof of the yellow building directly behind 1449, higher up on the hill.

Will's entire world collapsed into a single point of potential energy quaking in the space behind that door. The door was menacing and inevitable. It was the cause of all his anxiety. It was the object casting the shadows in his mind. It was the black fountain source of his haunting dreams and the strange "coincidences" he'd been experiencing. These truths were inescapable, and Will had never felt so afraid in his life.

Time slipped. Thunder cracked. He was standing in the pouring rain, staring in the direction of the door, now lost to the fog. He climbed down the ladder mindlessly. Inside the apartment, he peeled off his clothes and lay naked on the futon.

4

Will's mind defended itself. It had no choice. The episode on the roof was effectively swept under the rug.

The Ladies of the orphanage had raised him to respect his shadow side. George had taught him that dealing with the bad shit required thinking about it sometimes, and Elle had demanded this of him. He credited his ability to lead a relatively normal life with this consistent philosophy and his eventual acceptance that his parents were either assholes, dead, or for some legitimate reason had to give him up. But suppression was another arrow in his quiver, and there were times when it was the only option.

Will had reached the point of suspecting a door of infiltrating his life. This was not sustainable. He had one choice if he wanted to avoid unraveling, and that was to bury his strange thoughts and forget where he dug the hole.

A week went by, and he managed to live his life. He found solace and distraction in his film project. His angst lingered, but it was once again intelligible. He was leaving his friends, his girl, and his dog behind to start a new life. It was sad and uncertain, but it was normal. He was not losing his mind. He was having a quarter-life crisis.

In dreams, however, he was exposed. In the subconscious realms, his suppressed concerns maintained their energy and demanded attention.

And one sweaty night, something bigger, from somewhere deeper, rose
to the surface.

*When I was six, I had two lucid dreams within days of each other.
They became recurring, and I experienced both a handful of times
over the next decade or so before they went dormant sometime in high
school. They came back to me this week. I'm trying very hard not to
read into that.*

*I lie shaking in my bed in the orphanage. All the other beds are
empty. A figure looms over me, a shadow. I don't see it, I don't dare
look up, but it smothers me, squeezes, suffocates, feeds, sucks on my
soul, and I know nothing but terror.*

*The interpretation may be obvious. Fear of death, perhaps. And
that's normal, that's human. But what lingers, what stalks, for days,
sometimes longer, is a sense of premonition.*

*My lucid nightmare has an opposite. Its pain and darkness meet
their match in the joy and light induced by my other recurring dream.*

*I'm very young, two, maybe three. I'm lying on a stone floor and
looking up at a vague female imago. I don't know her, but I have
always known her. She smiles. She radiates strength and faith. I know
that whatever troubles we meet in this world, we will navigate through
them. But now is not the time to worry about those things. She kisses
me on the forehead, imprinting her soul on my soul, and I am filled
with love beyond description. She steps back and disappears, but I
know I will see her again.*

*I hadn't experienced these dreams in years, and they chose this
week to return. Dreams about defending L and being a hero are tied
to my insecurities, I know. But these two run deeper and may go
beyond me.*

*I know now what a goddess is, and that the woman is mine. And
the shadow, that fucking shadow is a god. And she has always come
back for me, but so has the other.*

5

Will and Raider scratched off all but a few locations on the filming list. He and Elle went on a handful of dates and got hammered with the crew in their apartments and favorite haunts. He had coffee with a few former coworkers and classmates. He saw just about everyone and every place at least one more time, all with mixed emotions. He wrote in his little blue spiral notebooks every day, mostly about his dreams. He had less than a week left.

He was riding the 34 bus downtown and sweating bullets. He still had a few loose ends to tie, and he'd set up a goodbye meeting with one of his former professors at CHS. He was now deeply regretting it. He'd attended the Center for Holistic Studies for less than a semester with aspirations of becoming an activist or psychoanalyst or *something* before about-facing and launching into his dubious pursuit of the greater comfort promised by a career in finance. Student loans were a legitimate concern, sure, but they were not the real reason he'd dropped out, if he was being honest with himself. He loved CHS, but it terrified him. These people were probing deeply into themselves and into the energy and systems in which they were embedded. It was beautiful, but it was also alarmingly self-analytical. Will just wasn't ready yet.

He stood on the corner of Mission and 10th looking up at the lone, four-story brick building that comprised the campus. He thought about hopping back onto the bus, but it pulled away and abandoned him. He dropped some change into the coffee can belonging to the woman who'd been sitting against the stop sign there every single time he'd come and gone over the last few months and probably every day for the last decade by the look and smell of her. She was passed out with her chin on her chest, dried puke on her filthy sweater. He knew he'd never see her again, and that hurt him more than was rational. He wished he'd asked her name. He wished her good luck.

The lobby settled him down a bit. It always did. The incense, the soft light, the low, ambient music coming from speakers he'd never been able to locate. He took the stairs to the second floor. Jazz seeped out of room 202. He rapped a knuckle on the door, and Jill invited him in.

She turned in her swivel chair as he stepped inside. Her loose clothes rippled, bracelets and necklaces jangled. Her cropped, fire-orange hair warmed him. Her artic blue eyes, dripping with unencumbered presence and genuine interest, scared him. He knew that look was not reserved for him but was the way she took in all the world and its inhabitants. Still, they were difficult eyes to meet.

"Hi, Will," she said. "Have a seat if you want."

"Great, thanks," he said. "Thanks for taking the time." He closed the door but not all the way. He sat in the only other chair.

"Of course," she said.

He risked her eyes, then looked away, racked with guilt. She embodied CHS to him. She was a change agent, a spirit guide, a scientist of the human mind, the final frontier. A couple of years learning from people like her, and Will would have been well on his way to self-realization, he hardly doubted it. But he hadn't lasted there, and he felt like a dipshit for showing his face again. He scratched the back of his neck and shifted in his seat.

"Thanks for coming, Will," Jill said. "I was sorry to hear that you're leaving, but I'm sure you're excited for what's next."

"Yeah, no," he said, eyes on his feet. "Definitely. Just wanted to stop by and say thanks." But uh-oh, oh, man, he realized then that he'd come up with other things to talk about since setting this meeting. He tried to hold them back, but he was powerless to, here in this institution under the penetrating gaze of a transpersonal psychologist. He blurted: "Jill, I had a strange dream about a bee not long ago. Does that mean anything to you?"

"Does it mean anything to you?"

"I'm not sure."

"You recall we read some of Carl Jung's work."

"Yeah."

"Do you remember the concept of an archetype?"

"I think so."

She straightened her back. "They're difficult to describe. Archetypes are expressions of unconscious contents or instincts or elements. These elements, call them, are independent from us but also a part of us. Our ability to connect with them and interact with them is innate, according to Jung."

"I remember now," Will said and wished he hadn't.

She nodded. "Who and what we are includes both our conscious and our unconscious selves, and so our relations to these elements are important. They tend to express themselves when there is an imbalance between the two selves. They show up as symbols, archetypes, often in our dreams. Can I get you some water? Tea?"

Will felt clammy from scalp to the soles of his feet. "Water, great, thanks." She left the room, and he thought about making a run for it. But he couldn't move. He was caught in some gravity, and there was no pulling out now.

She returned and handed him the water. "Would you like to continue?"

He chugged it. "Okay."

"It's important to understand that only you can decide whether the bee has meaning for you. Maybe you saw one during the day, and it showed up in your dream simply for that reason. But as a symbol, the bee has been depicted historically in a few primary ways."

Sweat trickled down Will's armpits.

"It's been a messenger for friends and relatives who have passed on," Jill continued, mercilessly. "It's predicted the arrival of someone important in the life of the person who sees it. The ancient Egyptians thought of bees as tears of their sun god, Ra. Most often, it's been a symbol of death and rebirth, according to Jung."

Will stood up and walked out.

"Happy to share more thoughts, now or another time," Jill offered.

"Yeah, okay, thanks," he said without turning. "I'll let you know. Happy early Saint Patrick's Day!"

He took the stairs three at a time. Crossing the lobby, he passed through a tight beam of light and stopped short. He didn't see it, but he sensed it, a tripwire in his mind. It shone through the peephole in the front door and cast a quarter-sized circle of royal-blue light on the back wall. The circle had a thin rainbow border and was filled with dark markings like craters on the moon. Will stood before it miserable and afraid and sensing some illusive truth. He tore himself away.

A woman stood at the bus stop wearing a black baseball hat with the word "Faith" written on it in silver letters inside a silver triangle. She looked at him, and he looked away. The bus pulled up. Will followed her on and took the only open seat. The guy next to him was mumbling to himself and scribbling gibberish onto a triangle-shaped numbers puzzle in a kid's magazine. He smelled of weed and garbage. Will got up and walked to the back of the bus, where he was confronted by a triangle-shaped warning sign instructing riders to use the marked windows in case of emergency. He stared at the floor for the remainder of the ride.

Cop cars blocked the intersection at Leavenworth and Sacramento at the top of Nob Hill. Several parked cars on the right side of the street were scraped, dented, and missing their left sideview mirrors. A black pickup was sticking out of the smashed, front window of the corner store. The boys and girls in blue were questioning witnesses. Everyone seemed bent out of shape. Will could sympathize.

Elle was sitting at the kitchen counter sobbing. She'd seen the whole thing. She'd seen a dog get hit.

They sat on the futon for some indeterminate amount of time. Elle cried on and off, not just about the dog but about "everything." Will held her hand and stared into space, thinking about archetypes. Raider lay with his head on Elle's lap and his tail tucked between his legs.

6

*Saying goodbye to her was the hardest thing I've ever done. The guilt
I felt getting in that cab and leaving her standing there on the sidewalk,
Jesus Christ. I knew she could handle it, but I couldn't. She'd be there
in less than a year when her analyst program ended, that was the plan.
But I knew it was the end, I just fucking knew it.*

*The airport was slammed. Everyone was in my way, cutting me
off, slowing down in front of me, moving left or right just as I was
about to. I got to the gate exhausted and disoriented.*

*The window was black, and the cabin was dark except for a cone
of orange light shining down on my hands and tray table and little
blue book. I pressed my forehead to the window and cried. I wondered
where I was and what I was doing.*

Will awoke and looked over at Elle. Her face was buried in her pillow,
but she was awake.

They got up and sat on opposite sides of the bed. He looked out the
window, at the yellow building with the door on top.

"Tough end to the day yesterday," she said.

"You said it, Elle."

"Can't let it get to us, though. We only have four left."

He scratched his nose. "I'm visiting in five weeks."

"You know what I mean."

"Yeah."

"You've been weird."

His chest tightened. He tried to look away from the door.

"Will?"

"Huh? I know. I'm sorry."

"That's it?"

"I guess, Elle. I'm struggling."

She took a deep breath. "I'd stay, but I have a meeting. Let's do lunch by the office today and talk."

"Okay," he said, still staring at the object of his obsession.

He went for a run by himself, leaving Raider at the door of their apartment wondering why he wasn't invited. He blasted heavy metal in his earbuds and pushed himself up and down the hills until his legs were rubber, his heart a jackhammer, and his mouth a bale of cotton. Back at 1449, he did five sets of sit-ups and chin-ups, took an ice-cold shower, dressed, and then pulled his camera case out of the trunk. He still had a handful of city shots left on his list, and he thought he'd bang them out before lunch and then lacrosse practice in Sonoma. He also had one major location left to shoot, but he was saving that for the end.

Digging for socks in the pile of laundry on top of his dresser, he unearthed a tear-sheet calendar that he hadn't looked at in weeks, a stocking stuffer Elle had given him last Christmas. Each sheet offered an astrological fact and a quote related to mindfulness. He tore off pages until he got to March 17. Some lama had said, "The forces that move the cosmos are no different from those which move the human soul." Below the quote was the day's "Celestial View," which called for a supermoon, the biggest since 1948. Will ripped the page off and put it in the back pocket of his earth-brown corduroys. A soft roar drew his eyes to the window and up to the sky as a plane flew straight across the morning moon. The calendar didn't lie. It was the biggest moon he'd ever seen. It was *too* big. It was swollen and ready to drop. Will decided to stay indoors until it was time to meet Elle. The last city shots could wait until tomorrow.

He sat next to Raider on the futon, lifted the lid of the trunk, and stared at his tapes stacked neatly in their plastic jewels. He'd enjoyed his project for the most part. The act of filming and the quality time with Ray had kept him sane during what insisted on being a bizarre, fragmented period of his life. But the idea of sitting on the couch and watching home videos depressed him, and he'd yet to look at any of his footage. Why he decided to do it that day he didn't know.

There were twelve tapes. He'd filled eleven. The paper inserts for those eleven listed the locations included on each, just like the music mixes he'd recorded as a kid. The blank twelfth was reserved for Angel Island.

He picked one at random, slotted it into the camera, connected camera to TV by way of black wire umbilical, and hit play. It opened up in Golden Gate Park on a gray morning sometime in the middle of the project. Coeds threw a frisbee. A guy pushed a stroller while leaning over it and shushing his kid. A couple argued quietly but bitterly on a bench between drags on their cigarettes. A woman slept like the dead beneath a cypress. Other little glimpses of humanity.

Cut to Ocean Beach blanketed with mist, ghostly, legless dogs and humans floating on top. Cut to driving through the Sunset during mild, lunch-hour traffic. Cut to panoramas of the entire Bay Area from Twin Peaks. Cut finally to Raider in the passenger seat sniffing the lens and blurring the picture with his wet snout. Will smiled, but it was forced. He put in a new tape.

Raider led the way over grass-covered hills somewhere in the East Bay. Sunny day. City in the distance across the water. A beat-up, rusted car pulled into the parking lot. Raider stopped, whipped his head around and pointed, crouched down and took off after a chipmunk. He sped past a grove of trees. Inside the grove a shadow shifted.

Will's heart stopped. His first thought was This is real. Someone is following me. His next was It's in your head, you psycho.

He was being stalked, or he was stalking himself. Pick your poison. He rewound the tape and hit play. Someone dressed in all black watched him from behind a tree, got camera shy when Ray ran past, and backed away into the grove.

Will rewound and watched it again, hoping it would change, not wanting it to change for some masochistic reason he had no interest in exploring. He'd known it in his gut from the beginning, from the first time he saw the stalker reflected in the glass refrigerator door in the market in Stinson, then again atop the Marin Highlands. No, three days earlier, in the passage beneath 1449.

The psychological explanation had seemed so plausible. The dreams and synchronicities had felt so real. But he'd been reading too deep into everything. He'd been driving himself crazy in defense against the truth, that he was being followed the entire time.

But that was also bullshit. The dreams had a purpose. They'd been warning him from the inside. And the synchronicities, they'd been his signs on the outside. And all of it—the stalker, the bee, the fucking giant white moon—had to do with the door. There was no reason why. There was just the door trying to suck him in.

They sat outside at a café in the shadow of Pac Bell Park.

"What is it?" she asked.

"Nothing. Stop asking, please."

"It's temporary."

Will looked away. "I know."

"It *is* temporary, right, Will? Are you thinking of breaking up with me?"

"What? You gotta let me—look, I'm working through this."

"I can help."

"You can't."

She shook her head. He clenched his fists. It tore him up to hide from her, but the last thing he wanted was to get her involved. The idea that she might somehow also be in danger, *this* he could not tolerate, *this* kept his head on a swivel and his mind clear for the first time since the bee dream. He had to cut this thing off at the knees, call the cops or confront the stalker at the next opportunity. He'd cancel his flight if he had to. He wasn't going anywhere until he knew she was safe.

"I didn't mean anything by that," he said.

She picked at her salad. "Yep."

"I've been weird and distant, I know. I'm sorry. I've been dealing with something that's hard to explain, but I made a little breakthrough this morning."

"It's been hard for me too."

He took her hand. "I know. I love you. I've been confused, but not about that."

She raised her gray-green eyes. "I know it," she said.

They were quiet. They were having the same thought. The crowd roared, and she spoke their mind. "It's just sad."

"I know. Less than a year, and we'll be partying our way through another city together. Plenty of steamy visits in between." He leaned across the table and kissed her. "I gotta go."

She glared at him. "Don't be late tonight. We're making green beer."

"See you around five-thirty."

"Go then, you crazy card."

He rose and walked away, strengthened by her love. But love was never the issue. It was life, and it was pulling them apart, for reasons and in ways he couldn't yet begin to fathom. He stopped and looked back. She sat alone at the table for two, framed by the ballpark and the café and the extras sitting around her. She waved. He kissed his fingers and held up his hand.

Walking to his car, he kept his eyes forward and his peripheral cast. Driving out of the city and up 101, he checked his mirrors constantly. He saw nothing suspicious except the supermoon keeping pace with him in the western sky.

He pulled into a gas station a few miles south of Sonoma Academy, a prep school where one of the crewmembers coached lacrosse and where Will trained the goalies once a week. He stood in the sun filling his tank and sweating profusely. It had been San Fran-chilly in San Fran, and he was overdressed for anywhere outside of the city. He wore his green shell over his green quarter-zip and a green T-shirt. The shades were all too earthy, but it was the best he could do for Saint Paddy's Day.

Someone slipped behind the station building. Will swallowed a lump, capped his tank, got in the car, and started it up. He couldn't do this. Whoever that was had to be ten times crazier than he was, and he had a better chance of getting his throat cut than resolving this thing.

Then he thought of Elle and of everything he'd been through over the past few weeks.

I shouldn't. This is insane.

But he did. He turned off the car, got out, opened his knife, and walked slowly toward the building.

He turned the corner and froze, caught in the double tractor beams of two very dark, very anxious, and very excited brown eyes looking down on him. They belonged to a middle-aged woman with crew-cut brown hair, strong arms. She was half a head taller than him, six feet easy. She wore a black tank top, fitted black cargo pants, and a black backpack. She stepped forward. He held up his knife, but he lacked conviction. She grabbed his wrist, lowered it, and hugged him. He stiffened, and they remained like that for some time behind the building, Will and the stalker.

She stepped back and took him in, brown eyes gleaming. She looked fascinated and miserable. "William Lark," she said.

"Huh?"

"Your name."

His chest ached all of a sudden. "Yeah, that's my name."

That simple response or just hearing him talk seemed to dazzle her. He supposed this was what it was like to have someone obsessed with you. He felt bad for celebrities.

"Wha does it mean?" she asked.

He couldn't place her accent. Scandinavian? Spanish? He looked from her eyes to her mouth, eyes to mouth. Maybe he recognized her. Maybe he'd gotten a look at her at some point over the last few weeks. "It's just a name," he said.

"Jus' a name?"

"Yeah. Well, no." Actually, the Ladies were very intentional when handing out names to kids who came to the orphanage without them. And he had. They'd found him in the forest. "A lark is a kind of bird. And the word lark is a combination of 'light' and 'dark.'"

Her smile was toothy. "William?"

"Will means mental effort or desire or something like that. You know, your *will*."

"I understand. Is a good name."

"You've been following me."

Her face hardened. "Yes."

"Why?"

"Your protection."

"Oh, yeah? From who?"

"Someone I'm convinced wan's to hurt you."

"Why would anyone want to hurt me?"

"I don' know," she said through her teeth.

"This is bullshit."

"Keep your voice down."

"Start explaining."

"The door."

Will seized, mind and body. Things just got very real.

"The door tha pulls you," she said.

"How do you know?"

"I've been watching, and I know how it feels."

A thought formed, a conclusion. It didn't make sense. He didn't want it. "No, no, no."

The woman said what he couldn't: "You have to go to it."

"Come on. It's just a door on a roof."

"It isn'. You'll see."

"I'm not going to see anything. I don't know who you are or what the fuck is going on."

She grimaced like he'd punched her in the gut. "Please, daw— William."

Cars pulled into the station. She shoved him up against the wall, reached behind her back, pulled a gun from her waistband, and peered around the corner. Her eyes were sharp brown steel. She turned them on Will. "Short and sweet you say, right?"

He looked down at the gun. "I guess."

"I think so. Lis'en, the men out there are here for you. I'm sorry, they were getting closer, so I took a chance. I don' know exactly wha they wan, but I know we don' want to ask. Walk out there calmly and go. The door pulls you for a reason."

"I don't know," he said. But he did. He had since that foggy, rainy afternoon when the pigeon revealed the door to him. "It doesn't make sense."

"It will."

"It doesn't go anywhere."

"It goes somewhere." She took a few pieces of folded paper out of a back pocket and handed them to him. "This is very important."

"Tell me your name, at least."

She put a hand on his chest. "I'm called Lorel. Find Ayn. Find Kade. Go to Mon Teles quick as you can."

"Mon Teles?"

"The door." She hung her head and shook it. "I love you. I'm sorry." She walked across the back of the building.

I love you?

Will was aware that most stalkers had strong feelings for the people they stalked. What surprised him was that he actually felt touched.

Walking to his car, he tried to act casual and failed miserably. Four rust-trimmed beaters, including, he was almost positive, the one he saw in the video that morning, were parked at odd angles around the pumps, engines growling. Three seedy dudes sat on hoods smoking cigarettes and watching him. He glanced through the shop window and immediately regretted it. A tall man in a trench coat was hunched over the counter holding the clerk up by her shirt. He looked out at Will through strands of greasy hair and smiled.

Will had his hand on the driver-side door handle when the bells on the shop door jingled. "Hey there, friend," the man called out in another accent Will didn't recognize. "Moment for a lost traveler? I'm looking for the 101." He stood six-six at least despite a bowed spine. He had a long, bent neck, collapsed shoulders, beady eyes, and a massive nose.

Will pointed to his pounding heart. "Who, me? Not sure, sorry."

The man, the Bird Man as Will thought of him, smiled again and spread his arms and coat as though displaying his wingspan. "You sure, friend? Around here somewhere. Where are you headed?"

Lorel stepped from behind the building with a machine gun leveled at her waist.

"Holy shit," Will whispered and hit the ground.

Bullets peppered metal. An explosion shook the ground and shook Will's brain. A wave of heat and shrapnel blew past his car.

He picked himself up, yanked open the door, jumped in, turned the key, and floored the pedal. In his rearview he saw the Bird Man framed by the flames of one wasted beater and pointing a handgun. Will's back windshield exploded as he tore out of the station.

He was miles down 101 before he blinked. The ringing in his head had faded, replaced by the hurried whoosh and whir of the early afternoon commute. He waited for the beaters to materialize in his mirrors. He wondered if they were all dead, if Lorel had killed them all. He wondered how he would feel about that. He wondered why his life had been thrown into the fire. He tried not to wonder, tried to focus on getting to the door as fast as possible without getting pulled over.

He was a few miles north of the city when he looked back and saw a gray SUV weaving in and out of the traffic behind him, followed by three beaters. They were all on top of him as he hit the tunnel. Gunfire and screeching tires echoed off the cement walls. Commuters cut and swerved, a panicked herd. Bullets tore through the right side of the hatchback and took out both windows. One of the beaters flipped and rolled.

Will flew through the toll without paying. Sirens blared, and the cops joined the chase. The good citizens of San Francisco, those who happened to be making their way home along this route at this time on just another day, thinking of that cold beer or that sitcom or that workout at the gym, yanked their wheels and pulled to either side of the big red bridge. Will took the center lanes, adrenaline jacked, wind whipping through his shattered windows. The traffic got thicker and the turns tighter as he sped into the city.

Lombard was chaos: gunshots, cars smashing into telephone poles and mailboxes and each other, pedestrians diving to the sidewalks, smothering their children, crouching in doorways. Will turned right onto Gough and gunned it up the hill. A beater crashed into an apartment building on the corner. The last one turned and climbed, followed by the SUV, followed by the cops. In the background, the Golden Gate, the mountains of Marin, San Francisco Bay, and Angel Island.

Will turned onto Washington, dropped onto a slope three blocks long, and looked in his rearview. The Bird Man was hunched over his steering wheel, head and shoulders pressed up against the ceiling. It was all red lights down into the valley beneath Nob Hill. Will didn't look both ways. He laid on his horn and prayed.

He saw the pickup at the last second, but he was going too fast to do anything about it. The hatchback spun like a top and wrapped around a pole.

He awoke to Lorel pulling him out of the driver-side window. He shook his head like a boxer shaking off punches, tested his fingers and toes.

"Have to move," she said as his feet hit the pavement.

It was two and a half steep blocks up Washington to 1449. They'd made it two when the Bird Man started firing. Will turned right. The yellow building was on Clay.

"No," Lorel said. "To yours. Underneath."

Beside the red door was the half-submerged one that led to the laundry room and storage spaces. Will stepped down and in. Lorel turned and pointed at the Bird Man with her thumb cocked and one eye closed. She jumped in as a bullet blew a hole in the door.

At the far end of the passage, beside the wooden staircase that led up to Will and Elle's apartment, was the narrow, fenced-over gap between 1449 and 1447. The fence had been cut. Will peeled it back and looked over his shoulder at Lorel. "It goes nowhere."

"It goes somewhere. Find Ayn, find Kade, go to Mon Teles, and keep that paper safe."

Will searched her brown eyes for evidence that this was all a sick joke. What he saw was true grit and immense pain. He turned and walked through the fence.

He crossed the cement patio outside the yellow building, inside the city block. Three stories above loomed the door that led nowhere or somewhere. Another door was open on the first floor. Inside it was a staircase.

He ascended in the dark. He reached the roof and opened the door to a view of the city, the bay, the bridge, and the mountains, the same view he'd basked in from his own roof a thousand times but for one difference. The yellow building was higher on the hill, just enough for him to see the top of Angel Island, the one spot on his filming list he never made it to.

Lorel and the Bird Man wrestled on the roof of 1449. The Bird Man caught sight of Will and screamed, "No!" He held Lorel down by the neck, raised his gun, and pulled the trigger. Empty clicks. "See you again!"

A flash of light from the Angel. The roof gave way, and Will plunged. He fell and fell into a growing orange glow. He was pulled apart, then pressed in a vice. Then he was out.

PART TWO

ANIMALS

7

Lightning cracks of pain split Will's head in a steady rhythm. Seconds passed as an eternity, and he prayed for death. Then the stabbing subsided, and he cried in relief and slowly became aware of himself.

He lay in the fetal position. He radiated heat like he'd been baking in an oven. The ground beneath him was stone. He could see nothing, remember nothing. He reached a hand through the dark and felt nothing. Panic crept in. He turned onto his knees and elbows, held his head in his hands, rubbed his eyes, opened them. Complete blackness. He gripped his chest, felt his shell and quarter-zip. His pants were corduroy.

Memories surfaced. He was under the building? He listened for voices, cars, a trolly. The only thing he heard was the blood pumping in his temples. He clawed at his pockets and took out his Zippo. Something was wrong, more wrong than people trying to kill him. He struck the lighter. He was in a cave. The ceiling and side walls were close around him. The curved back wall was blackened crystal. Ahead was an aperture, a nickel-size circle of daylight at the end of a thin, inclining tunnel. He scrambled toward the light on hands and knees.

It grew to the size of the supermoon. He pulled his knife and readied himself for the Bird Man, summoned his rage. He screamed and burst through the mouth of the tunnel—

—and tumbled down the side of a rocky, tree-covered slope. He smashed his right thigh on a trunk, spun, and slid gut-first into another. Threw up his lunch.

He wiped the puke from his trembling lips and the tip of his nose, pulled himself up, and straddled the trunk. What he saw, it wasn't good. He was a couple hundred feet up a hill in a forest. Outside of the city. As in not where he was minutes ago. The deep brown color of the bark bothered him on a very deep level. It reminded him of Lorel's eyes, and he remembered how they looked when he left her at the gap between 1447 and 1449.

Holy shit. She did this to me.

She defended him from the Bird Man. She said that she loved him. But it was all a hoax. She led him to the door, which was a trap all along.

He'd been knocked out from the fall and placed in a cave. In a cave in a hill.

"Gotta get out of here, man. Gotta find a road."

It was still light, so he couldn't have been blacked out long. San Francisco was visible from just about anywhere in the Bay Area—he'd filmed it from every angle. All he had to do was climb one of these trees, and he'd spot it over the next hill. The branches of the one he was straddling were too high, but he saw a smaller one sticking out of the hill at a shallower angle. He slid down and across the hill until he came to it, then started up.

Climbing, he noticed things. Like pinecones shaped like bean pods and made of thin, woven strands; and long, thick needles somewhere in color between hunter green and navy blue. Will was no horticulturist, but he'd camped in and hiked through many of the Bay Area's forests, and he was pretty sure he'd never seen this species before. Toward the top of the tree, he pulled back the branches and looked out.

There was no bay, no city, and no ocean, only large, wooded hills as far as he could see. But the sun was behind him. It was afternoon, and he was looking east.

The hill he was on steepened above him. The ones to the north seemed like easier climbs. He looked up, found the cave, then carved an "X" with his pocketknife into the tree trunk. He marked more trees as he worked his way to the bottom of the hill. He planned to go straight to the cops when he got out of there—no more do-it-yourself stalker confrontations, thank you—and they'd want to see where Lorel had left him.

Feet on flat ground, Will shed his earth-green shell and quarter-zip, tied them around his waist, and jogged north. The stringy, pod-like pinecones crunched beneath his feet. He named them *basketpods*. The trees he called *everbluegreens* for the color of their needles. This cataloging came instinctively. He'd done it often as a kid to make sense of a world that didn't make much sense, a world where some kids never got to meet their parents. Like his lucid dreams, this instinct had been dormant for a long time. Given the circumstances, he supposed the regression was understandable.

He came to a relatively moderate slope and started climbing. He'd taken two steps when a bird screeched from a branch directly above him. It looked like a hawk but was taller and thinner, as though stretched out. Its feathers were the same dark brown of the tree bark and Lorel's eyes, excepting a black mohawk that Will found arrogant and a little bit frightening. He and the bird stared at each other as he passed underneath it.

It wasn't a particularly hard climb, but it was a climb, and it came on the heels of a car chase, falling through a roof, and waking up in a cave. Will's mouth was good and dry when he reached the rounded summit. It was too quiet, so he knew before he crested. To the west was no bay, no city, and no ocean, but a wooded valley bordered by two tall ranges. Will fainted.

He awoke to a sharp pain on his left ear. He reached for it and was bitten on the finger. He jumped up. It was night. A squat, furry animal the size of a gopher snorted and shuffled at his feet. Another nipped the heel of his boot.

"Back off!"

He kicked one away. More circled. He looked to the trees and locked in on one sticking out of the western side of the hill. He gave himself a fifty-fifty shot of missing it, going down, breaking every limb, and getting eaten alive by these furry bastards at the bottom. But he had no choice. The bastards were multiplying. He ran, leapt, and grabbed onto a branch. The bastards jumped and snapped their teeth. He swung and punted one down the hill.

"Ha! Suck on that!"

He pulled himself up and watched with saucer eyes as the bastards scurried off into the inky night. Then he climbed higher and found a perch. He took out his cell phone, almost as an afterthought. It was dead, and he wasn't surprised, for this Saint Paddy's Day had gone to shit in a hundred ways. At least he had a chance now to breathe. To think. He was alone in a forest he didn't recognize. He'd spent plenty of nights in forests before but not, since the orphanage anyway, without George or Elle and the crew and an excessive amount of beer. Now it was just he and himself, and he had a decision to make. Civilization was on the other side of one of the two ranges. The question was which one, and the problem was that both were multiples taller and meaningfully steeper than the hills he'd just come over. If he expended the energy to climb the wrong one and didn't find humanity or water, he'd likely find himself in some real trouble.

He was desperate to start. Elle was surely shedding years off her life from worry at this point. Maybe they'd taken her too.

No, no, not that.

But hiking in the dark was a bad idea even without the furry bastards to deal with. He needed to get back, but he needed to be smart. He had no supplies and zero room for error. Tomorrow morning he'd choose the northern or southern range and climb.

He tried to quiet his mind and get some rest. There was nothing to piece together anyway, no clues, no conceivable reasons for any of this. He sat back in his perch, took off his belt, tied his left wrist to a branch, and laid his head down on his arm. He could see his breath, which pissed him off. It should have been warmer outside the city. A cold front was just insult added to injury.

He managed a few hours of broken sleep. At dawn, he climbed down to the lowest branches and looked and listened for the furry bastards. No sign. He crossed his fingers that his latest enemies were nocturnal, then jumped down.

There was a small clearing at the top of the hill. Will sucked frosty dew off the grass, snapped open a few basketpods, and ate the everbluegreen seeds. He noted the positioning of the rising sun over the rolling hills to the east, estimated where in the valley it had set the day before, and with this information tried to decide which range was hiding the city from his view.

It should have been obvious. He should have recognized something, anything. He looked back and forth between the two ranges and with every passing second became more clouded with fear and doubt. He thought of Elle alone in their apartment. He thought of dying beneath these trees he didn't recognize. The pressure of his decision mounted, and he couldn't make it.

But it was made for him. The sun peeked from behind a cloud, and a light flashed in the center of the valley, three, maybe four miles away. A small body of water. The ranges tapered off a bit at that distance. If he found the water, he could start north or south from there. If he needed to double back, he could drink again before trying the opposite range. It was the best option on a very short list of shitty options.

Down in the valley, it felt like there was nothing beyond the valley. The everbluegreens were dense, the shrubbery thick. Will did his best to stay headed in the general direction of the water by looking up at the sun through the needle canopy, but it was an inexact science. At midmorning, he came to a small rise where the branches of an everbluegreen hung over a boulder. He climbed up to get a read on his progress.

He hadn't maintained anything resembling a westerly course but rather had strayed to the base of the southern range, which now towered over him. He considered going for it, but the risk of being wrong was too great. He had to find the water first. Only now he'd be heading toward it from a different direction, and he'd just proven his inability to maintain a straight line through the forest.

He looked east in the direction of Cave Hill, as he called it, where he awoke the day before. He looked up at the bare, flat peak above him, then across the valley to the northern range, where he marked one forested, triangle tip. He figured that if he kept a line between his southern and northern marks, he'd have a decent chance of hitting the water. He resolved to climb trees and check his positioning more often.

Hours passed like a week. Will had seeds to eat, but his thirst was starting to scare him. He tried to block it out and stay calm. Most of the time, he felt like he was headed in the right direction. Other times, he was sure he was going in circles. And it became harder and harder to stay optimistic in the quiet solitude of this foreign place, with a brain and body increasingly deprived.

He came to a patch of younger everbluegreens with reachable branches. He pulled himself up into one, jumped to a larger tree, and climbed. He was in the center of the valley. He located his marks and felt confident that if he kept a straight line up the middle of the valley from there, he'd likely hit the water. He didn't waste time. He climbed down and continued on ...

... and on for the rest of the day and then another. Whenever he thought he was close, he was farthest away. Whenever he was ready to give up, he would climb and find himself centered again.

It was dusk on his third day in the valley. A brisk wind whistled through the trees: a late spring cold that smelled like early fall. Will came upon a fallen tree caught in the branches of another and decided to take the opportunity to get up before dark. It meant another night of terrible sleep in a tree with nothing but morning dew to drink and seeds to eat. And not a step closer to San Francisco. Elle had probably aged twenty years by now. Maybe she was in a forest somewhere too. Maybe she was dead.

But Will had a shred of hope left, even then. The fallen tree was a perfect path up to its neighbor, a bit of luck. He'd become a tree climber, and every adventure he'd conjured up as a kid while climbing trees in the forest surrounding the orphanage had had a happy and heroic ending. Maybe this one would be no different.

He stuck his head out of the branches with a weak smile. Fuzzy, green triangle mountains loomed. He was north again.

He shook. He tried to find his marks on both ranges, but his vision was blurred and his capacity for thought eroded by dehydration and sorrow. A bleary mohawk flew across the watery, setting sun, a silhouette against the great red-orange disc. It was a sign. He would die that night. He believed it with all his heart. Even when the Bird Man was firing at him on the streets of San Francisco and his faux protector was blowing shit up, death had not felt this close. Now there was no adrenaline left to mask Will's fear, and he could no longer suppress the truth: that Lorel and the Bird Man had wanted him dead and soon they would get their wish.

Reaching this conclusion opened his heart. Thin wisps of pink and purple cloud drifted across the royal-blue sky, the sun cast its final red rays over the darkening, fragrant pines, and for the first time since waking up in Cave Hill, Will noticed and savored the beauty of the ever-bluegreen forest. He imagined himself flying over it and across the sun, just like the mohawk. The world was a dream, beautiful and deadly. He took a last look, blew a kiss with a trembling hand, then climbed down to his final perch.

He held an image of Elle in his mind and called to her across space: *I love you, Elle, I'm sorry. I love you, Elle, I'm sorry. I love* . . . and drifted off to sleep, he hoped for the last time, to the sound of elks mewing in the valley.

Furry bastards, grunting and scrambling, woke him in the middle of the night. One squealed. Then silence. Then slow, barely audible footsteps.

A large shadow ambled toward the fallen tree and walked up it. A cat. Will had resigned himself to dying that night, but he would not be eaten alive. He gathered what fumes of strength and rage he had left and prepared himself to fight.

The cat stopped and fed where the two trees met, thirty feet below him. It tore skin and flesh, slurped blood, crunched bone. It turned and beamed its orange eyes up at Will. Will stared back, feigning courage and ferocity and holding his knife where the cat could see it. Unmoved, the cat finished its meal, walked down the fallen tree, and vanished into the night.

Will awoke again in the predawn, disappointed that he was still alive. He climbed to the top of the tree and watched the valley emerge from darkness. He wondered, not for the first time, if the world existed without beings to observe it. He hoped that the answers to that and the other big questions he'd been asking himself over the past three years were right around the corner. He climbed down and walked in no particular direction. In the end, he had one remaining connection to this world, the memory of the elks calling to each other in the night. They were his last threads of subconsciousness, the bells tolling, the dream he was trying to get back to, as he took his last sad steps and fell.

8

Will was a mouth that twitched. A sporadic patter on his lips was torturous, maddening. He forced them open and lay for several minutes unable to move his body, just a mouth drinking in tiny drops.

He rolled over and pushed himself up off the ground. His bones groaned. He cupped his hands and watched them fill slowly. He sucked small puddle after small puddle. He laughed and cried, spread his arms, looked up through the trees at the soft, benevolent, gray sky, and bathed. There was meaning in this. He was not just lucky. He was *saved*.

He chose a direction and started moving. An animal ran through the trees ahead of him, an elk or deer. But another sped past him, and he saw that it was neither. It was as tall as an elk but had thinner legs, a leaner body, and a longer neck. Its hair was the deep brown of the everbluegreen bark with patches of moss green. Two smooth pieces of bone curved back over its head, then forward again, finishing in sharp points. Will followed it, hoping that it was running *to* something and not *from* something. Like a large cat, for example.

The ground sloped downward into a depression blanketed with tall, lime-green, leafy stalks. The spaces between the trees widened. The ground ahead was dark. It was moving. It was water.

Will ripped off his clothes and dove in. He drank in buckets, squirted water through his teeth, splashed and spun. Never had he felt so alive, for never had he come so close to death. When his shrunken belly was full and ready to burst, he floated on top of it and drifted out of a small cove.

The pond opened up around him. Everbluegreens lined the far shore, a hundred feet across. To the right was a clay beach, to the left a rise and a sheer rock wall. In the wall was a very round cave. In the middle of the pond was a boulder.

Will swam back to shore, dressed, and considered his next move. Tomorrow he'd hike the northern range and with any luck see the city and make his way out. The cave was tempting—the cave was *manmade*—and he had a few hours of daylight left, but there was no climbing that wall. The only way in would be to hang from the ledge, drop fifteen or so feet, and try to catch himself on the floor. But a broken bone could cost him everything out there.

He put it out of his mind. He walked around the lake gorging on the stalks and looking for a tree to sleep in that night. A fallen branch caught his eye. It was as long as he was tall, thick as his wrist, and mostly straight, with a softball-sized knot at one end. He cut off the twigs and carved a sharp point on either side of the knot. He made a brief go at hunting a smaller *skinny-elk*, but he never got within a stone's throw. Even if he had, the horns were discouraging.

The sun set, the sky grew dark gray, and Will had yet to find a tree. He returned to the lake and stood with his arms crossed staring out at the boulder. He assumed the cats could swim but hoped they wouldn't bother with a supply of skinny-elk and furry bastards on dry land. Really, he had no choice. He undressed and swam out, holding his clothes and staff over his head.

He felt safe inside his moat, whether he was or not. He felt grateful too, indebted. He crossed his legs, closed his eyes, and paid homage to the sky and to the rain that saved his life. The Ladies would have called it a prayer, but he'd never taken to organized religion, and that word reeked of it. The idea of homage felt more appropriate to him, more organic. He paid it also to the forest and to his oasis, which he called Needle Pond, his proverbial needle in the haystack.

He laid down on his side, held his knife and staff tight against his chest, and stared at the cave until it blended into the surrounding dark.

The night passed without incident except for some stomach cramps, which came as no surprise to Will. Actually, they should have been much worse. Most pond water was undrinkable. The fact that he hadn't been shitting all night meant that Needle Pond was deeper than it looked (the boulder just the dull tip of some large hunk rolled here by a glacier a hundred thousand or a hundred million years ago) and sourced by a healthy flow of underground runoff filtered through the earth. Like the rain, Will did not consider this a circumstance of luck. He kissed the surface of the water, then swam ashore, intent on the northern range.

Maintaining his sense of direction proved difficult once again. It was afternoon before he made it to the base, and there wasn't enough daylight left to attempt the climb, but that was okay. He'd marked trees obsessively on the way. It was a crooked route, but tomorrow, if he followed it, he'd make it back in an hour or two. He returned to Needle Pond.

The sun was setting as he swam out to his rock, another day spent. Elle, George, and the crew were undoubtedly starting to fear the worst at this point. But it didn't help to think about such things. In fact, it hurt a great deal. So, Will busied himself by sharpening the points on his staff and cleaning his knife, his socks, and his underwear. He took his little blue book out of his back pocket just for something to read, something else to do. Maybe he'd find a clue in one of his dreams. What he found instead, tucked inside the book, were the pieces of paper that Lorel had given him. He'd forgotten about them, willfully perhaps. But it didn't matter. They were either blank or filled with lies. They were a prop, a part of the act to make him feel like she was on his side. Like when she said she loved him.

She'd written something after all, three pages of dense prose in foreign characters. The other three were covered in dots and lines, irregular shapes, and what might have been equations, geometry. Will didn't waste any brain cells. He refolded the pages and stuffed them back into his pocket. Anger and sadness flared, and he told them, "No."

He tossed a pebble into the lake and watched the gold-capped ripples roll toward the shore. He looked to the sky, to an arc of luminous clouds stretching into the west like the tail of a great comet with the sun as its head. He crossed his legs, closed his eyes, and focused on his breath. He'd learned mediation at CHS. He'd found it a painfully embarrassing thing to do in a classroom full of other people, but he'd dabbled in it at home, and it seemed a good fit for here and now.

He deepened his breath, slowed it. He observed, passively, the thoughts drifting in and out of his head. Energy formed in his open palms and swarmed in the darkness behind his eyelids. Time was different.

He opened his eyes. The sun had dipped behind the rock wall, and the cloud comet had broken up into dozens of pink and purple pieces, all reflected in the pond inside a frame of upside-down everbluegreens. A twinkle in the pond was a lone star floating directly above the cave. Will *was* that twinkle. He was utterly alone. He was the only person alive looking at that star at that moment. He did not know the source of this conviction, but it moved him and troubled him. He was suddenly very tired.

L and I are swimming for our lives in San Francisco Bay. The sharks are coming. We make it to the base of one of the Golden Gate towers, but it's too high for us to climb. We scan the rough waters and wait, knowing we have no chance.

We're swimming now in crystal, sky-blue, arctic waters surrounded by gleaming icebergs. We laugh and play with friendly strangers. A mud-green catfish bites onto a woman's leg, up to her thigh. I claw at its eyes and pull at its mouth, but it won't budge, and I realize we'll have to amputate the leg.

I'm standing on a hill. Below is a field of tall grass colored like the sunset—yellows, reds, oranges, and purples—so that I can't tell where the sky ends and the earth begins. Elle and the crew are with me, and they encourage me to go, be free. I drink in the color as I run down the hill.

A boy appears at the bottom just as I reach it. A boy with gray, cracked skin. A dead boy. The boy who killed himself with the bee. I try to talk to him, to comfort him, but he runs away.

We walk to the dead boy's house. We pick through boxes in his garage, looking for clues to who he is. He appears again, alive now but agitated, terrified. I hold him. He resists, but a connection grows between us, an energy. We exchange it. We resonate. Then all I see is the number three in blinding white.

Will awoke before sunrise and wrote his dream down in his little blue book by the light of the stars. The number three filled an entire page.

It was still dark when he swam ashore and walked up the rise to the top of the rock wall. He kept his staff cocked and his knife open, but no cats or furry bastards tried anything. He stepped up to the ledge and looked down at the cave. He was going in—the star that hung above it yesterday evening had insisted—he just had no idea how. He could weave a rope of the stalks, but it would likely take most of a day to make one thick enough to hold him. He could tie branches together with his clothes and belt, but then anchor that to what, and how? The only viable option was dropping off and trying to catch himself on the floor, but that was still too risky.

This time he tripped over the answer, a mound of dirt at the base of a tree a few feet from the ledge. He dug through the dirt and uncovered a wooden box. Inside the box was a decayed leather satchel. Inside the satchel was a frayed rope.

Will kissed his fingers and touched the rope, paying homage to whoever left it in his path. He tied it around the tree, gave it a couple of good yanks—it looked and felt about as old as the dirt it had been buried in, but it would hold—then walked back to the ledge and rappelled down.

The cave was tall enough for him to stand in hunched over. He took his silver Zippo out of his pocket and took a moment in the still darkness. Insects buzzed. Or was that coming from his head? He traced the engravings on the lighter with a thumb: his initials on one side and "Love, L" on the other. He struck it.

The walls were rounded, smooth, and lined with frescoes in black ink or paint or tar. The first on Will's left showed a man in a headdress standing above a crowd. Some people held their arms up to him as though in praise or worship. Others grabbed at his furs and tried to tear him down. He stood impassive and resolved with an eye floating over his left palm. Will named him the *Chief.*

In the next image, a step deeper into the cave, the Chief was leading his people across a tree-spotted plain. The eye hovered over him. Horned beasts carried large baskets on their backs, the people bore smaller ones on their heads, and all seemed to move with purpose and determination. But in the next image, their numbers had thinned, and they marched with heavy heads and slumped shoulders away from a stone mound, a grave. Still the Chief walked upright and led them on.

They were gathered now around a pond. The Chief stood on a boulder in the middle of it and pointed to the eye, which floated in the center of a rock wall. The last image showed a few of his people standing on a rope bridge strewn across the wall and digging the cave.

Will paused, shut his lighter, and breathed. He felt transported into the past, into the Chief's world. He felt watched. No, he felt *seen*.

He struck the lighter again. At the back of the cave, at the level of Will's waist, the Chief sat on the boulder and looked up at the cave, which was represented by a hole in the wall. On either side of the Chief was a crest, a hill. Within each hill was a dot. The dots were caves, Will knew. The one where he woke up and a third.

My dream of three.

The hole was the size of a half-dollar. Above it was a black asterisk, a radiating star, the star Will had seen last night hanging directly above the cave. He held his flame up to the hole, but it was too deep to see inside.

The drawings on the right wall were of a different energy or vibe or mana. Will didn't know how to think of it, but he sensed it immediately. The first, closest to the back wall, was of three concentric circles made of smaller circles, like stringless, beaded necklaces. The necklaces gave the impression of rotating clockwise, the beads of spinning. They gave the impression of time. The next image was of two planets revolving around the sun, one orbiting just outside the other. After that there was a man, shrouded in darkness, ascending a hill.

Will slapped the Zippo shut and stepped back. The dark man felt close somehow, felt familiar. It was like sensing the Chief's world only different. More present, or more future. The man would top the hill. It seemed inevitable.

The story did not end with the man but with something equally menacing and irrational: Needle Pond again, this time with large, shark-like fish circling the boulder.

Will's fear morphed into dizziness and déjà vu. The sun broke over the trees to the east and shone directly into the cave. From the back, from the hole in the wall, came a faint orange glow. Will went to it like a moth to the flame. He sat down, crossed his legs, and straightened his back. Deep inside was a symbol of golden-orange gems glowing like a hundred tiny suns: an eye inside a triangle inside a square. Within the eye was a wave with one trough and one crest. The gems, each smaller than a pinhead, shone so brilliantly and precisely that Will could have counted them. His mind emptied, and the symbol was burned into it forever. Moments later, the hole was dark again.

9

Will had known it deep down from the very beginning. The basketpods, everbluegreen needles, furry bastards, mohawks, skinny-elks—none of it was NorCal. It was denial that had allowed him to believe that he was within striking distance of home. He could climb the southern and northern ranges, but he would not see San Francisco. It was always a false hope.

But he'd been saved by the rain and then shown his path. He no longer doubted which way to go. He would follow the star, which had aligned perfectly with the cave and the setting sun.

The symbol of orange gems floated before him still as though lingering on the retina of his mind's eye. He suspected that he'd seen it through a small window of time. It might have shone at the same time the day before and might shine again tomorrow, but before long the angle of the sunlight would shift just enough to render the hole dark until next year.

Standing in the mouth of the Chief's cave, Will took a piece of paper from his back pocket, the calendar tear sheet for March 17th. At the bottom was the "Celestial View," announcing the biggest supermoon in over fifty years. Above it was the quote: "The forces that move the cosmos are no different from those which move the human soul." Will knew that he was meant to find the cave and see the symbol, and that his path was west.

The image of the Chief sitting on the rock showed three caves. The final symbol of Will's latest arcane dream had been the number three. The synchronicities he'd experienced in San Francisco before falling through the roof had all occurred in threes. A bee appeared in his dream, then on his window, then later crawled across the epigraph of a book proclaiming that a holographic model of reality could explain paranormal phenomena and synchronicities. The cat and snake both appeared three times. Within minutes of leaving the Center for Holistic Studies for the last time he saw three triangles, the last one the caution sign on the bus. All of this amounted to meaning. Will was still just as good and goddamn lost as he had been the day before, but for the first time since waking up in Cave Hill, he felt some sense of purpose.

There was one more image just inside the mouth of the cave: an etching of a bird in half a dozen curved lines: sleek body of negative space, wings back, sharp beak pointed to the sky. It had been made by a different hand. Someone else had been there. Will took out his knife and scratched his last name, a type of bird, into the stone beneath this bird mark. He then pulled himself up the rope, put it back in the box, paid homage to Needle Pond, and left.

Will understood, intrinsically, the duality of nature, its deadly beauty. He'd gotten himself into plenty of fixes in the forest surrounding the orphanage, and George had given him a hard lesson on where his meat came from early on in their relationship. But this duality had never manifested so profoundly as there in the everbluegreen forest, where Will nearly died of thirst and then was provided for in ways he could never mistake as coincidence. And as he walked west, thinking on these things, nature showed her teeth again.

Not a quarter-mile from the pond, he stumbled upon a puma-sized, coffee-colored cat, its snout buried in a fresh skinny-elk carcass. It was short and stocky, not unlike the bench Lab that used to live down the street from him and George. It looked up at him as though it couldn't quite believe this brazen interruption. It stood up on its hind legs and hissed.

Will backed up slowly and looked to the everbluegreen branches. They waved in the breeze, out of reach and apathetic: death is life. Between fight or flight, he had one choice. He raised his staff over his head, widened his stance, and screamed. But the cat was not discouraged. It walked forward on its hind legs like a bear.

Will swung his staff—*whoosh, whoosh, whoosh*—establishing a perimeter with the heavy, pointed head. The cat strafed, threw a light jab with one thick brown paw and then another, testing the force and timing of Will's swings. It lunged between them and slashed his T-shirt and belly. He stumbled backward. The cat pounced. He landed a Hail Mary on its lower jaw and bought himself some space.

The pain sharpened his instinct and anger. His senses tightened. Time stopped. He watched the cat's eyes and felt the cadence of its steps. When it leapt, he stepped into a swing and drove one pointed end of the staff into the side of its head.

It stammered off, stunned. Will came up behind it and brought his staff down again and again, splitting its head open like a melon. Warm blood splashed his face. His own seeped from the claw marks on his stomach. At some point he stopped, looked down at the gore at his feet, and retched.

Will was eleven years old the summer that George adopted him as his younger brother. "I'm not trying to replace your father, whoever he is, so let's just say we're brothers, I guess," George had said, and Will had agreed. A father was someone who disappeared before you had a chance to meet him, and Will very much liked the idea of a brother who was a man, wise in the ways of girls and other man things.

George had never been a father or a brother and had no intention of becoming either. He'd come to the orphanage by virtue of a flat tire in a storm and at an awkward point in his life. But Will was drawn to him from the start, to his straight talk and beard and calloused hands. The Ladies saw something in him too. That was clear to Will, looking on from a crack in the door, by the way they eyed each other as they subtly examined the man over dinner, or more to the truth, forced him to examine himself. George broke down over key lime pie—it was the only time Will ever saw him cry—and said, yeah, he'd like to meet the boy. They left in his pickup two days later.

It was a mixed beginning. George was at a loss for how to bond with or entertain an eleven-year-old. But when he offered to take Will hunting, Will thought he had died and gone to heaven. He had visions of stalking black bear through the Great Smokeys with bow and arrow while learning everything there was to know about his new big brother. It turned out, though, that hunting was a lot of sitting around in silence, and the idea of killing something for sport felt more and more wrong as time dragged on. When they finally saw a deer and George lined it up, Will's entire body flushed with hot guilt. When the crack went off and the deer went down, he humiliated himself by running away crying.

George broke the silence halfway home. "I'm sorry, I guess," he said. "That's life." As he dragged the carcass toward the shed, he told Will to go on inside, he didn't want to see this. But Will, determined as he was never to hurt another living thing, was only male, and he watched the entire procedure from the window of his new bedroom.

These were core memories, ones Will had kept safely buried for a very long time. He suspected now that they might save his life. To the west, according to the cave drawings, was a plain extending to the horizon. He figured it was possible that he'd reach a road or town in a day or two or three, but he couldn't assume it. So, he prepared. The skinny-elk and the cat, which he called a *buma* (brown puma, bench puma) would be his food and his sacks to carry water.

Watching a skinning from a distance and performing one, however, were different things. The sound of his knife tearing through the skinny-elk skin, the rubbery resistance, the rank, metallic smell of the still-warm flesh and blood—he was heaving within seconds, and he heaved a few more times before the end. But he got the job done, and he paid homage to the animals and the forest that provided them as he worked.

It was midday when he finished scraping the fat from the hides. He carried them to the pond, swam them out to the rock, and laid them out to dry in the sun. Back onshore, he built a fire and a high rack of sticks and hung thin filets of skinny-elk meat well above the flames where they would slowly dehydrate. He cleaned the cuts on his stomach, then walked back to the carcasses.

From the head of the skinny-elk he carved one sharp, curved antler for a tool and a weapon. From the mouth of the buma he carved a three-inch fang as a symbol of his crucible and his will to survive.

At sunrise the next morning, Will planted his staff, washed of the buma's blood, and left Needle Pond, this time for good. Hanging over each shoulder were two pouches of skinny-elk hide tied together with thick strips of the same. Three contained water, the fourth a few pounds of jerky. He carried the buma skin, rolled up and tied, under his left arm. He'd slept under it the night before out on the boulder and had his best rest since waking up in Cave Hill seven days earlier. The antler was tucked into his belt in the back. Around his neck he wore the fang tied to a thin strip of skinny-elk hide, and the karma stone.

10

He reached the tree line and waded into a sea of waist-high, mint-green grass peppered with gray rocks. The northern and southern mountain ranges, still towering, veered off in a V and receded into the distance. The sun was high. He passed his hands through the grass and took the first steps of the next leg of his journey slowly, mindfully, traveling in the direction of the star, which he called the Guide. He knew that wherever it led, Mon Teles perhaps, it would eventually lead him home to his love.

He walked beneath the low, sprawling branches of a gray tree with four thick, splicing trunks and a million spade-shaped, emerald-green leaves. There were trees every hundred or two hundred yards. In the cave drawings, the Chief led his people across flat, tree-spotted land. It was this land. The Chief traveled with an eye floating above him. The eye was his vision and his purpose. At the end of his march, he dug the cave, drew his history on the walls, and created the symbol of orange gems. And Will might have stumbled upon it. Or it might have been placed in his path.

There were celestial elements: the supermoon, the positioning of the Guide, the alignment of the two planets in the cave. Will didn't pretend to understand, but he didn't ignore the facts or signs either. The only two cave images still unexplained were the ones of the shrouded man ascending the hill and the sharklike fish circling Needle Pond. But that was all in the Chief's past, and Will was moving forward.

———

He marched for the remainder of the day. He sipped water from his pouches and nibbled at skinny-elk jerky. He watched and listened to the grass for signs of predators and heard only light rustlings. The sky clouded over, the temperature dropped, and this bothered him more than was rational. But he chalked it up to nature testing his resolve. He wasn't in NorCal, but it was spring everywhere in range of where he could be. The cold wouldn't last, nor the starlessness. He climbed up into a tree for the night.

He awoke to a world awash in starlight. He jumped down, raised his arms to the heavens, and cried. He understood for the first time, understood it in the depths of his soul, why different peoples throughout history and in far corners of the globe worshipped different gods for the sun and moon and stars. The sun brought the day, fed the world, burned it too. The moon and stars pierced the black of night, defied the emptiness. Very different sources of light with very distinct personalities.

But all light, he thought.

He lay down in the grass, pulled the buma skin over him, and stared at the Guide until he fell back asleep.

A cold wind whistled through the trees and grass the next day. The mountain ranges grew ghostly and distant, and with every passing mile Will sensed the increasing expanse of the Gray Plain. He named it that, this mostly green land, for the color of the tree bark and the sky that morning. He wasn't sure why he made that choice, and it troubled him. It troubled him too, the leaf that spiraled down out of a tree, dark blue and brown eating at the emerald-green edges.

He was scanning the ground through the grass for signs of water when something tore into his left calf. His knees buckled. He reached back and felt the sandpapery head of a snake. The body, juniper-green and thick as his neck, wrapped around his legs. He beat it with one hand and reached into his pocket for his knife with the other, but the snake trapped his arm, coiled around his stomach and ribs, and *squeezed*. His eyes bulged. The sky and trees blurred. He thought of Elle with excruciating regret.

A sting in his back was the antler. He reached for it, ripped it out of the snake's coils, and stabbed. Blotches of purple-red blood triggered the oldest parts of his brain, which he shared with this serpent: *Weakness, kill, FIGHT! KILL!* The blood sprayed and spread, fueling his rage. He stabbed and stabbed—*KILL! KILL!*—and hit a soft spot down by his legs. The snake released him and slithered into the grass. There was a bloody hole where its left eye had been.

Will pounded the pins and needles out of his legs, stood, backed up to a tree, and brandished his bloodied skinny-elk antler. "Try it again!" he screamed. "You can't kill me! None of you can! This is *my path!*" He screamed until he was satisfied that the snake, the cats, the furry bastards, Lorel, and the Bird Man had all heard him and felt his fury. Then he sat down and cleaned the two holes in his leg.

He rested for the remainder of the day, slept poorly in a tree that night, then continued on the next morning with a slight limp. His wounds had already begun to heal, and he knew that constrictors were rarely venomous. He didn't bat an eye when the first flakes drifted down. Snow at the end of March was nothing out of the ordinary in a lot of places, and Will no longer wasted brain cells speculating about where he was. He had other things to worry about, like food, water, and thirty-foot snakes. He stopped in the middle of the day and cut a hat from the buma skin, with flaps to cover his ears and strips of skinny-elk hide to tie under his chin. Staff and knife at the ready, eyes and ears on the grass, he carried on across the Gray.

11

Will carved a groove into a branch with his knife, then rubbed a smaller stick up and down it as hard and fast as he could. It smoked and charred. He placed a small pile of dried, dark-blue and brown leaves over his coal, then twigs over the leaves. He watched the fire grow as night descended, stroking his beard and buma hat.

He held his hands over two large, freshly skinned, ferret-like animals, closed his eyes, and mouthed words of gratitude for their meat and fur. He then set them on his rack above the fire, stood, looked to the western sky, and reached for a star. "The Guide shines for those with the strength to follow," he said, "and tonight it shines for me." He sat down to his meal.

After, he sewed the piebald furs onto a patchwork coat of two dozen others using strips of skinny-elk hide. Before going to sleep in a tree, he made a mark on the inside back cover of his little blue book, which contained his dreams. It was the fifty-fifth mark.

In the morning, he ate a breakfast of jerky, then stretched. As he took his first steps of the day, he said, "The light awakens the souls of those with the strength to see, and today I see my path."

Midday, he spotted a hole in the ground through the thinned, brown grass between two brick-sized rocks. He stood behind a tree and waited. A ferret scurried over, cheeks bulging with acorns, and disappeared into its den. Will cat-crept over. When the ferret popped up for another run, little snout sniffing at the electric air, Will broke its back with his staff. Soon after that, he came across a stream, frozen along the edges.

It was the first time he had killed in consecutive days. The sky was white, and the ferrets were out hustling. It had flurried a few times over the last several weeks, but Will knew, like the ferrets did, that a real storm was coming. Winter would soon announce itself.

He skinned and smoked the ferret while he had the chance. He'd built fires every third or fourth night out on the Gray, whenever he had fresh meat and always with sticks to conserve what little fuel he had left in his Zippo. This time he used the lighter for speed.

Waiting on the meat, he took off what remained of his buma fur and cut two socks out of it. He secured them around his feet and ankles with skinny-elk strips, then stuffed his feet back into his boots. He was left with a cropped buma vest, which he put on beneath his ferret parka. Thick snowflakes floated down from a heavy sky.

His spirits were low the next morning. The Guide had not shined for him the night before, and the sun was now hiding. He could not sense his path or feel his purpose. He trudged through the snow and wind with his head down.

Will always felt weaker when he couldn't see the celestial bodies. Their rise and fall had become the slow, steady rhythm of his being, their light his greatest source of energy. Cloudy days were soulless days, and Will kept moving on those days only because he knew that the sun and Guide would shine for him again. Today, however, he found his faith being tested. A new and harder phase of his journey had begun, and he had trouble believing that the sky had not clouded over forever.

He'd survived the Gray for fifty-seven days and nights by tapping his instincts, honing certain basic skills, traveling efficiently, and getting lucky. But survival also required emotional and psychological stability, and Will had maintained his sanity by way of suppression. He'd stopped wondering where he was, why he couldn't see the moon, and why it wasn't spring weeks ago. Elle hadn't shown up in his dreams since Needle Pond. Depression would have killed him as fast as the cold, so he'd buried all thoughts of his former life and followed the Guide. It was all he could do.

This marked transition of the seasons, however, this first real snowfall represented not just a break in his rhythm but the promise of a tomorrow without stars and sun. In his dispirited state, Will let down his guard, and memories of Elle broke through his mental wall.

She stood on the roof of 1449 looking out at the city and pointing at something; poured herself a drink in the kitchen at 2000 Post, surrounded by the crew but alone, thoughtful; strolled the beach at Chrissy Field without a care; tunneled through a crowd at a show, looking for him, worried. He called out, but she was gone.

A growl, and he snapped back to the merciless here and now. He dropped his pouches, leveled his staff, and scanned the trees. Two sky-blue eyes floated in the white, and a tall, white wolf emerged. Pups yelped from somewhere behind it.

Will swung his staff with strength and control, eyes dialed, heart pumping. The wolf crouched and crept forward on long, thin legs. Will watched its eyes. It was looking past him.

A white snake burst from the snow. The wolf leapt. The beasts collided in midair, jaws locking, and hit the ground. The wolf tore its snout from the snake's bite and ripped out one of the snake's fangs, now sticking out of the wolf's bottom jaw. Blood spilled from both animals and stained the white snow. The pups cried and howled from their hiding spot.

Will turned to run but stopped. The snake had one red eye. Where the other should have been was a brown patch of scar tissue. Will had ruined it weeks earlier when the grass and snake were still green. He pulled his knife and antler and stood behind a tree.

The wolf, foaming at the mouth, attacked. The snake struck like a hammer again and again. It drove the wolf back, clamped down on its jugular, and slammed it down into the snow. Will stepped from behind the tree, straddled the writhing, foot-thick body, plunged his knife into it, and pulled through the flesh. The snake turned on him and rose. He screamed, closed his eyes, and thrust the antler up and forward.

Crack!

His shoulder nearly popped. Warm blood spilled over his hand and down his arm. He opened his eyes. His hand was inside the snake's mouth. The antler was sticking out of the top of its broken skull. He dropped it into the snow, tore out the antler, and watched, grinning, as the scales slowly drained of white, faded to a lifeless green. He then cut out its remaining fang and wiped the blade of his knife on his earth-brown corduroys.

The wolf lay in the blood-drenched snow surrounded by three pups, who were frantically, desperately licking the wounds on its snout and neck. Will knelt beside them and lifted one of the larger wolf's hind legs. It was female. Their mother. He held his fang to the one lodged in her jaw.

"You fought hard," he said. "I'll never forget."

Her eyes rolled to him. She tried to bark, but nothing came out. Still, he understood, as animals somehow understand each other, what she meant to say. He responded by nodding and petting each of the pups in turn. But he was lying, and he knew she knew.

The mother died. Her children lay around her in shock. Will used snow to clean the snake blood from his hand and ferret parka, then took a piece of ferret jerky from one of his pouches and held it out to the pups.

"Here you go. Want to eat? Huh? Here, have a bite."

Two stared off into nothing. The third lifted its head off its paws and looked at him.

"Yes, come on. Over here."

It stood. It was lean like its mother, long legs and big, wide paws. Three, four months old maybe. Gray circles around its eyes like a raccoon. It came for the meat. Will sat down in the snow, fed it, petted it, and opened his knife.

"That's it."

He closed his eyes and paid homage to the Gray for its generous gifts of meat and fur. They seemed a form of compensation for the onset of winter. The world was just and balanced again.

But then, a whimper. Will cracked an eye. The other two pups were standing and staring at him with their tails tucked between their legs, pleading. He squeezed the eye shut and found Raider glaring at him in disgust.

God damn it.

He threw Racoon Eyes off his lap and stood. Reached down and lifted its leg. A boy. He approached the others. One, a gray stripe running down its snout, growled and backed up. Will grabbed it by the scruff and performed his examination. Another boy. The third, curved, gray splotches for eyebrows, lifted its own leg and pissed on a tree.

Will scowled at the wolf brothers. "You can hunt? I won't feed you. This is *my path.* You can walk it as long as you survive, but it's mine." Stripe On His Snout eyed him warily. Raccoon Eyes looked at his brother as though waiting to be told what to do. Eyebrows licked himself.

Will shook his head, wondering what he'd done to deserve this latest wrinkle. He walked back to the wolf mother. "Go chew a stick or something," he said to the pups. "You don't want to see this." But just as he'd watched George butcher the deer, they watched and howled as he skinned their mother and cut slices of her meat.

Gray, snowy dusk. Will wrapped the dripping filets in the dripping fur and carried his bundle away from the scene. He cleared the snow at the base of a tree, made a fire with his Zippo, built a rack, and hung the meat. He then made a necklace out of the snake fang and a skinny-elk strip, dropped it into his layers, and climbed up into the tree for the night. The pups curled up together beside the fire and cried themselves to sleep.

12

The horizon was a glowing rainbow stripe seen through the split trunks and sprawling, skeleton-finger branches of the gray trees. The sky above was a deep royal blue. The red sun rose, bathed the world, and Will paid homage by speaking his mantra: "The light awakens the souls of those with the strength to see, and today I see my path." He turned and continued west. The wolves followed. He wore the skin of their mother tied around his neck by the front legs, marbled skin-side-up so it could finish drying.

He watched them from the corners of his eyes, hoping they would fall off or better yet drop dead so that he could skin them without having to hear it from Raider. But they moved well through the deep snow on those big paws. Raccoon Eyes stuck to Will's side. Stripe On His Snout stayed level with them but kept his distance and kept an eye on Will. Eyebrows wandered off often, there one moment, gone the next.

Half the day was spent. They were still keeping pace and showing every intention of continuing to make Will's life more complicated, so he decided to give them some basic training. There would come a time out in this unforgiving nowhere, sure as shit, when he'd need them to do what they were told and stay out of his way.

"All right, assholes," he said. "I wasn't fucking around. If you're walking my path, you're gonna learn a few things. And get it through your skulls right now: I have no intention of letting you get me killed."

Stripe On His Snout tilted his head, Racoon Eyes wagged his tail, and Eyebrows sat down and scratched himself behind an ear.

"Okay, fine," Will said and took a few steps back, dangling a piece of ferret jerky. "Now *come*," he commanded. Starving after the morning's march, they nearly ran him over. He fended them off with a foot, put the jerky behind his back, held up his other hand, palm out, and backed up again. "*Stay*," he said. Raccoon Eyes came running, and Will smacked him on the snout. "*No. Stay.*" He backed up once more. This time, Raccoon Eyes, pawing his nose, stayed put.

"Okay, now *come*," he said, waving the jerky. But the pups, scared now of doing the wrong thing, didn't move. "It's okay, *come*. Come here."

Stripe On His Snout seemed to think very hard about it, smoke coming out of his pointed ears. Eyebrows yawned. Raccoon Eyes couldn't take it anymore.

"*Come*. Yes, good. *Come*." Will fed him a morsel. "*Now stay*." Will held up his hand and stepped back. Raccoon Eyes followed and earned another smack. Will tried again, but the pup, now thoroughly confused, sat down in the snow.

"That's *sit*, you dick. We'll get to that."

Will worked on Raccoon Eyes for a while with little to show for it. But Stripe On His Snout watched and listened from a safe distance and started doing what his brother was told. Then Raccoon Eyes started mimicking Stripe On His Snout, and suddenly they were getting somewhere. Eyebrows lost interest and took a nap next to a tree.

The sun was halfway down when they started falling behind. Big paws or not, they were just kids, and they'd walked for most of a day through deep snow with minimal rest. An hour or so later, they were gone. Will chewed their mother's meat and kept moving.

In the morning, he stood beneath the tree in which he'd slept the night before and whistled on and off as loud as he could. He passed an idle half hour and was ready to move on when he spied little white shadows flickering across the gray trunks. He whistled and yelled, "Come!" until they were at his feet panting. "That's the last time I wait," he said, and gave them each a handful of ferret meat.

They fell back again, and he almost felt sorry. He turned to wish them luck and saw them digging. They scattered, came together again, then ran back to him. Eyebrows and Stripe On His Snout each had baby ferrets hanging from their mouths. Racoon Eyes was beaming with pride.

Will shrugged. "If you keep that up, I don't give a shit how long you walk my path."

When they were done eating, Will grabbed Stripe On His Snout by the scruff, looked into his sky-blue eyes, and said, "*Stay*," then walked backward. Raccoon Eyes started to follow, but Stripe On His Snout growled and nipped his brother's ear. Will stopped a hundred feet away, waited, waited, whistled. All three pups came running.

That night, as they lay together beneath his perch, he decided to give them new names. Stripe On His Snout was a nervous kid but sharp and the clear leader of the brother trio. Will thought he deserved a strong name, and he called him Jackson. Raccoon Eyes was a fun-loving half-wit, the quintessential pup. Orly popped into Will's head and seemed appropriate. He struggled with what to call Eyebrows but finally settled on Fred.

It occurred to him only then, and it sent chills up his spine. He opened his little blue book to the dream of the dead boy, the one he'd dreamt out on the boulder in Needle Pond the night before he went into the Chief's cave. The number three covered an entire page. He looked up at the sky and said, "The Guide shines for those with the strength to follow, and tonight it shines for me."

Each day began with training at dawn and ended with a second session at dusk before dinner. Will reinforced the "Stay," "Come," and "Sit" commands with relentless repetition, smacks on the head, and small pieces of ferret meat. Jackson proved an excellent and eager learner, always anxious to do the right thing, as though his and his brothers' lives depended on it. Orly thought they were playing a game and learned more or less by mistake. Fred would ignore Will for entire sessions and then follow his commands at random just to prove that he could and to get a snack.

Will's life was his routine and his march, and he didn't have to change much about it. The pups were mostly transparent to him in the large spaces between sessions. They hunted for themselves, kept up (he suffered a slightly reduced pace), and generally left him alone. And so, this was all allowed to continue.

One dry, sunny, bitter-cold, morning, Will was settled deeply into the rhythm of his steps, staring ahead, waiting for the change in the landscape that never came, when something hit the back of his knees, and he fell. He turned, pinned the animal down in the snow, and pulled his antler. It was Orly. Fred and Jackson stood by with their tails tucked. Will, confused, stood up and walked away.

Orly cut him off, ran circles around him, and barked like an idiot. "Okay, enough," Will said. But Orly had the zoomies. There was no stopping him. He tripped over his own paws and face-planted into the snow. Will felt a spasm in his belly and heard a strange sound issue from his throat, some ugly cousin of a laugh. He chased Orly around a tree, kicked a buried rock, and fell himself. Orly pounced on him. Fred joined in. Will yelled to Jackson, "Come on, kid!" Then they were rolling in the snow.

It was beautiful, and then it was heavy. Will's laughter devolved from joyful and unfettered to forced and uncertain. He knew the danger here. He'd loved and lost and concluded that love wasn't worth the risk. But the wolves, their puppy breath, it conjured up Raider again. Then he thought of Elle, and that was it. Weeks of bottled emotions poured from his battered soul. Nothing stood in the way, no wall of suppression, no judgment about the utility of feelings in the wild. Just images of Elle, Raider, George, and the crew.

His crying sputtered out in broken breaths. He stood and looked west across the tear-blurred, snowy plain. "Come on," he said to the pups. "Let's keep moving."

He froze. He rubbed his eyes. He had trouble processing what he saw because nothing had changed for so long. A ravine and a round stone structure. His heart rate kicked up.

Okay, okay.

It was nothing. It was a ruin. But he couldn't assume that. He had to assume that he was about to make contact.

He bent down and grabbed Jackson hard by his striped snout. "Okay, man, this is why we train. You have to *stay*. Understand? *Do not move. Stay.*" He looked Fred and Orly dead in their eyes. "You heard me. *Stay.*" He turned and walked to the structure.

It sat just off the edge of the ravine, an igloo-sized dome made of the gray rocks that Will had stepped over and stubbed his toes on a thousand times out on the plain. He slowed to a stalk and came up from behind it. "Hello?" he called out. There was an opening on the western side and a staircase leading down into the earth. "Come out. Hello?" He inched closer, peered inside. It was dark. No chimney, he realized. No evidence of life. He was crushed. He was relieved beyond measure. He struck his Zippo, lowered his head, and stepped in.

The floor and walls were dirt. Thick, arched branches held up the rock roof. In the middle of the room was a column of flat stones about waist-high. On top of the tower was an eye drawn in black paint or ink or tar.

The Chief was here, Will thought and shivered. The drawing in the cave of the thinned migrants: this was a gravesite for those of the Chief's people who'd perished on their journey across the Gray. Maybe there were more along the path.

He knelt before the tower, kissed the tips of his fingers, and touched the eye. On the floor at the edge of the halo was a shrunken leather boot. A skeleton lay against the back wall. Will crawled to it and held his flame up to the dark holes where the eyes had once been … and wondered about the mind, where it came from, and where it went when people died.

The skeleton held something to its chest beneath a leather coat hardened by time. Will peeled it back, and the bones crumbled. In the rubble was a leather satchel. Inside the satchel was a small leather book.

Will lifted it very carefully. He stroked it. He held it to his heart.

There could be answers inside, he mused. *There could be* thoughts.

Another man's thoughts. Another man who'd walked the path. This could be his journal, his little blue book.

Will place a hand upon the skull on the floor, then upon the eye atop the stone tower. He asked forgiveness for his trespass, then walked up into blue sky.

The wolves were sniffing around outside the grave. Jackson lowered his head and sat down in the snow as Will approached. "I told you to *stay,* Jackson," he said and smacked him hard on the nose. He then walked past the mound to the ravine, sat with his legs hanging over the drop, and opened the book. The first several pages were covered in a dusting of black dots, some of which were connected by lines to form patterns, shapes. Will recognized one as a constellation that hung just north of the Guide. The man had mapped the stars, it seemed, and likely traveled by them, just as Will was doing. They were kin, Will and the traveler. They were brothers of the Gray, separated by time.

He turned the page, and a lump formed in his throat. He turned to the next and the next. The writing was in foreign characters. But Will recognized them. He pulled the pieces of paper that Lorel had given him out of his back pocket and held them beside the book. They were written in the same language. And she too had drawn constellations.

On the last page of the leather book was a bird symbol, a bird *signature*, the same Will had seen etched into the Chief's cave in a different hand than the one that had drawn the frescoes. He placed Lorel's note inside the book, held it in his lap, and stared into the ravine. The traveler had been to Needle Pond and left the rope. He'd walked the Gray, died, and left his journal. Left it for *Will*. And Will would not read the traveler's thoughts today, but he knew now that wherever he was, Lorel was from the same region. He was getting closer, to getting out, and to this place. His suffering would not be in vain. The Guide was leading him true.

He stood. In the morning's excitement, he had not noticed the ghostly, crooked line stretching across on the western horizon. He saw it now, and a thin plume of smoke rising into the setting sun.

13

Will paced the edge of the ravine. Walking west, he eyed the smoke with hope and dread. Coming east, he looked down at the wolves, avoiding Jackson's eyes.

He wanted to believe that this was the beginning of the end. Civilization had to be within striking distance or there wouldn't be people out in this wintry desert. Maybe there was a town at the base of the mountains. Maybe it was Mon Teles. But whatever the case, Will thought it highly unlikely that whoever built that fire was out for some adventure and soul-searching. No, he assumed ties to the ones who shattered his former life.

Jackson stood with his tail straight back and his gray-striped snout pointing west. Fred sniffed in all other directions as though making sure there were no more surprises creeping up on them. Orly looked from one brother to the other, waiting to hear what was next. He wasn't going to like the answer. They'd proven themselves coachable and mostly obedient, but they were just kids, and they'd made a crucial mistake minutes ago. They hadn't stayed. Will had one choice, and he didn't waste any more time struggling over it. He removed stones from the top of the dome and filled the entrance, leaving a hole in the top. He picked up Orly, kissed him on the nose, and dropped him in. Fred nipped him on the hand but submitted. Jackson waited his turn with a knowing, sad expression. Will got down on his haunches in front of him and patted him on the head. "I'm coming back, Jackson," he said. "I mean to. Tomorrow morning, I figure. Take care of them." He dropped Jackson in and tossed in a couple handfuls of ferret meat.

He went slow. He let it get dark. Faint voices carried on a cold wind. A campfire flickered through the trees.

He got as close as he dared and looked on through the split of a trunk. Three men in fitted white suits sat on stools around the fire. One tapped his wrist like he was typing, then held it up to the sky as though searching for a signal. He shook his head and cursed in a foreign language. One of the others said something. Their accents matched Lorel's. Something European.

The suits. Maybe they were rangers or scientists. Maybe they weren't out there for Will. It had been two months. Why would his enemies send anyone out there now? He watched. He listened for his name or Lorel's. He heard neither. And he was nearly convinced that they were worth the risk of approaching when they jumped up from their seats and pulled weapons from their sides. A fourth man, tall, broad-shouldered, bearded, fur coat dragging through the snow, stepped into the firelight. The men in white holstered their weapons and proceeded to fidget around the camp.

Will started back in the direction of the grave. It was possible they wouldn't find his tracks in the morning, or if they did that they wouldn't care. But he couldn't count on any of that. Hope was not a strategy. And he wasn't giving up his path, not for anything. He'd make a wide arc around the camp and then continue west. By morning, if they slept, he'd have a solid head start.

He kept a strong pace for an hour or two, alone with the restless wind at his back. Then, crunching footsteps far behind him. He turned. A shadow moved against the shadowed trunks. The three men in white would have looked like ghosts. This was the other one.

Will had stood his ground against the cat and the snake, but he knew that flight was the right choice this time. He picked up his pace and maintained it. He aimed to outlast the man, and he did. After another hour or so, it was just him and the wind again.

He rested and drank. He pounded his chest, full of primal pride. The endurance he'd built up over weeks on the Gray had been tested, and he'd survived again. He considered when to rest going forward and for how long, when they might rest, how to throw them off his trail.

Then the footsteps again, closer this time. Caught, after all.

No, not yet.

He breathed in through his nose, out through his mouth. He rolled his neck. He took his knife out of his pocket and clipped it to the back of his underwear (an insurance policy, a gut decision that would pay off in spades), and felt for the traveler's journal tucked into his belt against his stomach. Two hands on his staff, he continued west and waited.

A rush to his right. He turned and swung and took a brick-hard fist to the temple.

He awoke to someone or something jabbing him in the ribs. He opened his eyes. It was morning. He was lying on his back in the snow. One of the men in white stood over him, holding his staff and smiling. His head pounded. His hands were bound behind his back by a ring of hard rubber. He rolled over on his side and used his face and head to push himself up to a seated position, spat out some snow. The guy laughed. He was missing a few teeth and, Will judged, more than a few brain cells. Will decided then and there to be very careful.

The other two were stuffing camping gear into white backpacks beside a charred hole in the ground. They were all roughly his height, comfortably below average. One, with long brown hair and hollow cheeks, looked over at him and looked away. The other, short black hair and a cleft lip, walked over. He seemed off in a way Will couldn't finger. It wasn't just the lip. He had deep blue eyes that seemed dialed in and somewhere else at the same time. He said something in their language.

Will shook his head. "You speak English?"

All three brows furrowed.

"My name is Bob," Will said. "Bob Williams. Please. I'm sure this is just a misunderstanding."

Cleft Lip opened his deformed mouth, paused as though searching for the right words. He was there and not there. He was probing his thoughts or listening to a voice in his head. "English talk?" he said.

"Yes, English! You speak English?"

He held his left thumb and pointer an inch apart to show that he knew a small amount of English. "From wha place?"

Will gave him the first city that came to mind other than San Francisco and immediately regretted not picking some place farther from home. "Greensboro."

He shrugged.

"North Carolina," Will added. "You know, the United States."

He looked to his associates, who shook their heads. "Wha corim?" he asked Will. "Greensboro Norf… Norf Carolina, Unita Stase?"

Will played it cool. Had these men been donning furs and face paint, carrying spears, and not speaking English, well, he might have entertained the idea that he was in some remote corner of the world where small groups of people still didn't know of the United States. Sure, why the hell not at this point? But these dudes wore computers on their wrists, fitted white suits that were way too thin for winter, white metal belts, and black metal barrels attached to their hips. They wore technology. They came from the developed world. They knew of the United States and probably of North Carolina. So, why such a blatant lie? Was it a mistake or an attempt to throw him off? Was he dealing with idiots or sociopaths? Either way, Will intended to keep his own truths safely hidden until he knew more about his new friends.

"Greensboro, no?" Will asked.

"No," Cleft Lip replied. He looked troubled, like something didn't fit.

Will was suddenly dizzy. Everything around him seemed very unreal. The endless plain, the moonless sky, the shortish men and their accents. He shook his head like a dog. They stared at him. They were real. He was real. He was in trouble, and he needed to keep his shit together. He motioned back east with his head. "Greensboro. Long way. My name is Bob Williams. What's yours?"

All at once the men looked behind him, then all at once turned and continued cleaning up their camp.

Will swallowed.

Jesus, here we go.

He shuffled around to face the other.

But this was a sick joke. He had a head like a cinder block. His face was flat and pale nearly to the point of translucence. No neck. Round ears sticking out of a mane of gray hair. Thick, gray beard. Icy-blue eyes. He wore a dark-gray fur coat with wooden buttons. A black strap crossed his chest from left shoulder down to right hip, and a worn, wooden handle rose up from behind his right shoulder.

Will lowered his head and squeezed his eyes shut. He was afraid to his bones and deeply fascinated at the same time. He felt crazy. This was too much.

This is happening, whatever it is. It's happening. Open your eyes.

The man, the Goon, the Gray Goon, walked off on legs too long for his body. He walked west. He carried an axe on his back, five feet long with two copper heads bobbing against the small of his back. Will wanted to laugh and cry.

———

They didn't talk to him, and he didn't say a word. He watched the men in white from the corners of his eyes and listened to their occasional terse exchanges in a foreign tongue. He didn't see the Goon, for the Goon had taken the rear. But he heard those footsteps.

He developed a tick, an occasional spasm in his left cheek that yanked that side of his mouth up into a half smile. He'd smack himself in the face whenever it happened, then look around to see if anyone noticed. Longhair always pretended not to. Cleft Lip sometimes did and sometimes twitched himself. Smiles, the one short on teeth and gray matter, took each of these opportunities to jab Will with his staff.

They stopped at dark. Longhair took a foldout stool out of his pack and set it down beside Will. Cleft Lip came around behind him, removed his rubber bind, then backed away and patted the black barrel attached to his white belt in a warning to Will to behave himself. Will rolled his wrists, thanked them both, and sat. Smiles dropped what looked like a hockey puck into the snow, then held the back of his hand to his barrel. A black band slid across his palm, and another wrapped around his wrist. He lifted the barrel, now an extension of his arm, and touched the tip of it to the puck, which threw up a thin, upside-down cone of fire. He then slapped the weapon back onto his belt.

Will watched this procedure from under his brow. He scratched his beard, mumbled, blinked, and wrinkled his nose. He was playing the loon, but he didn't have to try very hard. He'd been alone for a long time in a place he didn't know during winter when it should have been spring. Now he was being held captive by an axe-wielding Goon and three uniformed men with *Star Trek* weaponry. They were leading him west along his path, presumably for some reason, but this land had never felt so foreign to Will and his mystery so impenetrable. Whatever answers they might be making their way toward, Will felt like he no longer knew the questions. He battled with his emotions and let the men see him struggle.

Longhair passed him a canteen and a small piece of mud-green taffy. Will took a sip, passed the canteen to Cleft Lip, then popped the taffy into his mouth. It tasted like vegetable soup, not bad, but not ferret jerky, and he lamented the loss of his pouches. Apparently, the men had felt it unnecessary to bring those or his antler along. Just his staff for poking him. He resolved to make them pay for that.

He waited hopefully for another taffy but found his hunger relieved within seconds. The men in white also seemed satisfied with just one. He wasn't sure if the Goon ate, because the Goon sat behind him; and out of respect and fear that was only partially feigned, Will didn't look back but acted like it was just him and the others sitting around the campfire. He opened his mouth, hesitated, pretended to muster up some courage. "Please, what's your name?" he asked Cleft Lip.

The fire sputtered. Cleft Lip mouthed something. His brow creased. He looked like he was debating with himself whether to respond. "Faril," he said.

Will nodded and turned to Longhair. There were deep, deep shadows in the man's sallow cheeks. "You?"

Faril translated.

"Mick," Longhair said, looking down and looking like he very much regretted being out there.

"Heely," said Smiles with a smile.

"Where are you all from?"

"No Greensboro, Norf Carolina, Unita Stase," Faril replied, and it was clear from his tone that he suspected Will of inventing those places.

Will dropped his face into his hands and considered his next move. They stared, he could feel it. He let them.

Inspiration stabbed him in the chest. He lifted his head and threw Faril a wild look. "Want to know why I'm out here? Huh? I had a girl. You know, a love, a girl?"

Faril, compelled or confused, by Will or by something else entirely, nodded and translated for Mick and Heely.

"She was beautiful," Will said. "Blonde hair, yellow, yes? And tall and smart. She had fire, great spirit." He smirked at Faril and cupped his hands in front of his chest. "Great tits too, yes?"

The men in white leaned in. Will shuddered and smiled and told them about this girl. "We lived in Greensboro. You don't know that place, it doesn't matter. We had a house on a hill not far from the city. A good house." He fell silent. His chest felt like it was tearing open. He blurted: "We would go for hikes! Yes, hikes. Most days we would hike. She loved to hike even more than I do. She was better, more athletic, more knowledgeable. But she shouldn't have gone that day, and I let her go."

This time Will did not fall silent. He was *silenced*. He was losing control. The story was bullshit, but his love for Elle and the pain of losing her infused every word.

"Late fall," he said, tears streaming. "There was energy in the air. I told her that. A short hike, she said, a short hike before dinner. You shop and cook, she said, and set the table, and I'll be back by the time you're done. Yes! Yes! I said. I'll set the table, I'll do it! I'll cook for you and set the table. I'll wait for you. But the storm came quick. They always do that time of year. There was energy in the air, I told her. But I didn't tell her to stay."

Will keeled over into the snow and wept.

A soft orange light spills from the grave. I step down. The symbol of orange gems, ominous, beautiful, the reason for and the answer to all my troubles, floats above the tower of stones with the eye on top. The light goes out, and I turn. The traveler is standing in the entrance, a shadow against the starry sky. He points west and walks away. I try to follow, but I trip over the bones of the wolves. I crawl up the steps, but the wolves, now live skeletons, bite my ankles and drag me back down. I try to tell them that I'm sorry, but nothing comes out, and they're eating me alive.

Will awoke to Heely poking him in the stomach. His hands were bound again. He was wrapped in a thin, white sleeping bag and sweating profusely beneath his furs. The sky was white.

"We go, Bob," Faril said, and helped him up.

Will hung his head. "I'm sorry," he said. About his episode the night before. But he wasn't, now that it was over. He was getting to them. They looked at him differently now, like they'd lost their patience, or were disappointed in him, or weren't quite sure they had the right guy. Heely wasn't smiling anymore. "I still get sad sometimes," he said, telling the truth and fucking with them at the same time.

"We move, Bob."

They did, in a very uncomfortable silence. Will basked in it. He let it stretch, and then he broke it. "You're looking for someone?" he asked Faril.

Faril seemed to consult with himself.

"I'm sorry," Will said. "It's just that I might not be him. I've come across other travelers, one just recently."

Faril twitched. Will let him stew on that for a while, then changed the subject. He motioned back over his shoulder in the direction of the Goon. "Who is he?"

Faril chose not to answer.

"Not like you or me, huh? We're going to Mon Teles?"

"We're no going there."

"But it's in this direction?"

"Of course."

A vein pulsed in Will's neck, a blood-pump of hope. Hope of getting out. Of seeing Elle again. Of getting revenge on those who tore his life apart. He'd harbored these passions in his subconscious during his trek across Gray, for they were distractions from the everyday physical and psychological work of survival, and thus a threat. Even now he fought to keep them at bay. But there were cracks forming in the wall in his mind.

And there was energy in the air. The white sky was pregnant. Will smiled with his teeth and mumbled under his breath to no one in particular, "The Guide will not shine for you tonight."

14

Will had suffered great loss with no idea why. He'd buried his pain and his need to get home. He'd regressed to a more instinctual being, an animal concerned with warmth and sustenance but with a spiritual instinct as well, oriented toward the sun and the Guide.

But the moment he saw that thin stream of smoke rising into the setting sun, images had begun to stir in his subconscious, ghosts of his former reality lurking near the surface. They were now starting to demand attention.

The snow started light the next morning, then dumped, and the bleary white landscape became a canvas for the specters and scenes flowing of their own volition through Will's mind: the Bird Man chasing Lorel up Washington Street, flapping his trench coat wings; the supermoon hanging over 1449 like doom; Lorel watching Will from behind a tree—*the door*—Raider swimming for his life in San Francisco Bay; Elle stumbling toward him in the living room the morning after his bee dream and her nightmare about him committing suicide, arms outstretched and eyes googly—*the door*—the Great Chameleon Snake spraying warm, purple-red blood out of its mouth and all over his face; brains spilling from the split head of the buma—*the door.*

I'm standing on the roof of the yellow building. It sags beneath me, splinters. Something is trying to pull me down, something that has been pulling me for a long time, though I didn't know it. The sun sets red through the towers of the Golden Gate. The city, bay, and mountains take on the colors of the clouds and sky, all phases of matter blended into one. Except the golden green of Angel Island.

Lorel and the Bird Man stand shoulder to shoulder on the roof of 1449, staring up at me and waiting to see what I'll do. I look to the Angel, but it's gone now, swallowed by a gaping white hole that grows, sucks the water down, eats the city and the mountains. The wind picks up, strong and cold.

And I hear Elle, clear as a bell. "Will! Are you there? Will!"

"She's here!" Will screamed. "I heard her!"

He was lying in the snow, hands bound. Faril was bent over him and smacking him in the face. "Bob, wake up! Get up! No girl. She's gone."

Will whipped his head around, searching for his lost girl. He remembered where he was. It was midday. He'd passed out walking? "I heard her," he whispered.

"We move, Bob," Faril said, and pulled him up.

The snow dumped in quarter-sized flakes for the remainder of that day and then the next. Will had three more episodes during that time. While immersed in them, he was wretched and incapacitated. Between them, he watched the men closely from his peripheral. They fought amongst themselves. They were sick of Will and sick of the weather. Even the Goon's block face showed signs of thinning patience and doubt. He took the lead and set a hard pace, looking back at Will often as though grappling with whether or not to cut his losses.

Will's mental state continued to deteriorate, and it served him well. He was broken in their eyes. He was a burden but not a flight risk. But he grew more comfortable with his budding lunacy, because *she* was at the bottom of every spiral. He didn't hear her again—she didn't notice him—but he knew that her scared, sweet call had not originated in his mind like the other sights and sounds.

They kept on. Will's mind would split, and he'd fall to the snow, and he wasn't pretending. But back on his feet, he observed his captors with keen senses. He saw more and more clearly in the white world, though he never let on. He used his illusions and tried to appear insane even when he wasn't feeling it. And he waited—until the real storm hit, and he saw those floating, sky-blue circles.

The wind and snow lulled. The men in white pointed to the spectral mountains and claimed the end of the weather. But Will knew like any other animal of the Gray Plain that the sky was only gathering its breath for the bigger blow. Electricity raised his flesh. He kept his head low and his eyes up.

The wind picked up to gale force before the men had a chance to complain. Visibility plummeted. Faril grabbed hold of Will's right arm, still bound to his left behind his back. Mick and Heely moved into a tighter formation on their left, and the Goon dropped back to a few steps in front of them. Heads down, they drove through the sideways snowfall.

Faril stumbled and lost hold of Will. The others didn't see. They kept moving, disappeared. Will unclipped his knife from the back of his underwear, turned, and saw a sign as profound as the Guide and the symbol of orange gems. Behind Faril, now getting to his feet, were three pairs of sky-blue eyes hovering in the white. This was Will's path, and the time had come for him to take it back.

He cut at the rubber bracelet in tiny, two-handed strokes. It went limp as though he'd severed its spinal cord and slipped off his hands. He turned to face the wind and collected snowflakes on his tongue. His blood warmed. One deep breath was all the noise in the cosmos.

He locked eyes with the center blue pair, pointed in the direction of Mick and Heely, then turned and drove his knife down into Faril's thigh. Faril fell, his screams drowned by the shrieking wind. Will ran after the wolves. The brown line of his staff materialized. He ripped it out of Heely's hands and thrust it up into his chin—he dropped like a sack. The wolves tore at Mick's legs and took him down. Will sat on his chest, pounded his face until his neck went limp, planted a kiss on his split lips, then stripped him of his pack and fled into the white with Jackson, Fred, and Orly.

He led them at a full sprint in some direction. He looked back every few steps expecting to see the Gray Goon emerge, expecting to have to fight for his life one more time. He pushed and pushed. His heart slammed against his ribs. His legs finally gave, and he fell to his knees and held his arms out to the pups. "I'm sorry!" he cried into the storm. "Please, I'm sorry!" He bear-hugged Orly. Fred and Jackson circled and sniffed, tongues hanging out.

Will corralled his breath and his mind. He risked a minute more of rest, two. The burn in his legs and lungs settled into a deep ache. The guilt in his heart stung, but the past was past, and he had the future to prove his love and loyalty to the pups.

He kissed Fred and Orly on their snouts, took Jackson's head in his hands, and said, "Gotta move, man. Stay close."

He lost himself in maintaining efficient movement. He willfully reduced his brain to a simple computer chip sending the signal to *step, step, step, step,* and occasionally to *eat* and *drink.* He overrode all signals to *sleep.* The world grew dark, stayed dark for a long time, then grew white again. He moved like a machine. But there was a ghost inside.

At times he was so immersed in his visions that he believed he was back in his previous life. But for the most part he knew, or at least suspected, that he was hallucinating or dreaming. It was curious to him.

He asked himself what a hallucination was, what a dream was. He lost all sense of boundaries. States of consciousness melded together.

He followed Raider along a trail through the everbluegreens. They came out of the trees onto Stinson Beach, where the crew was dancing around a fire. "Where's Elle?" he asked, but they whirled past him as though he wasn't there. The wind picked up. The sand was fine and white. Something brushed against his leg as he walked out onto the frozen ocean, and he remembered: *Oh, yeah, the pups. Step, step, step, step.*

He stood on the roof of 1449 scanning the streets of Nob Hill, searching for Elle. The boy who killed himself with the bee, the same boy from the dream of three, stood beside the door on the roof of the yellow building, which bent the space-time around it with its gravity. Had Will always felt it? He reached for the boy, but he jumped to the next building and was gone. George pounded on the red door, down on Washington. "George, up here!" Will yelled. "It's snowing in San Francisco!" Something bit his hand. That was real, he knew. So was the Gray Goon. *Step, step, step, step. Keep moving, man.*

He walked into their bathroom. She was there, hunched over the sink and crying. She froze as though she sensed him. She lifted her head.

"I'm here!" he said. "It's me! I'm alive!"

He crashed backward through the wall. The world was white and empty.

Step, step—Get up, get up!

He lay moaning in the snow. The pups were licking his face, and he tried to claw his way back to the world where they existed. But his mind went away, or perhaps it was taken.

I'm lying in the fetal position, helpless and hopeless. A dark being stands over me, smothers me, slashes me. I know nothing but terror. I am not awake and not dreaming but trapped in some purgatory from which there is no escape, at the mercy of this being who knows none.

I'm floating in dark water. Large, gray-black sharks circle me. One brushes my side. I see rows of razor-sharp teeth. I see a single, cold, black eye. The sharks attack, and my mind unravels.

I lay writhing on a hill, clawing at my face. The sharks froth in the water below. I sense, before I see, a shrouded man climbing the hill: a dark, featureless head bobbing, shoulders and arms swaying, legs marching. This man is my fate, my death, and the death of the world. He stands over me, sucking on my fear, the air he breathes! I will die, but that will not be the end. I will live forever in this limbo hell.

Will shot up from the snow and screamed: "It's him! I'll kill him!" He did not understand these words and did not know where he was. Then he was flooded with black intuition. He grabbed Jackson by the scruff. "The Chief," he said. "He drew my nightmare on the wall. The man coming up the hill—the shadow from my childhood dream. The Chief drew my death!"

The hair stood up on the back of his neck like tiny antennae. He picked up his staff and rose as the Goon materialized out of the thinning snowfall. The others were white shadows on the white background.

Will's soul shook with the reverberations of his lucid nightmare. Invisible sharks brushed against him still. The shadow haunted, now and forever. But of those standing before him he was unafraid. He knew that these men posed no threat to him anymore, for he had seen his death and the man-god who would deal it.

The pups barked. The Goon started. His square, bearded jaw dropped open. He lifted his axe and turned.

Copper streaks in the white world. Splashes of red. Faril, Mick, and Heely barely had time to protest.

Will changed then and there. The Goon had gashed him too, heart, mind, and soul. There had existed some connection between him and these men, now severed. Three human lives extinguished right in front of him, and he felt the loss.

This heartbreak, this evidence of his humanness, was supplanted by the reptile in his brain. *Step, step, kill, kill!* He walked forward. The Goon pointed his axe and chanted in a buzzsaw voice: "Morrarru Dondante. Morrarru Dondante!"

Will didn't speak Goon, but he picked up on the sentiment just fine. Still, he knew he had the advantage, for his fate would play out somewhere else with some other enemy. "Sorry," he said. "It's not my time."

Orly charged. The Goon punted him away. Will swung his staff once, twice, testing. Fred threatened and drew a swing from the copper axe. Jackson took the opening, lunged, and clamped down on one too-long leg. Will drove the pointed end of his staff into the other, and the Goon dropped to his knees. Will swung for the block face, for blood, for the win, but the Goon threw up his axe, lopped off the head of the staff, and drove the handle of his axe into Will's gut. Will hit the ground and puked up taffy.

The Goon stood.

This isn't possible, Will thought.

His nightmare had been too real. The Chief had drawn it!

He wiped the puke from his mouth and threw his headless staff at the Goon's legs. It bounced off harmlessly, but it was the thought that counted. "No, no, see," Will said. "I'll be wearing your fucking teeth around my neck." He pulled his knife and got to his feet. If he could get inside the axe's reach, get up close and personal . . .

A brown figure entered stage right. The Goon turned. Will walked backward to where Jackson and Fred were tending to Orly. They watched together as the gray and brown shadows danced in the white world. Copper streaks met curved, electric, blue-green flashes. Sparks flew. The Goon fell, and his grinding voice cut through the dying storm: "*Morrarru Dondante!*"

Then the world was deathly quiet. The man in brown stood over the Goon's body for a minute, two, three. He then walked to the men in white, dropped something into the red snow, picked up Will's staff, and turned toward him. Will held up his knife. "Slowly," he said.

The man stopped. "You speak English?" he asked, startled. He had the same accent as Lorel and the men in white.

"Yes, Christ, I speak English. Who the fuck are you?"

"English?" the man said, looking down at the snow and shaking his head. He wore a fitted brown suit, a dark green metal belt, and a dark green metal disc on his left hip. He had short brown hair, brown beard, white, wind-burnt skin, and very dark, very deep brown eyes that wouldn't stop moving.

"You need to tell me who you are, and quick," Will said.

"Wha?"

"Who. The fuck. Are you?"

He was confused. He was wracking his brain. "Wha? Wha am I called? I'm called Kade."

Will swooned. "Kade?"

"Yes."

"No, no, no, Kade?"

"Kade."

Will pointed his knife. "She told me to find you. Lorel."

Kade put a hand to his mouth.

PART THREE

FOUND

15

The wind howled, the flyer shook. The map in Kade's helmet fizzled and flickered out. He smacked it. Gone. Dead. He had nothing now but Peis Ota's words to guide him through the white winds. He repeated the first of them in his head as the engines failed and the flyer dove into the mountains. In English: *The boy lives. The boy lives...* He yanked the ejector lever, burst into the open air, and tumbled backward. One tick, two, three. The flyer hit the mountain with a dull, distant thud. He stabilized, opened the wings of his suit, and lifted as fast as he'd been falling. He rode the wind hard, furious with himself for being in this position. Eighteen turns of waiting for a boy who may or may not be alive only to die himself?

Gray rock, needled trees. He caught an up current, crossed a ridge, and was blind again. He dropped through an air pocket, leveled off, exhaled.

The boy lives, the boy lives.

Now, at least, was a time to believe.

Leafless trees and flat land.

The Shole.

A branch severed his right wing. He spun, landed hard in the snow, and rolled.

Lying on his back, he slowed his heart and confronted what had just happened. The pop beneath the dash. The backup systems completely unresponsive. This didn't just happen. This was sabotage.

They've been waiting too, and they're ahead of us.

He stood, took off his helmet and tossed it, shed his wings. He pulled his glasses out of his pack, put them on, turned them on. No com signal, no surprise. Wrist device, same thing. The flyer's more powerful computer had been able to access the nearest satellite and had beamed him directly into Ayn's office. He'd just been telling her that he wasn't worried about the storm. She'd just been telling him that he was out there for good reason. But the flyer was scraps in the mountain.

They'd made a crucial mistake. They'd been lulled to sleep, and it was his fault. He'd been responsible for keeping an eye on the Fenti. He'd been back to Fentum several times over the past eighteen turns to chase the rumors and faint trails that too often felt imagined. He never learned the Fenti's motivation for coming after the boy, nor whether they thought they'd finished the job, nor whether it even mattered to them. And there was no real reason to think he was alive, only the "vision" of a street performer, a mother's intuition, and an understanding that the Mind sometimes had strange dreams. But the mother died long ago, the echo of Peis's words had faded, and it became increasingly difficult as time went on to believe that this had been anything but senseless loss from the beginning. Kade always knew he would go searching eventually, if only to honor them both and finally put their souls to rest.

But the Fenti had resurfaced. It was the only plausible explanation. Maybe they were chasing a ghost too, or maybe Peis was a prophet after all. If so, then the boy was out there somewhere, and Kade wasn't the only one looking for him.

To return when the Pymm hangs Trimus. Across the Shole toward the city of seven.

Now was the time, and here was the place. One way or another, Kade would soon finally learn the truth. The boy would be moving east to west if Peis was right, and Kade was just inside the West Range. His scanner had a reach of forty kels, but the Shole was ten times that wide and twenty long. So, he turned once again to the street performer's words, spewed from a foaming mouth eighteen turns past, and to his own instincts. If the positioning of the Pymm determined the timing of the boy's return, Kade would use it to guide him.

He blinked open the green box in the top right corner of his right lens and scrolled with his eyes. He didn't have a signal, but he had deep memory stores. He opened a map of the stars in his left lens and a map of the Shole in the right, then programmed a line across the plain that matched the Pymm's path across the night sky. The line was seventy kels south of his current position. He switched to thermal vision, felt for his xim on his belt, put on his hood, and started off.

The storm raged. He cranked the heat in his suit. He was well aware of his latitude and how bad it could get out on the Shole during the cold season, but he'd expected to experience it from the inside of a flyer. He was warm enough and dry and didn't doubt his own ability to survive out there, but the boy? He'd be a man now, of course, and he'd have found a way, if Peis was right. He'd also be walking, and it was not lost on Kade, the irony that he too was now marching across this frigid wilderness. It seemed appropriate that he should travel as the boy was and endure the same conditions. It seemed *by design*. But of course, he had no idea what the boy had been through over the past eighteen turns. Maybe he'd wandered the world as Kade had.

Sent by the Mind to know this far place.

He thought back to the flyer again. The Fenti could not have done it alone. Access to the hanger required guard clearance. Knowing when and how Kade planned to set out required tapped links and knowledge of private conversations held between him and Ayn as the Pymm drew Trimus. Maybe he'd been followed more often and more closely over the turns than he'd realized. Maybe they'd learned of Peis's vision. Whatever the case, they'd returned to Damarra at the right time, they were getting help, and Peis's final words loomed large: *Trailed by a great shadow.*

A heat signature appeared at the left edge of Kade's right lens. Then four more. He held his breath and waited for the readout.

Human.

"Alive!" he screamed into the storm.

Peis had seen, in a still, black lake, a blur of a man, who he said was the boy, walking alone across the Shole beneath a starry sky. That there turned out to be multiple people and that it was light out did not inspire doubt in Kade. No, he knew that one of the five was Dawlis. He'd never in his life felt such a resonance of truth, so beautiful and ominous. The Mind's wisdom in showing Peis the Pymm hanging above the boy so that they could locate him out on the plain spoke of universal connection and communication. Its concern with the boy's shadow portended a powerful antithesis.

Kade thought of the boy's mother and father.

Not in vain.

The five were forty kels away, downwind. He'd rest some. He'd not approach these people and this moment exhausted. He'd reach them early in the arc of the second spin.

But rest was elusive. Quieting his mind was a delicate task for Kade under normal circumstances, and here he was realizing a prophecy eighteen turns in the making. There were a hundred questions without answers. About the boy, where he'd been all this time. About the mother, where and when and how she'd died. The Fenti, their motivation. The guard's. *The father on his way?* Kade speculated. He probed every granule of his memory. He got nowhere. He did not feel tired.

It was deep into the ninarc, and his mind was starting to fry from the circular thoughts when three new heat signatures appeared in his right lens: a pack of groos moving toward the humans, who had stopped to sleep. There was no real danger. The groos were eighteen kels away, and the humans would pick them up with any decent scanners and be able to defend themselves with any decent weapons. But it was easy to make a mistake in this weather.

The five started moving again at first light. The storm lulled and then grew violent. The groos closed the gap. One human split off and was chased.

Not Dawlis!

They caught the person. All four heat signatures blended into one. But Kade didn't believe it. He refused to. The Mind would not bring the boy back exactly in keeping with the vision that it had incepted into Peis Ota's head only to deal him a quick, cold, and painful death. And indeed, something odd. They sped off together, the groos and the human.

They kept a strong pace through the arc and then the ninarc. So did the other four, and so did Kade. It grew light again. The pack rested. Kade was one kel away when the others caught up to them. One attacked, three dropped dead in the snow, and Kade's heart froze. His eyes darted in their sockets. He high-knee sprinted through the deep snow. The pack and the last two humans came together. A groo went flying. Kade turned off his glasses, saw the tall, gray figure, and all anxiety and anticipation left him. He placed the back of his hand to his xim. The black metal handle slid across his palm, cold and comforting. The energy enveloped his hand.

A bearded man in mixed furs backed away into the white. The Fenti charged, and Kade killed for the second time in his life.

The darkness spread through him, the emptiness and misery, the seduction. He'd forgotten how gutless and powerful it made him feel, how omnipotent. And if that was Dawlis standing there with the three groos, then the prophecy was fulfilled but for the last line, which called for—Kade was convinced in that bleak moment—more fighting and death.

So be it, he thought, knowing that it was not that simple, and knowing that what was done could not be undone.

Three guards lay in the snow, split open. Beside them was a wooden staff that Kade was sure was not theirs. He picked it up, dropped a beacon into the red, melting snow, and walked toward the man in the furs.

"Slowly," the man said. In English.

Mind, it isn't him, was Kade's first, sickening thought. There was only one place in this wide world where English was spoken by other than historians and linguaphiles, and he would have known if Dawlis had been there.

Why send Peis a vision of another and call him the boy?

It defied the mysterious logic. It called the connection into question.

"You speak English?" Kade asked.

"Yes, cryst, I speak English. Who the fuck are you?"

"English?" It didn't make sense.

"You need to tell me who you are, and quick."

"Wha?"

"Who. The Fuck. Are you?"

"Wha? Wha am I called? I'm called Kade."

The man swooned. "Kade?"

"Yes."

"No, no, no, Kade?"

"Kade."

The man pointed a small blade. "She told me to find you. Lorel."

Revelation.

Dawlis! Lorel, alive!

Kade breathed through the fingers of his right hand. Instinct told him to tread lightly. This moment was thin ice: the way Dawlis said her name, like it was someone he hardly knew. "Where?" Kade asked.

"Where what?"

"Where did you see her?"

"Sanfransisko. Where the hell is here?"

Kade, eighteen turns a global nomad, off and on digging in the world's corners for clues as to the location of the lost boy, had never heard of this place. "Sanfransisko?"

"Don't tell me you don't know where Sanfransisko is."

She did it. She found him.

"Wha else did she say?" Kade asked.

"Very goddam little."

Kade saw the resemblance now, through the beard and dirt, the feral anger, the eighteen turns of time. But he stayed cautious. He had the heartbreaking impression that Dawlis didn't know who Lorel was, that she didn't tell him. It was not a decision she would have made lightly. "Wha do they call you?"

"Call me? My name is Will."

You're called Dawlis.

"How many turns do you have?"

"I'll ask the questions!" Dawlis yelled.

"Keep it calm. We have to help each other understand. Where is she now?"

"She did this to me. Her and the Bird Man. Look at me."

"Wha did she do?"

"I had a life. She destroyed it. Followed me and sent me to the door and left me for dead."

"She didn' leave you for dead. She said to find me. Wha else?"

"Find Ayn. And Mon Teles. She said she loved me. But she killed me."

"She would never hurt you."

"You don't know what I've been through."

"I know her."

"Who is she? *Tell me.*"

Kade put up his hands and slowly lowered himself to a seat in the snow. "Please. First tell me where you came from. How you got here. We'll both understand more tha way."

Dawlis crouched and pointed his blade. His eyes were wild, mad, desperate. "You have to tell me."

"I will."

Dawlis sat. One groo laid down on either side of him. The third stood at his side and stared at Kade.

Traveling with groos, Mind.

They made it all the more unbelievable.

"I had a dream about a boy," Dawlis said. "Elle was there. The boy killed himself with a bee. He showed up later in another dream, walking dead, and I think he's me because I'm going to die soon. But wait—let me back up. I had this nightmare when I was a kid—no, wait. Hold on."

Die soon?

Kade went cold: the emptiness, the nothing born of killing. They should wait, he thought. Rest before diving into this mystery, the abyss of lost time. But Dawlis seemed to find his bearings. "I have a girl-friend," he said. "Her name is Elle." Then he poured out a strange story.

The wild flitting of his eyes as he spoke. The volatility of his emotions. It was like there were two of him, one hopeful and strong, the other on the brink or already fallen. He spoke in awe of a cave and a symbol made of gems. He spoke with fierce pride about his march across the Shole. His voice dripped with bloodlust as he relived his escape from the guards and the Fenti. It cracked, and the color drained from his face at the mention of another dream, which seemed to ruin his interest in sharing. He stood, walked away with the groos, and climbed a tree.

Kade recorded it all through his glasses. He waited until Dawlis and the groos were asleep and then listened. Then again. It was hard to follow and harder to believe. There were chunks missing, like Dawlis's time between this place Sanfransisko, real or imagined, and the mountains east of the Shole. But of all the confused and disquieting things the boy had said, the worst was near the beginning: "He showed up later in another dream, walking dead, and I think he's me because I'm going to die soon." Kade finally slept that ninarc, but not much and not well.

16

The next day began like so many others on the Gray Plain. Will awoke, climbed down from his perch, tossed a meal-bite to each of the boys, ate one himself, and stretched. The sun was shining, so he spoke his mantra. Then to Jackson he said, "We're out of jerky. Find us some ferrets." He set his eyes on the peaks to the west and quickly fell into the rhythm of his march.

He did not acknowledge the other. He sought, in the repetition of his steps, the hard but simple life that he and the wolves had led before contact. He would not admit that this man associated with that woman had played a meaningful role in his fate. He'd taken out the Goon, sure, but it wouldn't have mattered. Will would have found a way.

But ignoring him proved difficult, for Jackson watched him like a hawk, Orly crept up to him and sniffed his legs every thirty seconds, hoping for a pet he never received, and even Fred glanced over at him from time to time. Eventually, reluctantly, Will did too.

He was Will's height, give or take. He had legs in proportion to the rest of his body and a normal-shaped head, things Will no longer took for granted. His eyes, though, were disconcerting. They *didn't move.* They were set against his pain. Will believed he knew the source. "You killed that man."

Kade looked at him. Looked west. "He died so you could live."

Will was timeless. He sensed the universe, there and gone. Those words spoke of meaning, maybe even of purpose. This was Will's path, and Kade was now walking it. She said to find him, and here he was.

"Did you recognize him?" Will asked. "Or the others? Their names were Faril, Mick, and Heely."

"I ... didn'."

He was withholding, it was clear, but Will let it go for now. "I've been lost a long time. Tell me where I am. Where is Mon Teles?"

"You really don' know it."

"I sure don't."

"Mon Teles is where we're headed. Is a city, over the range."

"Where is Mon Teles in relation to the United States?"

"I don' know the Unita Stase."

Will didn't like that answer, not one bit. He slapped his staff against his palm. "Don't you lie to me, man."

Kade stopped walking, locked his dead still, miles-deep brown eyes on Will, and said, "I don' know the Unita Stase, and you don' know Mon Teles. I told you we have to help each other understand."

Will clenched his teeth. "I have to take a piss." He stepped behind the nearest tree and pulled the traveler's journal out from beneath his furs. It left a cool rectangle of absence on his stomach. He took the note Lorel had given him out of the journal, tucked the journal back into his waistband, then walked to Kade and handed him the note. "I left a couple of things out of my story. I can't read this. I'm guessing you can."

The wind whistled.

KADE COULDN'T THINK. The electricity in his brain was misfiring. He started to read it to himself again. Dawlis's voice was far away. This was a dream. This couldn't be.

Dawlis grabbed him by the neck of his suit. "Kade, I need you to read it."

"I'm not sure—"

"You *have* to read it to me."

It's not possible.

He blinked. He grabbed Dawlis's hand gently and removed it from his suit. "I'll read it. I will. But I'm going to tell you about Lorel firs'."

I'm going to tell you who you are.

He started. It was the only thing to do, just start. "We lived in a town called Trill, two hundred kels south and eas' of here."

"Kels?" Dawlis asked.

"Kel, a measure."

"Like a mile, I guess."

Kade didn't know that word. "I haven' seen her in over fourteen turns."

"Turns?"

Kade swallowed, pointed up at Nurin, and made a circular motion with his finger.

"Years," Will said.

Kade ignored it. "Lorel has a man, Shaw. They have a son. Something happened to the boy when he had two turns. A Fenti, a man like the one we fought, tried to kill him. Shaw wasn' there. Lorel took the boy into the forest. She hid him in a cave and led the Fenti away." Kade breathed into the darkness crystallizing in his chest. "Killed the Fenti. Then the ground shook, and the hill with the cave collapsed."

He took a sip of water from his canteen, then offered it to Dawlis, who shook his head very slowly. He continued, "A man in Trill called Peis Ota performed in the square for his food. He could juggle eight balls while standing on one foot. He could climb buildings. He could guess our ages, weights, our thoughts sometimes. He spoke in rhymes often, simple ones, never very good." Kade searched for the right words. He'd never rhymed in English. "Things like 'He likes him, I can tell, he'll be his bell,' and 'She's worried too much, don' carry tha crutch,' and 'He's happy today, le's keep it tha way.' He could always sense a storm."

Dawlis stared at the snow. He was starting to suspect certain things, Kade was sure of it. Others, Kade was equally sure, were yet beyond his ability to imagine.

"Peis disappeared after the boy died. It was hard to believe, but we thought he might have had something to do with it. He came to Lorel and Shaw's house three spins later. I was there. He was raving. He said tha the boy was alive, tha he'd seen him in a vision. He said, exactly: 'The boy lives. In the future, eighteen turns. In a city built on hills. Blue building, red door, red bridge. Sent by the Mind to know this far place. To return when the Pymm hangs Trimus. Across the Shole toward the city of seven. Scars of beast and serpent. Trailed by a great shadow.'"

Dawlis put a fist in his mouth.

He's here, Kade thought. *Right in front of me.*

"You came from a city built on hills?" he asked the boy. "A blue building, red door?"

"Huh? Yeah," said Dawlis.

"You have the scars?"

"The scars? Yeah, sure." He tried to smile. It was painful to watch. A tear dripped from each eye and streaked the dirt on his cheeks. "She's my mother. My mom. She said she loved me." He grabbed one of the groos and hugged it tight. "I doubted her and hated her this whole time. But when she said it, behind the gas station, I felt something too. It seemed crazy at the time, but now I know it was real."

Kade gave him space. This was enough for now. The letter could wait.

"Will I see her again?"

"Hard to say," Kade replied, and was sure he'd never uttered a greater understatement.

"It was such a short time. It's so unfair." He hung his head, lifted it suddenly. "She saved me, Kade. You should have seen her. My mother … And my father? Can I meet him?"

"He may be on his way already, but he lives very far from here. A very remote place."

"My father …" Dawlis said. He petted the groo in his lap and looked out across the Shole. "This Peis Ota. He saw my future."

Energy coursed up Kade's spine, over his head, and out to his limbs. "We never knew for sure until now."

"What did he mean by the mind? Whose mind?"

"A deeper intelligence. We call it the Mind. The Mind dreamt life, and life was manifested."

"Religion or whatever. The Pymm hangs Trimus?"

"The Pymm is a star."

Dawlis's eyes widened. "A star."

"Trimus is the Pymm's position in the cycle," Kade said.

"The Pymm is the brightest star in the sky." Dawlis pointed west above the mountains. "It will shine about there tonight."

"Yes."

"Kade, that star led me here."

"Incredible." But there was more, and Dawlis sensed it. It made the lines in his brow. Maybe he'd been sensing it since he woke up in that cave.

"He saw my future, saw where I lived, and said that I would be out here and when. That's how you found me?"

"Largely, yes."

Dawlis took a deep breath. "Read me the letter."

Kade sighed and nodded.

17

Will stood on a threshold. On the other side was knowledge, answers to many questions at once, like how snakes could change color and be warm-blooded, why it wasn't winter, why he hadn't seen the moon, and what could cause a hill to collapse, to name a few. Like the door on the roof of the yellow building, this knowledge called to him and scared the life out of him. And like the door, he knew there was no turning back once he crossed over.

"Read me the letter," he said.

Kade translated:

Shaw, Ayn, Kade,

If you're reading this, then you know that Peis was right. I did it. Shaw, our boy lives. I found him in a city built on hills, in a blue building with a red door. Red bridge. He'll have crossed the Shole toward Mon Teles. Peis saw it all across time and space.

Dawlis fell through a hole in our world and traveled to another. Believe it. The hole was inside the cave where I left him. I found another in my fourth turn searching for him on Qol, in southeast Damarra. Shaw, what you saw in your delirium, in the mountains where I almost lost you, what you saw in the stars, that led me to the passage! What do you remember? You were trapped inside your fever, inside your mind. But you pleaded with me to go. So I left you in the care of the Gontoma, and I went.

I did it to keep moving. I didn't expect to find anything. I expected to be back with you before long, and we'd continue on together. But there were clues as I got closer, in local histories, legends, landscapes. When I found it, I was across the world, and I had no way of getting a message to you in that place. And I couldn't turn back once I felt it and saw it. It had gravity, Shaw. An orange glow deep down in a crevice inside the cave. Dawlis must have seen and felt the same. Lover, I had to go. Right then. I'm so sorry. I've missed you every single spin of this world.

This could be another dimension, a different version of our world. They speak English in many places. How else is that possible? But it has to be another system. There are more than seven billion people. There are eight worlds, one with human life. This is Earth. It has a satellite, which they call the moon. I've studied the stars and searched for ours in this space and never found it.

I've been here for seventeen turns of Earth, fourteen Qol turns if Peis was correct in his timing. Well? It seems to spin faster than Qol, but not by much. I came out over a thousand miles from the city, a story for another time. I found the city and the red bridge early on, there's no other bridge like it. The city is vast. I walked every inch of it multiple times. I found every blue building with a red door, but there were several, and new ones were built or painted at times, others were painted over. I know now that he wasn't here when I arrived, but I couldn't have known it then. I couldn't have known where he came out. The passages align with constellations—Shaw, that's what you taught me! I followed the Bolt in our sky to get here, but I didn't have enough information to know which constellation here to follow to look for him. He came here a lost child who didn't know the language. He could have been anywhere.

I searched far, aimlessly, multiple continents. I hoped something would surface somewhere, anything, his picture in a paper, on a website. I searched for passages and found none. I went back to the city many times. I stalked red-doored blue buildings for ten spins at a time, twenty, then I'd leave, too painful to be there. And it crushed me one ninarc in the middle of the second turn as I stood in the ocean looking up at stars I didn't recognize: I wasn't meant to see him until it was time. I broke down on that beach, but it was the first step on a long path to acceptance. I asked myself then and have asked myself a thousand times since—you should ask yourselves!—What is time to the Mind anyway?

I never doubted he was alive. No, when I crawled out of a cave on the slope of a forested hill and saw the moon for the first time, a different sky—there's no explaining it. This was the far place. I was living part of the prophecy. My boy was here somewhere. But I had to wait to see him.

I lived a kind of life. Half a turn in one place, half a turn in another, on to the next. Back to the city for a few spins, as much as I could bear, less and less as time went on. It got harder and harder to be here. I traveled constantly. I couldn't sit still. I felt crazy at times, miserable, bitter. The Mind was hiding him from me, cruel, heartless, timeless! But was it cruel, or was it wise?

I was attacked half a turn past. A tall man, deformed, hunched, slick, violent. He overheard me asking questions about Dawlis. He and his men beat me for information. I had none. He set me loose and has been my shadow ever since. An enemy on another world, Mind! An enemy I know nothing about. I only know that he wants my son. Like the Fenti. Kade, what more have you learned about them??

'In the future, eighteenth turns.' That's how long the Mind made me wait. Then the Mind showed me.

Four weeks past, I risked the city again. I stalked red-doored blue buildings. It was late. I wandered into Golden Gate Park. A woman wearing a gray suit and a mask split down the middle into two different faces was standing on a bench reading from a book about gravity. Reading to people who weren't there. I was lost in a crowd to her—she didn't see me. She spoke of her people. She spoke about black holes. She ended her lecture and left. I followed her home.

I recognized the neighborhood—I know them all—but I hadn't been to this one in many months. I watched her walk into her apartment, then I walked around the block toward the blue building that I knew was there. The red door opened as I rounded the corner, and you stepped outside with a woman. My knees buckled. You walked the other way, you didn't see me. I couldn't speak. Eighteen turns! My son! I knew it was you! You still smile the same! Oh, I left you in that cave!

I got up off the pavement and ran after you, my child, but it still wasn't our time. He drove through the intersection, our enemy. I ducked into a doorway. You turned the corner and disappeared. It took every ounce of my will not to follow you, but if he saw me … It was the hardest thing I have ever done.

He sensed the change in me. I saw his men everywhere after that. I got close to you again, very close, a few times, but I always drew back, terrified of leading him to you. I couldn't risk it. I watched you and waited for a clear opening. I watched the woman too, the one from the park, the one living on the other side of your block. I went to her apartment one night. She let me in as though she'd been waiting for me. I felt the gravity the instant I stepped inside. Mind, Dawlis, you'd been living beside it for three turns! And we'd been living not far from that cave! Did you feel it? Were you drawn? How did you end up there? She showed it to me, the passage.

She calls herself Mana. She was once a professor of physics, a scientist. She owns half the block. Her people have been on this land protecting the passage for twenty generations. Waiting for someone. For us. For you, Dawlis. For me to tell Mana that it's you and that it's time. She is old, her memory is mostly gone. She built a machine in the basement that she says will keep the hill from collapsing. She built a trap door in the roof and a cement tube leading down into the passage, though she doesn't remember why. For the energy to escape, I assume. A great deal will be spent when the passage closes behind you. But it also means that your only way in is down through the roof, and I've seen you staring up at the door, yes! You've felt something! When did it start? The Mind has strange dreams.

I don't know if two can pass at once, and I won't take that risk either. This is being read, so you know the pain of traveling, like being pulled apart and squeezed to death. And Peis called for your return, not mine. I won't tempt prophecy. That was your passage. I'll find another.

I also decided not to tell you who I am. If you knew, you might not have gone, and I needed you to go home. I understand the severity of everything you're going to discover. I understand too what you've left behind, and I'm sorry, Dawlis, but this was all meant to happen. Perhaps you see that now. I trust the others to manage their own shock and disbelief and read this to you when the time is right. I'll find another passage. I suspect that Mana knows which constellation to follow and that I just need to help her remember. Maybe your passing will jog her memory. Regardless, it will take time. I've given you charts, equations, and notes, and Shaw holds the knowledge in his way. Dawlis, you may go looking for one. I understand you didn't ask for this. I understand that your life is here. But wait for me, please. Give us a few spins together, a few phases maybe, the three of us. Please.

'Sent by the Mind to know this far place.' Why? I only know that the worlds are connected. Through passages and through our minds. How else could Peis have seen the boy's future here? How else could I have known that he was still alive?

I won't remind you of Peis's last words. I will only command you, Shaw and Kade, to keep him safe while I make my way back.

Dawlis, I always knew. A world apart, and we were reunited. I'm sorry we missed so much of each other's past, but we have the future.

—Lorel nu si Hayden

Will couldn't move. A thought bludgeoned him: *That is not my sun. That is not my sun.*

"Okay," he said, frantic, trying to blot it out, "what"—*that is not my sun*—"now?"—*that is not my sun*—"what?"

"You should see him."

"Who?"

"Peis Ota."

"Peis Ota. But Elle. I gotta get back."

"Ayn and I will start researching. We can go looking for one, or we can go see him first. You'll have to decide."

"Yeah, just gotta find"—*that is not my sun*—"another hole." Will snatched his headless staff out of the snow and stood. "Let's keep moving." He retreated into his steps and did not speak for the remainder of the day. That night he slept draped over the branches of a tree and dreamt that he was in a plane crash, over and over.

They marched in silence. Late morning, they came to a river at the western edge of the plain. Everbluegreen-covered foothills rose from the far bank and led up to sharp, gray, snow-capped peaks. Will knelt at the river's edge and stared at his blurred reflection. His lips trembled and tried to turn up. He'd done it. He'd crossed the Gray, the Shole. He'd survived. But who was *he*? And where in space was that sun blazing over his left shoulder?

Kade led them north to a narrow bend. He stepped into the frigid water up to the dark green metal disc attached to his dark green metal belt and waved the wolves in. "Come on, this way. Dawlis, wait there."

Will shoved his boys into the water, then turned and stared up at a large, brilliantly white cumulous cloud floating alone. It seemed to grow very slowly, to bloom. It seemed carved out of the blue by a scalpel, not a wisp about the cauliflower edges. But Will understood that if he flew up close to it, he would not see a boundary.

He closed his eyes and watched the pixels flow in dark space. Images formed and faded away into the fractal flux. He pondered boundaries. His mother had written: 'I only know that the worlds are connected. Through passages and through our minds. How else could Peis have seen the boy's future here? How else could I have known he was still alive?'

How else could I have heard Elle's voice? he thought.

He opened his eyes.

"Ready?" Kade asked in English, that language-thread between worlds. He seemed perfectly warm and dry in his fitted brown suit and boots. The wolves waited anxiously on the far bank.

"I guess," Will said, and jumped on Kade's back.

The everbluegreens were shorter and thinner west of the plain than east of it. The foothills were steeper and rockier. The wind had swept the snow into waves, and Kade led them on a sinuous path up through the troughs. He put on his wraparound sunglasses now and again to check a map, which he uploaded and manipulated with what seemed to be an invisible ball in his right hand. They hiked without speaking or barking for the remainder of that day. Jackson and Orly stuck close to Will. Fred guarded the rear.

They stopped for the night. They ate meal-bites from Mick's pack and drank water from Kade's canteen, which melted snow instantly. Will took a hockey puck out of the pack and threw it down in the snow, eyeing the disc on Kade's hip. It was about the size of a CD and only half an inch thick, but it looked heavy in more ways than one. "Your weapon?" Will asked.

"Yes," Kade answered, and there was a great weight in his voice, even in the one word.

"How does it work?"

Kade looked down at it as though at an evil he had no choice but to confront. In one smooth, cold motion, he stood, dropped his left hand to his belt, and threw a haymaker at the air. The disc, which had attached to the back of his hand, fired a thick half-circle of blue-green energy. He slapped it back onto his belt, and a black metal handle retracted across his palm. He sat down.

Will frowned. "Not a lot of range, huh? Why not carry a gun? Those guys back there had guns or something."

"Is called a xim," Kade said in that accent that Will would have had if not for, well … "Protec's me from most fired weapons."

"How do you figure?"

"It emits a field the size of the user tha cools heat charges and deadens projectiles."

Will shook his head. "We don't have that tech where I come from."

You come from here, said a voice in his head.

"Leave me alone," he responded.

"Wha?" Kade asked.

"Huh? Nothing. Wanna light this thing?"

Kade shot a thin sliver of arc at the hockey puck, and up rose an inverted cone of fire.

The hills steepened. The snowy, gray peaks towered. They hiked hard for another day without speaking a word. As the last blue faded to black above them, they slid down a sharp slope into a valley, where they walked along a stream.

Will watched the stars come out in the water. They followed him downstream. He wondered aloud: "How is it that we both speak English?"

Kade just nodded.

Will reached down and patted Orly's head. "Why are the worlds connected?"

"Yes, why."

Two boulders leaning against each other at a bend in the stream formed a triangle cave just big enough for the five travelers. They tucked in. Kade placed a puck in the mouth, lit it, put on his glasses, and took hold of the invisible ball. He tapped and rolled. One of his lenses filled with the map and the other with text or data. He took the glasses off. "No signal still. Soon, I hope." The fire burned in one heavily bagged, still brown eye. The other was in shadow, the eye of a skull.

"You should get some sleep," Will said.

"I came in a flyer, but it crashed. I'm sorry."

Will made wings with his arms. "A flyer? A plane?"

"Yes."

"Jesus," Will said. He'd yet to consider what Kade had gone through to find him; he'd had enough of his own shit to deal with. But according to the story, Kade had spent some meaningful portion of his life looking for Will, or waiting for him to return, never knowing if it was a waste of time. Then it happened just like some street performer said it would eighteen years ago, and Kade was forced to kill someone, and before that, apparently, survive a plane crash.

A poisonous curiosity climbed Will's spine. He shivered. "What's it like?"

Kade stared at nothing. "Ironic."

"Ironic?"

A bird cried.

"There is some unity," Kade said, shoving his thumbs into his eye sockets. "The irony is tha you never feel it more than when you take a life. You rip the fabric tha you are made of. Is pure power and pure misery. You feel the fabric less afterward. But you *need* to feel it."

Will considered suicide for the first time since Needle Valley. He was the cause of this man's suffering. And there was more to come.

Trailed by a great shadow.

"I think this is a beginning," Kade said.

"Of what?"

"I don' know."

"What about Peis Ota?"

"We'll see."

Will lay down on top of Mick's sleeping bag and pulled Orly close. Kade crossed his legs and soon passed out with his head hanging. Will had more trouble falling asleep.

They hiked for two more days and slept poorly for two more nights. Late afternoon of the third day, they crossed above the tree line, topped a rise, and came to a field of boulders that blanketed the mountain for a mile or so beneath a high ridge. The wolves leapt from rock to rock on skinny legs and broad paws. Will followed, draped in their mother's fur. He stopped and looked back at the foothills and the Gray Plain. He searched the horizon for the range at the far end, the one that contained Cave Hill and Needle Pond, though he knew that it was far too far away to see. He felt nostalgic despite it all. The sun that was not his warmed the back of his neck. He turned and pointed up at it. "What do you call it?" he asked Kade.

"Nurin," Kade said.

They crossed the boulder field.

They sat on rocks at the edge of a sky-blue lake beneath the gray ridge. They drank from Kade's flask and ate meal-bites. An icy wind blew across the water as Nurin dipped behind the ridge just a hair too slow. 'It seems to spin faster than Qol, but not by much,' Lorel had written about Earth.

"How much longer?" Will asked.

"Over, then down into the trees again. Three spins."

"Days. To Mon Teles?"

"Yes."

"A city?"

"Yes."

"What is it like?"

Kade breathed heavily. "Is beautiful. We'll be there soon."

"What are you not saying?"

"Another time."

"No," Will said. He wasn't sure how much more he could handle, but he also didn't particularly love having no idea where he was, who, how, or why. He chose an evil. "Just tell me."

"Mon Teles was built in the image of the city Teles."

"Why build a city like another city?"

"Teles is where Gideon the astronomer discovered humans on Gog. There are two planets with human life in this system."

Will had buried it in a hole in his mind, that little nag of a sentence in his mother's letter: 'There are eight worlds, one with human life.' He'd had enough to digest at the time. But Kade had just given him the rude reminder, and he'd asked for it. "Discovered? You didn't populate it?"

"Discovered," Kade said.

"The Goon. He didn't look like one of us."

"Gog doesn' have the technology to get here. The 'goon' was Fenti."

"Gog, Gog." Will tried it out in his mouth and didn't like the taste. Saying it felt like choking. He was about to ask where he could find it in the sky but decided he didn't want to know. "No one from Gog has ever been here?"

"Before I learned how you got here, I would have said absolutely no."

"The holes, Kade. There could be one connecting Gog to Qol."

"The passages Lorel described connect the two systems, not planets within the same one."

Will felt a brand-new kind of pain.

Otherworldly.

He had no idea who he was.

So goddam lost.

But he had to keep going. He had to rip the bandages off these festering, impossible realities. "What happened when Gideon saw?"

"He was burned. The devout would not accept tha the Mind dreamt of a world outside of Qol, cer'ainly not one with humans. But he had an assistant who also saw. Jus' a young man. Very brave. He spread the truth. It was an important time in our history."

"Kade?"

"Yes?"

"They evolved there?"

"Tha is the theory with the most evidence. They have a deep history, though much of it was lost, and we only have pieces of it."

"How could—? Forget it." He wasn't up for tackling that little wrinkle at the moment. "Then what?"

"All resources wen' toward getting there. Wars ended, large ones anyway. The continen's raced each other over generations and ultimately came together. We sent the first satellite seventy-three turns pas' and the first ship nineteen turns after tha."

"*Contact.* Tell me."

"They killed the crew and destroyed the ship."

The wind burned Will's face. He hugged himself. "Why?"

Kade's eyes shook and then froze again. Will wished he hadn't seen it. "They believe they are owed another world. Theirs was hit by a meteor, three pieces, all very large, a little over a thousand turns pas'. Dried a sea. Wiped out all life on one large continent. Eventually wiped out the atmosphere. Slowed the spin slightly, which wreaked havoc in the core, volcanoes erupting everywhere. Altered its relation tc its five planetoids, moons, which wreaked havoc with gravity and tides. The survivors—there weren' many—were forced underground. There are pocket populations now in hives on the other two continen's: a few quiet, religious cultures, a few violent ones, a few slowly fading away. They lead hard lives, all of them. One built massive temples roughly six hundred turns pas'—tha's what Gideon saw—pointing at Qol when they are closest in their orbits, a blue star to them at the time, an afterlife. One group nurtured this faith into an obsession with reaching the star in *this* life. They were vindicated when our satellites arrived. Is them. Is where we firs' made contact and where our efforts have been con-centrated since. Their leader is ambitious, fierce, capable, and deeply loved. She's convinced them tha we have no interest in helping them fulfill their destiny, which is true of half of our population. Negotiations always start up and always fail, and we're as much to blame as they are. But they don' have the technology to get here on their own."

"How do you know all this?"

"We've landed ships since the firs'. We have informants and satel-lites."

Will lay down on his rock. He felt untethered, schizophrenic. His identity was being torn apart piece by piece and replaced with fragments of a fantasy life. He was unknown in an unknown world. "Jesus," he muttered.

"Jesus?"

"Like the Mind, I guess."

"'Sent by the Mind to know this far place.' Think about wha tha could mean, what you saw tha's important."

But Will didn't feel like thinking about it. He stared at the lake until the Guide appeared over the ridge, then stared at the Guide until he fell asleep.

Strange dreams. Obsession over a door. Torn from his life and love.

Woke up in the wild. Nearly died of dehydration. Cave drawings, a symbol of gems, a star.

Attacked and scarred by beast and serpent. Taken captive. Winter when it should have been spring. No moon. A lucid nightmare he was convinced revealed his death. Found out who his parents are. Found out that he disappeared as a child and was prophesized to return by a rhyming street performer. Found out he was on another planet. Found out there were human beings on two planets in this system.

A lot for one mind to handle. Maybe that was why he experienced his lucid terror and heard Elle calling to him out on the Shole. Maybe that was how any mind would react.

He'd been flirting with insanity. Now insanity was flirting back. He'd flown too close to the sun, and his wings were on fire. He'd dug a mass grave in his unconscious for mental zombies that were now eating their way to the surface. He could feel their manic hunger, their psychotic excitement. They threatened as he slept on the rock beside the blue lake.

All the fiends from my worst nightmares are contained in a frozen pond, and I'm walking across it. They swim down there. They play. They eat each other. They torture fish and turtles and snakes. But the ice is thick and covered with snow.

The snow is gone. I slip. A skeleton nymph raps a bony knuckle on the ice and waves up at me. Another scratches at it with finger-knives and cackles. Others attack it with scythes and axes. I run for the shore, but it recedes with every step. A rock drops out of the sky and smashes into the ice—a sound like a gunshot—and lodges inside a spider web of cracks. Another one falls, another. The webs splinter and spread. I run and run, but I'm only waiting for that final rock to hit.

Will awoke in the dark. He wondered how long his dream had lasted in real time, how long his heart had been beating this hard, how much more it could take. Kade sat cross-legged on his rock reading from his glasses. The wolves stirred. They ate meal-bites. Will carved a sharp point onto the end of his staff where the head had once been. When there was light enough to see a few feet in front of them, they worked their way over the boulders to the base of the ridge.

Kade led them up a switchback trail, the first manmade anything Will had seen since the grave where he found the traveler. He might have considered it a good sign if he'd had the capacity to consider anything good. He would have been wrong.

They reached the ridge at noon. Death drop on either side, they hiked north single file toward the trail down. Will looked west and saw nothing but more hills covered in everbluegreens—no city, no Mon Teles—and he didn't care.

The ridge widened around a jutting, angled rock resembling an arrowhead. They rested there and passed the canteen around. Will scratched his names into the rock with his knife: William Lark and Dawlis. Beneath them, a question mark.

Kade gripped his shoulder. Jackson flew into a rage. Three gray-maned, neckless, square-faced men bearing copper axes were running toward them on legs too long for their bodies.

Kade's dark-brown eyes shook in their sockets. They were filled with murder. The ghost of a grin on his blood-flushed lips? "Stay here, Dawlis," he said. "Do not move—do not. Keep them with you." He turned and walked with terrible calm along the curved ridge.

Will held Jackson by the scruff and peered over his head. "Stay."

Kade lowered his left hand to his side, took his xim, and raised it above his head. He brought it down and across his body in a smooth arc, firing a blue-green half-circle. The first Goon raised his axe and charged. Kade threw his arms out, and the man flew off the side of the mountain.

What the hell, Will thought.

No energy arc. No physical contact that Will could see. He snarled at the sound of the Fenti's buzzsaw voice, echoing as he fell: *"Morrarru Dondante!"*

The second Fenti went high, the third went low. Kade defended with deadly composure. His xim was a blur. Copper on blue-green yielded orange sparks. A red line formed on the neck of one of the Goons, and Will's heart broke anew.

"I'm sorry, Kade," he whispered.

Jackson tore himself from Will's grip. A Fenti stepped from behind the arrowhead. Orly clamped down on one ankle, Jackson on the other, and Will stuck him in the chest with his sharpened staff. The Fenti grabbed the staff with one hand and swung his axe with the other. Will ducked and pushed. The staff slipped through his hands.

Fred, raving, spit flying from his mouth, backed down another Fenti, who tripped and fell and clung to the edge of the ridge. Will didn't think. He lifted a large rock from the base of the arrowhead and brought it down on the block face, cracking it open. The bodies tumbled like ragdolls down the side of the mountain, flipping, rolling, breaking.

"Stop!" Will yelled. "Fucking stop!"

They came to rest, and Will fell against the arrowhead and buried his head in his hands. The wolves sat down around him. Kade came back and stood over them.

Some time passed. Some black hole in the present. Will rose mindlessly and walked along the ridge to where Kade had fought. He looked east toward his past, then west toward his dark and uncertain future. He walked back to the arrowhead and scratched two lines, one for each of the men he killed, below his names and the question mark. He offered his knife to Kade, who carved his name, Kade ru sy Bhomik, and seven lines, four for the deaths he'd tallied and three for the guards in white.

18

Will did not speak or eat for two days. He slept very little. Kade poured water into his mouth from time to time and made him swallow.

Every branch that snapped beneath his feet was the Fenti's face cracking. Every shadow was the devil from his nightmare. He kept his head low between his shoulders, his eyes up, and his knife open as they hiked.

Kade set a hard pace. His dark brown eyes had stilled again—and darkened, if such a thing was possible. Will didn't notice much, but he noticed that. The memory of them shaking was etched into his mind forever.

Kade broke the silence on the third morning. "Eat something," he said and held out a meal-bite.

Will flinched. Kade stepped in front of him, clasped a hand on the back of his neck, and pulled him close. "You'll never be rid of it."

Will's eyes welled. "Then I'll die."

"And never see your girl again, or Lorel, or Shaw."

"Let me go."

"Stare it down. It was you or them."

"It doesn't matter."

"No."

"Then how do we live like this, Kade?"

Kade shook his head. "Maybe we saved lives. Maybe we killed so tha others won' have to."

"We killed ourselves."

"A part of us. Not all."

But Will didn't believe him.

From that point on, the pain was sharper and the flashbacks more vivid and menacing. Will tried to collapse into numbness. He tried to confront what they'd done, to stare it down as Kade had said, but there was no healing this and no reprieve. He drank on his own, but he kept his fast, his hunger strike.

They came to a hill taller than any they'd crossed since the ridge. It was late in the day.

"Mon Teles is on the other side," Kade said.

Will looked up. "'Trailed by a great shadow.'"

"You don' cast it."

"You don't know that. There are things I haven't told you."

"Tell me now."

They started up.

"I heard her voice on the Gray, the Shole," Will said.

"Your girl?"

"Yes. Not a dream. Not a hallucination. It didn't come from my head. I know that's impossible."

"Rare, not impossible."

"ESP? I've never had that ability. Neither has she."

"You're sure?"

"Yeah, I'm—" But then Will thought of the bee dream and of Elle's nightmare from that same night, the one of him slitting his wrists in a motel room. Dreams dreamt side by side, signaling the beginning in their own ways. Synchronicity. "No, I'm not sure. But between worlds?"

"The worlds are connected, and there are humans on both. If you heard her, then she could have heard you."

Will stopped. If she sensed him too ... She'd called out: 'Will! Are you there? Will!' If she sensed him ...

But no.

"You can learn to harness it," Kade said. "Peis Ota can help."

"I imagined it."

"Maybe not."

"If not, then she knows I'm alive."

Will took the lead and picked up the pace. He tried to outrun these thoughts, this hope. He could not allow it. The greater his hope, the greater his fall, he knew, for there was another he connected with. "Kade, I've seen the shadow."

"Keep it calm. Tell me."

"Sharks in the water. A man ascending a hill. I can't shake 'em!" The fiends burst from the void, screamed and slashed. Will clawed his way to the top of the hill and fell over into a narrow pass. He squirmed on his back and tore at his eyes.

Kade grabbed his arms and pinned them down. "Steady, Dawlis."

He screamed. A shark brushed his side. The man was close now!

He came to in Kade's arms. The sky had clouded over. The fiends were gone, but they'd be back.

At the far end of the pass was a dull, dark-blue glass egg buried in the snow. Will stood and walked toward it. It grew into the rounded tip of a glass skyscraper, a giant, dormant Christmas bulb sloping down into a snowy forest of everbluegreens. Another emerged from the slanted rock wall on the right, a thick parallelogram of light-purple glass. Farther right and closer to the hill was a sky-blue rectangle with a garden on top. Beneath this was a rose-colored cylinder. On the left was a soft-orange trapezoid, a dark-purple cylinder, and a thin, lime-green parallelogram. Six glass skyscrapers arranged in an irregular hexagon around the center blue one.

"The Seven Spires of Mon Teles," Kade said from behind Will.

The buildings reflected off each other into infinity, a never-ending glass city rising from a never-ending, white-tipped forest. The clouds parted, and Nurin lit up the skyscrapers and set fire to a wide, sinuous river to the south.

Will dropped his head. "It's beautiful," he said, and lay down in the pass. "Let's rest first. Just a while."

He put an arm under his head and looked out. Each building held, in its own luminous hue, the sky, the clouds, the trees, the river, the other buildings. It was resplendent and hopeful and thus it was menacing. Will closed his eyes, opened one, shut it.

He slept hard and awoke before dawn. Jackson was staring at him. Orly licked his face. Fred stood at the other end of the pass keeping watch. Kade was reading from his glasses. There were a few dozen random lights on in the otherwise dark Spires.

"Did you sleep?" Will asked.

"Are you ready?" Kade replied.

A shadow moved across one of the lit windows. A human being. "No," Will said. "But let's go before they all wake up." A brand-new species of anxiety flared in his chest. "Kade?"

"Yes."

"Is anyone expecting me?"

"Only Ayn."

It wasn't much, but it was something.

The trail down was steep, the edge close, the starlight weak, but Will led at a reckless pace. He feared seeing other humans more and more the closer they got to level earth. But there was something other than dread in him. There was a lingering rainbow glimmer, the memory of the city at sunset. The rose aura of the nearest Spire blossomed through the trees as light crept into the world.

A heated stone path, glistening with melted snow, ran along the base of the hills. Will tested it with one foot and then the other. The wolves too hesitated to engage with this bit of modernity. Kade stepped around them and led them north.

A light in the forest drew Will off the path. "Stay," he said to the boys and crept up to a wooden structure built around an everbluegreen. It was two stories tall, narrow, hexagonal. The light inside shone down on a small table set against the trunk and an old man eating breakfast. The man turned. Will ducked, waited a few seconds, then walked quiet and low back to the path.

"A house?" he asked Kade.

"A terub."

Will saw them now, the dark outlines of terubs wrapped around every tenth or twelfth tree, each two or three stories tall. Another light flicked on, deeper in the woods. A network of paths developed. More lights. More shadows inside the terubs moving at the pace of routine. Men, women, and children starting their days. Human beings, here on the planet Qol.

"How many?" Will asked.

"Hundreds," Kade answered.

"All built around the trees?"

"Yes."

An egg-shaped, glass-roofed, puffy-tired vehicle sized for one whizzed toward them from the left and stopped on a dime. A woman in a crimson jumpsuit was sitting inside watching a hologram. She looked up, locked eyes with Will, and seemed to regret it. Kade took him by the arm and shepherded him across the intersection. The egg's wake swept across the backs of their legs as it sped off.

A man in an all-purple suit with rainbow cuffs and a young girl in green with a yellow flower over her heart walked out of a nearby terub.

Two egg cars pulled up, connected like segments of a centipede. The man sat down in the front car, the girl got in the back, and off they rolled. The girl turned, pressed her face up against the glass, and waved. Orly wagged his tail. Will lifted a hand down by his side.

"Where are they all going?" he asked.

"Many to the river, the labs," Kade answered.

Ahead was a dark-blue glass wall, the center Spire. Commuters in jumpsuits, fitted or loose, each a uniform color but for some small piece of personal flare, a blue flame over a red breast, a red bird on a blue sleeve, a green wave across a burnt-orange back, trickled toward the Spire from all directions. Real-life, tired, annoyed, happy, ambitious, lazy humans with things to do and places to be. Will envied them. He wanted to join in their flow and begin the day as they were, with normalcy and habit. Maybe he could start a life here in Mon Teles. Maybe he could learn the language, rent a terub, wait tables, swim in the river when the weather turned.

But of course none of that would happen, for he'd never be normal again, and there was something coming for him anyway. Maybe for all of them.

He stared at his blue reflection, more animal than man. He looked up through the thin band of space between the towering trees and the Spire, up and up to where it scraped a cobalt sky. Tears dripped down his dirty cheeks and into his beard.

Kade placed a hand on his back. "Le's go."

The commuters stared, muttered, parted for the odd party of five. The Spire had no door that Will could see, just a large rectangle of darker blue. Someone snuck past them and disappeared into it.

"Stay tight," Will said to the wolves.

It felt like passing through a thick bubble. They came into a circular lobby with green stone floors and a green stone ceiling three stories high. A column of green stone as thick as a space shuttle rocket was surrounded at ground level by darker green energy doors. Kade pointed to one. The startled crowd made another path for them, and they stepped through the door into a round, silver-plated elevator car, where Will was once again confronted by his reflection, this time very close and very clear.

That is not me, he thought. *My name is Will Lark. I live in San Francisco. I have friends. I go to parties and concerts. I work in a restaurant.*

But there was no trace of that kid here. The furs, the beard, the sallow, dull eyes. Will Lark was dead, had actually never been. It was always a false existence. And whoever Dawlis was, he wouldn't be around much longer.

The green door turned silver. They rose.

"You have to accept what you've done because you've done it," Kade said in a tone of speaking to both Will and himself. "And tha you're here because you are."

Will knew that was true, and he felt worse.

They walked down a curving, wood-paneled hallway lined with cloudy glass windows and arched doors, real ones, painted in various primary colors. They walked long enough to have circumnavigated the Spire twice, it seemed to Will, before the hall split. They took the right fork and stopped at the fourth door.

"Ayn is here," Kade said. He knocked. The door slid open.

She stood up from a large, green, sea-glass desk. Like Lorel and every adult female Will had glanced at on their way through the city, she was at least a few inches taller than him (and Kade, and the men in white, and that guy who got into the egg car with his daughter, and the male commuters, etcetera). She wore a loose-fitting, night-blue jumpsuit with three stars on the inside of her right wrist. Her eyes were large, violet, crow-footed, exhausted, and smiling. A mess of thick black hair tied atop her head drooped to one side. She came around the desk and held a hand out to the wolves. "Wha do you call them?" she asked in English tinged by the local accent, that something European that definitely wasn't.

"That's Fred," Will said, pointing. "Orly and Jackson."

Orly stepped forward and accepted a scratch behind his ears. Jackson sniffed her thoroughly while deftly avoiding her hand. Fred walked to a corner of the room and plopped down beside a smaller sea-glass table and two sea-glass chairs. There were no windows.

Ayn touched her forehead with the tips of her right thumb and fingers, then held her hand out to Will palm up as though offering something. "To see you, Mind," she said. Her eyes widened and twinkled like amethysts catching some internal light. "To find out that Lorel is alive and tha she led you here."

So, she knew that he'd seen Lorel. Which meant that Kade had been in touch.

"I found a signal a couple of spins past," Kade explained without having to be asked.

"Did you call for a ride?"

"I called it off. You needed time."

"What if there were more Fenti?"

"I took the risk."

"I'm sorry for what you've been through," Ayn said.

So was Will. He took a seat in a glass chair, but he didn't take a load off. The load was good and on. "Look, I did what she said. I found you both and made it here. But I gotta keep moving and eventually get back. If this guy Peis Ota knows anything, let's just go."

"Is all arranged," Ayn said. "But have a real meal firs'. A shower."

Will could suddenly smell himself. "Shower?"

"Follow me."

They rode an elevator up and stepped out into a small village of shack-sized, opaque, sapphire-blue, glass boxes. Muted music leaked from one on their left, chimes from one on their right, voices from another. Ayn led them to one near the wall of the Spire. Inside it was a sink, a cushioned chair, a small table, and a shower stall. Will didn't look back. The wolves followed him in.

"Take your time," Ayn said. "When you're done, I have something to show you, and we'll eat." The door slid closed.

Will took off his buma hat and patted his filthy, matted hair. He stroked the mother-wolf fur, then shed his skins and Earth clothes and buried the traveler's journal in the pile. The shower turned on when he stepped in. He sat down in the warm water and held his knees.

19

Ayn tracked the storm in one lens and Kade flying straight toward it in the other. "What do you think?" she asked in Korial.

"A few bumps," he replied.

"Careful." She breathed. "Soon, Kade. He's out there."

"We'll know for sure."

He'd had his doubts from the very beginning, which was entirely understandable and forgivable. But he hadn't seen Lorel in that moment eighteen turns past. They'd been digging for three spins with no sleep. They'd long since given in and were just trying to find the body. When something came over Lorel. Or got her attention. Or touched her. Ayn saw it happen, saw her face twist in confusion and hope. Then the bang on the door. And when Peis burst in and told them that the boy was alive, it was like Lorel already knew.

Ayn had gone back to that scene in her mind many, many times during the long wait, whenever she needed a reminder of why she'd chosen the life she had. She went back to it more and more as the Pymm drifted closer to Trimus in the eighteenth turn. Now the Pymm was in phase.

"He's out there," she said again, when her glasses went dark.

"Kade?"

Her chest tightened.

Mind.

She slumped in her chair.

Is this . . . ?

Guard satellites didn't just black out. Her feed was cut.

Trailed by—

She called Mays.

"Overseer," he groaned in Korial, rubbing sleep from his eyes.

"I'm blind."

He was awake now. He swallowed, blinked. His fingers flew over his keys. "Which one?"

"Number four."

"This is too much."

"Be light on your feet."

"I'll clean it up."

"It's very important that you do."

"Are you going to tell me why? I'm in harm's way, Ayn."

"Soon. Find me another eye please."

He shook his head. "I can get views of Mon Teles, nothing west. They're locking down over there."

"Find something not guard. Whatever you have to do."

"Just like that? It'll take time, maybe a lot, and no guarantees."

"I need it as soon as possible."

He switched off.

Ayn had been living a lie. There was not a soul in Mon Teles and very few anywhere else who knew her real reason for showing up there eighteen turns past. What they thought they knew was that a friend of hers and that friend's son had died and that she'd left home to distance herself from the tragedy. It was a sad story, perhaps truer than she hoped, and she'd leveraged it very effectively. But what Peis said that ninarc stayed between those present. Lorel made sure of it. She put a knife to his throat and promised to slit it or anyone else's if they spoke those words again. No one outside of that room could know her boy was alive.

It was the first spin of the rest of their lives. Lorel, Shaw, and Kade took off that very ninarc on the long trek to Fentum to find those responsible. Maybe they'd find Dawlis there. Maybe Lorel and Shaw wouldn't have to wait eighteen turns to see their child again. Ayr stayed in Trill. She knew virtually every man, woman, and child within a hundred kels. She could trade drinks for information with any number of questionable characters. If there was anything to learn at home, she'd learn it. But no one and nothing surfaced.

The others, though, found clues. They made it to the northern cap and were attacked during their second ninarc in the port city. An old Fenti man hid them out and helped them escape. He told them that they weren't the only foreigners to have come there recently. Another had been seen hiking in and out of the hills over the past turn. There were villages up there still, he said, though very few since the meteor.

They went looking for this other, a bald woman with a limp (that was everything the man knew about her). She left a trail that smelled faintly of something to do with the attack, a trail that crossed continents and led them nowhere. There was always something that turned out to be nothing. Lorel would never stop, and Shaw, though he didn't believe as she did, would never leave her side. Kade went back to Fentum several times. He lurked about the villages in the hills. He found nothing but the crater.

Ayn spent two restless phases in and around Trill asking questions and running searches. In vain. And it came to her one ninarc as she put the first drink to her lips. It seemed obvious in hindsight: she should go to where Peis expected Dawlis to show up in eighteen turns. Check it out, at least. Maybe she'd find something important there. She didn't expect to plant roots and wait.

But that first ride down the river infected her, the glowing Spires rising from their forest garden. She started slow. They all wanted answers, but the hard truth, if Peis was right, was that they had an excruciating amount of time to wait; and Ayn had to live a life, even if she was now partly living a mystery.

She worked as a fisher and kept close to the river for most of her first turn. She fixed terubs for a while after that, farmed a bit. Eventually she made her way into the labs, where she worked maintenance and was introduced to the other half of the Mon Teles population, the scientists. She made friends wherever she went and left her employers disappointed every time she changed jobs. She drank with whoever was drinking.

She didn't have a goal, not at first. She built relationships and kept her eyes and ears open. She did favors as often as she could and never asked for any. It wasn't until Lorel disappeared, four turns after Dawlis, that Ayn finally chose a career and moved closer to the Spires.

Kade said that it was time to move on, that Lorel was dead and for nothing because the boy was too. But he hadn't seen the change come over Lorel that ninarc. Ayn had. Lorel *knew*. The boy would find his way to Mon Teles, somehow. And Ayn would be running it when he did.

Three spins, and she was still blind. She hadn't slept more than a few thin wedges of arc. She hadn't been home to see the girls. Mays worked tirelessly, but there was nothing he could do. There were no private satellites within range of the Shole, and the guard's were now impenetrable.

But something was off. The code, Mays said. The updated defenses. They were anonymous. All guard code bore the signature of the coder so that they could track who was responsible for what. But not this code. And no one seemed to know about the hack. No one in May's former-guard tech network and no one in any of Ayn's. They fished carefully. They came up empty. It begged a number of questions. Corruption in the guard? Someone on the inside who'd also been watching and waiting? Someone who knew the timing and was trying not to draw attention?

Mind.

It didn't make sense, but none of it ever did.

We were always in shadow.

And Ayn felt it growing inside of her as she waited and waited.

Seven spins and nothing. She left her office in the Spire Stilter to use the bathroom, shower, and have her nightly drink in the Spire Yune. She kept her meetings but changed them all to virtual. Ayn, a woman who valued in-person conversation above all else in politics and management, didn't trust herself to be face-to-face with anyone. Her staff were confused and concerned, but she chose not to trouble herself with that. She had enough trouble.

Mays still wasn't getting anywhere. She told him to keep trying, but he finally lost his patience. He got angry on the seventh ninarc and demanded to know what was going on. He hit her right in her weak spot with those pouty brown eyes, that scowl, those full lips, and that tousled brown hair. She'd been taking and giving nothing. She needed to take a little bit more. She told him to come to her office. She forced tears into her eyes, made love to him, and said she'd tell him everything very soon.

Maya and Zee had devolved from worried to worried sick to just plain scared. This according to Mycah, who was now threatening to take them to their father's. Ayn had left them alone plenty of times before but never for this long. She went home late in the arc on the eighth spin, ate a few bites of the dinner that Mycah had cooked for three, held Zee in her lap for comfort and protection from her older sisters, apologized and deflected and told them all many times that she loved them. Then she climbed up to her room and passed out. Mycah was sitting in the chair beside the door when Ayn came down in the early arc. She stared hard at the floor, tapped a foot, and waited, without hope it seemed to Ayn, for an explanation. Ayn said that she loved her and to tell her sisters as she walked out.

The head of her local guard made his regular report for the third time since she'd lost contact with Kade. For the third time he said nothing about a flyer going down in the mountains. It meant that no satellite had picked up or that one had, and it was being covered up. Maybe he was in on it and maybe he wasn't. She didn't know what to think or who to trust. She needed more information. She needed to talk to Kade. Except Kade was dead. It was the only explanation for him not being back yet, with or without the boy.

But that potential devastation had a dangerously sweet-smelling mercury lining. It seemed in support of the prophecy, the final dark line. It began to feel very real to her: a budding fear and exhilaration, a loaded spring, a weapon cocked. Every time she imagined seeing the boy again, she imagined what followed him. She imagined that she was marked for death too, Shaw as well. She indulged in the darkly romantic idea that they should all four die in service of keeping the boy alive. Maybe that was the meaning of the shadow.

But on the eleventh spin since losing her connection, Mays broke through.

"Ayn."

"Yes?"

"I don't have eyes, but I have data, and you have messages from someone called Kade."

A blue square appeared in her right lens. She sucked in a breath, held it, blew it out, blinked open the note, and read in Korial: "I have him. Peis was right. He's seen Lorel. She found him, sent him here. I don't know the place he came from or where she is."

Ayn threw off her glasses and crumbled, imploded, burst into tears. She laughed uncontrollably. All of this time she thought she believed, but nothing could have prepared her. All of this time working for her dead friend only to find out that she too was alive and had been the one to find her only son.

She wiped the snot from her nose. She eyed her glasses warily, put them back on, and kept reading: "My flyer was sabotaged. The Fenti figured out the timing somehow. They've been waiting too. They're working with guards, Ayn, be careful. The guards may be pawns. Three of them and one Fenti found Dawlis before me. The Fenti killed the others, turned on them, I think when he confirmed who Dawlis was. I killed the Fenti. Four dead already. Dawlis told me how he came to the Shole. I recorded his story. Listen for yourself. It's three spins since I left. This will send when I find a signal. We're on foot. Send a flyer. We're on the line of the Pymm."

The sound of Dawlis's voice sent Ayn into another fit of crying laughter. The boy now a man! And the way he started, with mention of his love! But how erratic his tone and emotion. How crushing the brevity of his time with Lorel. But: "Alive!" Ayn screamed, without a care for who might be passing in the hall.

Nearly killed in this place called Sanfransisko. A door, a forest, a symbol of gems, three groos, the Fenti, the guards. Ayn was consumed. She should have sent a flyer immediately, but she would have to be very careful how she went about that, and she couldn't bear not listening to and reading every note first.

The next file contained a picture of a note, six pictures, six pages, accompanied by a one-line preamble: "It explains certain things, perhaps."

Ayn read Lorel's note. She shut her eyes, rubbed the knot in her chest, and breathed. It was always going to be this way if Peis was right.

Unfathomable.

But another world? It wasn't true. It couldn't be true. Could it? She'd start learning everything there was to learn. She knew which scientists to ask, and they didn't have to know why she was asking. She sped through the rest of Kade's messages, updates on their position, speculation on the Fenti-guard connection, scattered thoughts on what to do next. And then: "Attacked again. Five more Fenti dead. Dawlis killed two. He's nearly lost his mind. Don't send a flyer. We're two spins away, and we need time. We'll get there."

She took her glasses off and laid her head down on her desk. Her head throbbed. Her face and eyeballs were burning hot.

The Mind has strange dreams indeed, she thought, a line from her friend's letter.

She fell asleep but didn't dream. She woke up deep in the ninarc to another message from Kade, this one current: "We're in the pass. He wants to rest first. We'll be there first light."

20

The water pelted, sharp and warm. Will listened to its soft hiss and stared into the blue-tinted, sparkling spray bouncing off his head.

He got out, dried himself, and dressed in every layer of his clothes and furs down to his buma socks. He held onto his buma hat. The wolves stood, yawned, and stretched. There was a dark circle beside the door. Will passed a hand over it, and the door opened. Ayn and Kade were standing beside the nearest sapphire box.

"Hungry?" she asked.

Will nodded.

She led them to the elevator. Inside, she put a hand on his shoulder. "Kade told you tha Mon Teles was inspired by another city, Teles," she said.

"Yes," Will replied, and held her violet gaze. She was exhausted and afraid, but she was fighting it. She was a friend of his mother's, and she'd waited for him, here in the city of seven.

"The original Seven Spires are towers of a brown, stone cas'le on a hill," she said. "Inside the cas'le is a very large hall lined with colored glass windows depicting the history of the world as understood at the time. A creator is portrayed as an eye, a consciousness without form tha we call the Mind. When I was made Overseer, I had the images re-created on the top floor of this building, our Spire Stilter."

The elevator stopped. A green door appeared, and they stepped through into crystal, midnight-blue sky. A twenty-foot-high wall of stained glass circled the silo, a mosaic in one color, tens of thousands of pieces teeming with internal light. Floating at eye level was an eye in darker blue, fist-sized, simple curves, looking internally or seeing through. Will stepped forward and touched it, touched the sky. He wanted to fall into the blue and float off into oblivion. Ayn took him gently by the arm and led him along the wall.

The sky brightened as they rounded the silo. Nurin blazed from on high and poured a great, diffuse triangle of light down on primordial soup. A story of evolution followed, a version any earthling would have understood: microscopic animals, rains and floods, green plants, larger animals, extinctions, resurgence, metamorphosis, all glittering and radiant and all culminating in the shadows of a man, a taller woman, and a child contained within a circle of light. The eye peered from each of their foreheads.

A gap in the wall led to a second circle of mosaics, these pixelated images of migrating peoples, wars, harvests, famine, ships, theater, music, other hallmarks of civilization and culture, and last, the Seven-Spired brown stone castle standing on its hill and surrounded by a walled city. The story ended here in the original Spire Stilter, Ayn explained. But she'd commissioned the last three hundred turns of history for this installment.

The first image on the third wall was of an old man with wild gray hair, wild eyes, and copper spectacles standing at the base of a telescope. Gideon the astronomer. His assistant, a lanky tween with twinkling brown freckles and eyes stood beside Gideon studying a map of the stars. Above them was what they'd seen in the lens: a cragged coastline, a churning gray-blue ocean to the west, a colorless continent to the east, three volcanoes down the coast, and six square structures arranged in a semicircle around the center volcano. Will had never seen anything so unreal.

They continued on. Molecules vibrated. Constellations scintillated. Nine crests, the emblems of Qol's island continents, made a circle in starry space peppered with satellites. A silver triangle spacecraft approached Gog.

A fourth wall glowed white from floor to ceiling and around the curved edges. It felt like walking along the edge of infinity. "For the future," Ayn said.

Will twitched.

"Is not your shadow," she said.

"You don't know that."

"Maybe you're back to help us figure out what it is. Tha makes more sense to me. Maybe is our responsibility, yours, Kade's, mine, Peis Ota's, Lorel's, Shaw's."

A shrouded figure formed in the white nothing and marched up a hill toward Will. He bit his lip until the pain broke his stare, and death disappeared.

"Let's eat," he said.

"One more thing."

Outside the blank white canvas was the blue outside wall of Stilter. Will walked to it and pressed his forehead to the glass. The light-purple parallelogram (the Spire Yune, Ayn said), the sky-blue rectangle (Jhule), and the rose-colored cylinder (Qwi) stood sentry over the snowy ever-bluegreen wilderness, reflected it back, and shone with the late-morning light of Nurin, the sun that was not the sun.

"I'm sorry for wha you went through," Ayn said. "But you're here. You survived."

Will looked at her and felt something other than pain.

This is my path.

She pointed to a table covered in food.

Will gorged in silence. He then stood up and walked along the wall, found a couch, and lay down. Orly jumped up and settled between his legs. Fred and Jackson curled up on the floor. He closed his eyes and hugged the traveler's journal, snug against his stomach beneath his layers.

KADE WATCHED DAWLIS DISAPPEAR around the curvature of the building. He stood up to follow, but Ayn grabbed his hand. "We're alone," she said in Korial. "I closed this floor."

He sat back down and nodded gingerly. His head felt like it had been split down the middle by a Fenti axe.

She leaned in. "You did it, Kade. Thank you. I'm sorry for what it cost."

"I'll be fine," he said, though he was very unsure about that. "It's him we have to worry about."

"She's alive. She found him and sent him back."

"Incredible."

"On another world?"

"She said she jumped into a hole in the ground. She went somewhere. And I've never heard of Sanfransisko."

"I've run searches through a hundred databases. It doesn't exist."

"We need to understand if it's possible. She said the passages align with constellations—the Bolt—and have gravity. We have her charts and notes."

"I think I know where to start, but I'm going to have to break our promise."

"Who?"

"Mays. We can tap satellites and search for gravity... aberrations. We can tap guard records on other planets. He has a gift, and we need it, and I can't lie to him much longer."

Kade knew she was right. "Only Mays. At least until we see Peis."

"Agreed."

"We also need to know the origin of English."

"*Yes.*" v

"I'll talk to the Nimar."

"Good."

"And the symbol that Dawlis saw in the cave."

"I'll take that. Don't worry. Rest."

He squeezed her hand. He stood and walked around the building until he could see Dawlis and the groos. He sat in a high, glass chair facing them, put his head back, and closed his eyes.

21

Ayn took a single drink each ninarc in a small, warmly lit restaurant called Alden Lu situated just above the tree line in the Spire Yune. Alden Lu was shaped like a wave. Tables lined the inside of the crest, which was covered in an ocean mural, an underwater scene chock full of colorful life. The base was the flat, light-purple glass wall of the Spire. Hanging on the wall were three rows of green glass shelves lined with clear bottles arranged by the color of the liquor inside, a sepia rainbow. Beneath the shelves was a pristine wooden bar. Yune was all offices and labs, and so Alden Lu, a bustling establishment during the arc, got very quiet once Nurin dipped behind the woody horizon. The few dinner patrons were scientists working late on any given ninarc. Ayn was the only regular.

The first drink she ever had there was her first in six turns, four turns past. She'd just been named Overseer, a development that was causing her no small amount of chest pain. She'd accomplished her goal, but *now* what? *So* what? What had she been doing all this time? What was she going to do for the next four turns? Would it even matter? What would her supporters think if they knew she was waiting for a boy whom she had told them was dead? What would they think if they saw her now with a drink in her hand? The fact that she'd lived at the bottom of a bottle for a time and then achieved and maintained sobriety was something she'd convinced them to appreciate about her. But she stepped up to the bar in Alden Lu that ninarc knowing it was over.

The bartender was a dark-haired, dark-skinned girl of twenty turns named Ruve, born and raised in Mon Teles. She was beautiful, too beautiful to be working ninarcs in a mostly empty restaurant for scientists. "What are you doing here?" was the first thing Ayn ever said to her, in their native Korial.

"Helping people," was Ruve's response. "What are you doing here?"

"I need help," Ayn said.

Ruve recognized her, of course. "It's my first spin on this job too. What a coincidence. But I've helped people at other establishments all over this city." She started wiping down the already immaculate bar.

Ayn looked over her shoulder. They were all alone. She got up, closed and locked the door, then sat back down and looked up at the rows of bottles. "It's been a long time."

"I know," Ruve said. "Take it easy. I've got something for you. You only need one."

Ayn exhaled.

Yes, just one.

That made it seem not so bad. "I'm in your hands."

Ruve lifted two sparkling glasses from beneath the bar and placed them on top. She walked to one end and came back holding a small bushel of herbs, a green stone dish, and a green stone muddler. She turned the bushel over in her hand and plucked a few choice leaves, flavoring the air with fresh mint. "It's called a Bell," she said. "It'll warm you and clear you up."

Ayn felt it happening already. She felt her guilt lifting.

Ruve placed the leaves into the dish and mashed them with smooth half-twists of the muddler. "Three ingredients," she said. "Fin, which can be harsh, I know, but I source quality. Juni, which you can get anywhere. And tree sap, in this case local surim." She let the juni pulp sit. She turned and took a bottle of brown liquor down off the top shelf. "They combine in a beautiful way if you get it perfect. But you don't want a lot of this, trust me."

"Whatever you say," Ayn said.

Ruve took a spoon and a knife from a holster on her belt, rinsed them, dried them, scooped the juni pulp from the dish and scraped a carefully sized dollop into one of the glasses. She then opened the bottle of fin and poured it in a thin stream around the inside edge. Smoke, wood, and mint flooded Ayn's nostrils. She stared at the tiny scraps of green leaf floating in the liquor and salivated.

"The flavor and effects of a Bell can vary a lot," Ruve said as she conducted her chemistry in the other glass. "Depends on where you get your fin and your juni, to an extent. Really, though, it's about the sap. Some cause hallucinations, for example." She reached beneath the bar again, lifted a small jar of amber surim, put it down, and placed her hand firmly on top. "Listen. You commit to only one, and I'll help you. I think you'll find one is perfect, but I need to hear you say it."

Ayn didn't hesitate. "I promise." It was the only answer.

Ruve mixed the final ingredient in silence. She let the drinks breathe, then, at long last, pushed one of the glasses to Ayn. Ayn picked it up, hesitated, drank.

Ruve must have gotten in perfect. Ayn felt settled, calm, and stimulated at the same time. She felt no shame. She confronted, in her mind, the bizarre source of her apprehension. She'd been building up to this for fourteen turns. She'd run for Overseer so that when the time came, she would have this city at her disposal, and she'd done it. She'd put herself in position. The boy was out there somewhere, and he'd make his way there in four short turns. And Lorel, who had always known her son was alive and had died trying to find him, would sense his return from the other side and be at peace.

Ruve leaned on the bar and took a sip of her own Bell. Ayn smiled and thanked her. Ruve blushed. They talked for the time it took them both to finish their drinks, then for a short while longer. They came to know each other one drink at a time over the next four turns in the mostly empty, warmly lit, wave-shaped restaurant.

A single drink each ninarc. Ayn had made that commitment to Ruve and never once had a problem keeping it. Even as the Pymm drew Trimus in the eighteenth turn since Dawlis's disappearance. Even when Kade was out of touch.

But early in Nurin's arc on the spin that Kade and the boy arrived, Ayn felt the true urge coming on, the old, familiar demon. She was physically, mentally, and emotionally spent. The wait was over, but it seemed like they were just getting started. Peis Ota had actually seen the future. Lorel was *alive.* Corruption in the guard. The Fenti. The shadow? Ayn wondered if it was contained outside the borders of Mon Teles, or if it had already crept inside, for something was creeping around in her mind.

She slept the arc away in her office and awoke in the dark. She messaged Kade. Dawlis was still asleep, he said. So she went to Yune, to Alden Lu.

She stared at the bar as she approached it, avoiding eye contact with the two women eating dinner and the glass bottles watching her from their perches. Ruve came out of the kitchen door in the tip of the wave and cleared the women's plates. Ayn stared into the gleaming wood and summoned patience.

"You don't look so good," Ruve said, suddenly there. The two women were gone.

"No?" Ayn asked.

"No," Ruve confirmed, wiping the bar.

The bottles glowered.

"Lots on my mind," Ayn said.

"That's two of us."

"You first," Ayn said. It came out desperate. She scratched her nose.

"Me first then," Ruve replied, placing the glasses on the bar. She walked away and returned with the juni, the dish, and the muddler. She selected her leaves and started crushing. "Well, my famous friend, I'm not quite sure how to say this, so I'll just say it. I'm thinking of getting out of here." She turned and reached for the bottle of fin.

Ayn played it off internally as meaningless coincidence. She suppressed the *feeling,* because she didn't like it, not one bit. "Timely," she said.

"Timely how?" Ruve asked, scraping the juni into the first glass, then pouring the fin.

"Leaving me? What am I going to do? But no, that's good. It's great. I'm proud of you. You were always too beautiful and talented for this place."

Ruve cleared her throat and reached down for the surim. "It's not a big deal."

"It is. I'll miss you."

Tears welled in both women's eyes.

"Yeah, me too," Ruve said.

"Where?" Ayn asked.

"I haven't thought that far. I kind of like the idea of just going."

"When?"

"Soon. It's scary though."

Ayn pictured herself alone at this bar, alone in Yune, alone in Mon Teles. Everyone gone, including her daughters. Everything empty. Just her and these gawking, whispering bottles. "Change is good," she said without conviction. She was ready for her drink.

Ruve dipped her little spoon into the jar of surim, lifted it, and held it over the first glass. The amber goo slid slowly to the end, hung there, dripped. She twisted the spoon, severing the string and dosing the drink. She dosed the other. "I hope you're right."

Ayn raised her glass. It felt too heavy. "To change."

The glasses clinked. Ruve took a sip.

Ayn nearly did. "What made you decide? Why now?"

Ruve's cheeks reddened. "You know me. I'm a practical girl. I don't believe in anything I can't touch. But I had a dream recently. Kind of scared me. Made me think about dying here without ever seeing any-place else."

Ayn went cold.

It's here, in this very room.

It was seeping into their minds, like the surim infusing the fin.

How deep does this thing go?

Ayn was no longer interested in the wakeful buzz of a Bell. She didn't feel like opening up and confronting her fears. She wanted to drown them and feel the burn. "Ruve, I'll take it straight tonight." She tapped her fingers on the bar until the drink was poured. She had three in total, straight hard spirit for the first time in ten turns. Ruve drank both Bells out of obligation; she wouldn't leave a perfect Bell sitting on the bar. They made small talk. Ruve complained about a stomachache. From having two, she said. But one sip would have done it, and Ayn had put the glass to her lips

PART FOUR

THE ISLAND

22

Will passed from some unconscious realm. He'd been dreaming of something important, though he immediately forgot what. A man, a shadow—Kade?—stood over him and said, "Time to go." Will closed his eyes, lowered a hook into wherever he'd come from, tried to fish out the dream, sighed as he realized it had swum away.

One wolf slept on either side of him, another under his legs.

"Time to go," the shadowman said again.

"Okay, I got it." He tried to get up, but Orly crawled on top of him. The man leaned closer, breathed heavily. "Please." The wolves pinned him and growled. He fended off the shadowman with his mind, as sharp, cold teeth bit down on his neck.

He awoke to footsteps. It was dark. The wolves stood beside the couch pointing, sniffing, quiet. He hugged his knees. "That you, Kade?"

"Le's go," Kade said and dropped a pack on the floor. "Different clothes, put them on."

"I'm not—"

"Do it. Something's happened. I'll explain."

Will went along. He didn't love the murderous calm in Kade's voice. He traded his furs and Earth clothes for a fitted microfiber hoody, pants, and gloves, all black to Kade's brown, all light and heavy at the same time. He changed behind the couch so Kade wouldn't see him pull the traveler's journal from his waistband and bury it in his clothes in the pack. He slotted his knife and lighter into opposite inside breast pockets, then zipped up the hoody.

Kade led them quickly and quietly around the circle mosaic walls, hand on his xim. They spiraled down through the nothing white future and through history toward the elevator. Before passing through the energy door, Will looked back over his shoulder at the first mosaic, at the eye floating in midnight-blue space.

The elevator dropped. Will tightened the straps on his pack. The wolves' claws clicked on the metal floor. Jackson stepped up next to Kade as the wall turned green. They ran down a winding hallway, through an empty common room, up two flights of stairs, and then down another hall, which dead-ended in a white door with a small triangle window. Kade touched the door with the thumb and four fingers of his right hand, circles of light appeared around each digit, and the door slid open. It closed behind them, and they looked back through the window at the same time. A spindly man in a polished green jumpsuit and a brown, round-brimmed hat stood in the intersection. His eyes were hidden by the brim. His smile was not. He waved and put a thin-fingered hand around his throat.

Will pulled his knife. The wolves took his cue: sniffed and growled. Kade stared, weighed. His eyes trembled. "No," he said. "He can' get through here." He spoke a message in Korial into the computer wrapped around his wrist, turned, and took off.

They sprinted down a wood-paneled hall lined with red, elliptical doors. Kade chose one and opened it with his fingers. They stepped into a small white chamber where columns of blue light came up out of the floor and surrounded them. Will touched his and got zapped. Orly yelped. The columns disappeared, and the far elliptical door opened.

They slalomed through a maze of cloudy glass cubicles, all white, all empty in this early hour except for one where a guy was sleeping with his head on his desk beneath a hologram of what looked like a particle spray. They passed through another white chamber where they were surrounded by blue light again. They ran down a narrow, curved, bright-yellow hallway lined with square, sky-blue doors, each adorned with the same small painting of an everbluegreen. The doors and paintings streamed by endlessly, and Will started to lose his cool. "I need some air."

Kade stopped and opened one of the doors. Inside was a clone of Ayn's office. Kade sat in one of the two glass chairs set around the glass table in the corner. "Get them under and keep them close," he said.

Will didn't ask questions. He grabbed Orly by the scruff and dragged him under the table. Fred and Jackson took the hint. A set of light keys appeared on the surface. Kade tapped something. "Hold on," he said.

They dropped into a silo. Will held his head in his hands.

"Almos', Dawlis."

They stopped dead. The door slid open. They were in an underground bunker. An orange metal pill the size of a small train car floated inside a frame of silver beams, which disappeared into tunnels on either side. A gap opened up in the beams, and an energy door in the pill. They passed through the bubble.

Will tossed his pack on the floor and collapsed onto a couch. The wolves sniffed around for danger. Kade walked into a booth at one end, and a few seconds later the pill started moving in that direction.

He came back. "They tried for Ayn," he said. "A girl was killed."

Will told himself that he didn't hear that. If someone was dead, then it was probably his fault—he should never have dragged his shadow through Mon Teles—and so no one was dead. He sat up, banged his elbow on the orange metal wall, and an oval "window" appeared. Blurry silver beams streamed through the dark. "Where are we going?" he asked, though he didn't really care.

"To see Peis Ota."

"Oh, yeah. Then you'll help me get back," he said, though he knew that wasn't going to happen.

"If tha's what you decide."

Will pretended that he was inside a blue cocoon of energy and that no more bad could get in.

"Is a long trip," Kade said. "This is the firs' leg. There's food and water there."

Will didn't see where Kade pointed. He watched the silver beams and scowled when the pill lifted and shot out into sunshine—*Nurinshine, starshine, whatever,* he thought—flying through a silver trestle, snaking through bare, snow-covered hills made bleary by their speed. He hated it. It was cheating. He wanted to be out there on foot, just him and his boys. He wanted to go back to the time when all that mattered was food and water and warmth, the time before prophecies and murder. He touched the wall, closed the window, and pulled Orly up onto the couch.

An hour later, maybe two, maybe three—time was strange and useless— the pill slowed. Will sat up and opened the window again. A mile or two off was a sheer, green rock wall split by a canyon. In the snowy mouth of the canyon was a dome of rainbow glass. Will had a second to wonder what the hell he was looking at before the pill slipped underground.

Kade stepped out of the booth. "We're coming to a station. There'll be people."

Will sighed.

The pill stopped, the energy door appeared, and the sounds of bustle assaulted: a washed cacophony of footsteps and voices and machines going *phoom, phoom, ph-ph-phoom.* Will stood, put on his pack, tapped Jackson firmly on the nose, pointed at Fred and Orly, and said, "Stay tight."

They fell into foot traffic. Travelers jumped, stared, sped up, or slowed down upon seeing the wolves. Will kept his eyes on his feet. He saw through the wood floorboards to another trestle. He looked up at a layered web of silver connected by wooden scaffolds crawling with humans. Pills of different metallic colors, some singles, some strung together by invisible bonds, magnets maybe, pulled in and out of the station through tunnels in the green stone walls or zipped through without stopping like electrons through wires—*phoom, ph-ph-ph-phoom*—leaving chemtrails.

They climbed a wide flight of stairs and walked diagonally toward the center of the station. Thick rays of primary and pastel light shone down through a column of space in the web. They reached it and looked up, all five of them, at the underside of the glass dome set into the yawning cavern ceiling like a giant's jewel. Light painted the edges of the silver beams and poured down onto a sitting area three stories below, benches surrounding a box of water walls surrounding a metal bird sculpture, all tinted rainbow. Two little girls ran through one of the walls, squeaked and squirmed with delight, touched the bird, then ran out again. Will wanted to cry. He wanted to go down there and sit on one of those benches, bask in that colored light and soak in that joy. He wanted to get out of there as soon as possible. Kade took him by the arm.

They reached the outer wall, turned left, and walked along it beneath floating holograms: abstract art, nature scenes, news maybe, ads maybe, Korial streaming in closed caption. One showed an enormous oval fish tank filled with people wearing wet suits and fins and swimming through an obstacle course or playing a sport. Fans watched from stands outside the bowl. Will tossed it into his box of Qol curiosities in the back of his mind and shut the lid.

A guy about Will's age stood beside a single blue pill just inside the mouth of a tunnel. He wore loose, hemp-like pants, leather boots, and a thick leather jacket that was too big for him. He looked as out of place amongst these several hundred monochrome-jump-suited travelers as the wolves did and as Will would have if he'd been wearing his furs. He had caramel skin, long, dark hair tied back in a ponytail, a widow's peak, and small eyes. He seemed more than a little uncertain about the five coming his way, and Will couldn't blame him.

Kade touched his forehead with the thumb and four fingers of his left hand and then held it out to the man, palm up. Ayn had made the same gesture to Will in her office. It meant, she'd later told him, *My mind is open to you.* Or, *I present my mind to you.* The man reciprocated, though his heart didn't seem to be in it.

Kade looked at Will. "He's called Baly. He's native to where Peis Ota lives."

Baly presented his mind to Will with a terse tap on his forehead and a flick of his hand. He already didn't like Will, and he didn't try to hide it. He'd clearly come here with priors. Maybe he knew the prophecy. Maybe everyone did where they were going. Will didn't offer his mind in return. He was sure that Baly wouldn't want it.

"This is Dawlis," Kade said.

"Will," Will corrected.

"These are his, ah, groos."

Baly looked down at the wolves, shook his head, and cocked a thumb at the pill. "Ready, yeh?"

Will took a seat in the back. Kade leaned against the wall next to him. Baly went in the booth, came back, stepped around the wolves, and stepped up to Will. "Nima declined the Cooperative," he said. "Never forget it, yeh. It's very rare we have foreigners." His accent was some island mix of New Zealand-ese and Jamaican. His tone was threatening.

Will put his elbows on his knees and rubbed his forehead. "Maybe we should just start moving."

But Baly wasn't done. "Disturb nothing while you're there," he said. "Leave with nothing but your memories, yeh, which stay between you and the Mind." He stood with his arms crossed, expecting some sort of response apparently. But what exactly was Will supposed to say? It wasn't like he had friends on this planet to blab to, and he'd be dead before long anyway.

"Okay," was all he offered.

Baly took a step closer. "We know that Peis has waited for you. We're not afraid, yeh, but you should know that many voted against taking you in."

Will stood up, looked Baly deep in one of his little eyes—green—and thought he would very much like to destroy it like he did the chameleon snake's. "I'm not exactly thrilled about any of this."

Kade put an arm between them. Baly walked off into the booth and shut the door behind him. Will sat down, opened a window, and stared out at the rainbow light beams pouring down through the silver web. He thought about the little girls and hoped to God or the Mind or whatever that he hadn't pulled them into his wake. He held his breath as the light and the station were sucked away into the shrinking eye of the tunnel.

"Is not just talk," Kade said. "The Nima rules."

"That's fine," Will said. He very genuinely didn't give a shit. One thing did bother him, though. "He speaks good English."

"The Nimar have for roughly three hundred turns."

"We should look into that."

"I plan to."

"Maybe I wasn't the first," Will said.

Kade's eyes were cold brown marbles. "Is possible."

As in possible that English didn't spawn on two worlds. Possible that it was passed between them.

Kade pointed to a waist-high column in the middle of the pill. "I wan to show you something." Five circle keys lit up on top of it as they approached, four in an arc and one below for a thumb. Kade tapped, and a white hologram cube popped into existence above the column. He tapped some more, and the square became a large, piebald landmass surrounded by ocean. A continent. "Damarra," he said.

It looked to Will like the crowned head of a cyclops. A bulge in the middle of the hilly east coast was an ear. A dark-blue lake just west of the range and roughly the size of Massachusetts, if Will's sense of scale was at all attuned, was the eye, droopy, off-center, and staring at him. Above the eye were two scars, tall mountain ranges that extended west out of the hills, diverged, and faded across a snowy brow. Red forest filled with a couple hundred green lakes made a festering rash on the left cheek above a thick, tan stripe resembling a bandage. It had a blue, V-shaped smile and a broad chin covered in thin blue veins. Another range ran in a wide band up and down the entire curved western coastline. Snow-capped mountains dwarfing all others formed the crown.

A red dot appeared in the eastern hills.

"You started about here, I think," Kade said. "Not far from Teles, Dawlis."

Teles, the home of Gideon and his assistant and the big brown castle.

The dot slid right to left, out of the hills and through the valley created by the scars, Needle Valley. It crossed the brow, the Gray Plain, the Shole. It paused at Mon Teles, just inside the western mountains, then passed through them to the pill station near the coast. It was eleven hundred kels across the northern region, Kade said. Will asked him how many kels he thought he could walk on a good day through deep snow. Based on the answer, Will guessed that Damarra was something like fifteen hundred miles long. He'd walked more than half of it. He'd endured. And perhaps it couldn't have been or shouldn't have been any other way. Perhaps all the pain had been necessary. If Kade had been there to greet him outside the cave, flown him straight to Mon Teles on a warm plane, and broke the news to him gently over a couple of beers that, *Hey, you're on another planet,* and, *Hey, that stalker was your mom,* and, *Hey, there's this prophecy about you,* he wouldn't have believed any of it. He had to sleep in the everbluegreens, get bit by a furry bastard, and get slashed across the belly by a buma. He had to experience winter during spring, sense the loss of the moon, find the wolves, find the traveler, and find the symbol of orange gems.

But then, there could be no purpose in killing. He'd never be able to justify *that*. Self-defense or not, he still heard the Goon's head cracking.

His hand hurt. He was biting it. Kade pulled it away from his mouth and said, "Now I'll show you where we're going."

Will ran a finger over the teeth marks. "Okay, Kade."

The dot moved south through the western range, turned in along the bend of Damarra's jaw, then followed one of the two primary rivers that formed its sharp smile down into the veiny chin, where it stopped.

"Here in the delta," Kade said.

"Zoom in."

The rivers converged just north of a lone, cone-shaped mountain, flowed around it on either side, and then splintered into dozens and hundreds of tributaries.

"Where exactly?" Will asked.

"Only the Nimar know where their villages are."

Will reached out and touched the delta. Somewhere in there was the man who saw him coming.

Why did you go down there? he asked the prophet. *Into that maze?*

"Zoom out," he said. "All of Qol."

Kade tapped. Damarra rushed away. Nine island continents floated on one half of the planet like puzzle pieces separated by curved and crooked bands of sea. Damarra was farthest north and east. The largest was twice its size, the smallest the size of Texas. Ice capped the poles. The rest of the planet was covered in a single immense ocean.

Will flicked the hologram and sent the world spinning. "Further."

Qol flew backward into space: a marble of blues, greens, and browns wrapped in a patchy white blanket.

"So much like Earth," Will said.

"It couldn' be any other way," Kade said.

Sure, Will thought.

It made sense that two planets supporting human life should be very similar. It made a lot less sense that there were two planets supporting human life. And actually there was a third, though that one had apparently not been fit for some time.

"The others," Will said.

Nurin burst from the left edge of the hologram, a burning half-circle a couple of shades lighter than the sun. White semi-circular lines marked the orbits of six satellites, three of which were visible. One, the farthest from Nurin, was a swirling blue and purple gas giant. Qol was second from the star. The third was a gray rock. Qol and this dull world hung beside each other at the end of their ellipses.

"Gog," Will said.

"Yes."

"What is it called?"

"Wha?"

"The system."

"Mantari Nurin."

Mantari Nurin.

Will walked away and lay on a bench. He shut his eyes and was back in the Chief's cave looking at the black drawing of two planets close together in their orbits. Beside that was the one of the harbinger of his death walking up a hill.

23

The pill flew through a trestle across an ocean of grass coated with starlight. A glimmering river bent away from the trestle, toward it, away again. The pill slowed and stopped. Outside, two rails of blue light lit the underside of a small plane. The energy door appeared. Baly walked out. Kade went next. Will breathed and looked down at his boys. "You know the drill."

They relived themselves in the grass, the four of them side by side. The grass came up to his knees and their bellies. They'd sprouted. They resembled young men. He was painfully proud of them. He knew they'd be fine without him, and that hurt very badly, but it was good too. It was as it should be.

He searched the western sky for the Guide. It took him a breathless moment to find it, for they'd turned from his path, but it was there. Then, slowly, carefully, sweat popping out on his forehead, he scanned the dome of space from west to east and found the other star in his life, a grayish one bigger than all the rest—the size of a pinhead instead of a pinprick—floating alone in a black pond. It had been behind him the entire time, from Needle Valley to Mon Teles. Trailing him. He never knew. The spear point of his obsessive focus had been pointed west. Well, he saw it now, Gog.

The plane was green metal with a wide, flat body and a fanned tail. Twin hulls floated above the blue tracks. Baly was already inside. Kade lifted the wolves and passed them through the energy door one by one, their heads disappearing, then their bodies, then their tails. Kade grabbed hold of handles on either side of the door and pulled himself up and in. Will took a moment. Breathed. Smacked himself in the face and jumped aboard.

There were three seats on either side of a narrow aisle now clogged with wolves. "Sit," Will told them, though only Orly complied. Fred and Jackson tried to push past him and get back out. He shoved them down the aisle, took the seat across from Kade and behind Baly, and opened his window. The plane started up with a gentle hum, and they were off, flying low across the land of Nima.

It was patches of black jungle carved by starlit waterways. It was large swathes of land, islands as big as Alcatraz and as small as cars, wiggling streams, foaming rapids, and calm, glassy rivers. An immense triangle shadow in the distance, framed by star-dusty sky, was the lone mountain. Will hunted for and found not a single building or light. It was vast and dark, Nima. Its vastness and darkness oppressed and saddened him. This was a one-way flight.

Somewhere in here, he thought.

He was resigned to it, but it was hard. He was scared.

The plane dipped a wing, and a pair of blue tracks lit up in a field below. A trio of torches represented three lives Will was about to touch.

They landed. Baly jumped out. Will put his head back and took a few deep, shaky breaths. Kade stood in the door looking at him. "Give me a second," he said. He clipped his knife to the back of his underwear, dug through his furs in his pack, touched the traveler's journal, then buried it again. He listened through the door.

"Tigo, Baly. Everybody's here?" a man asked in English. "Call it out, man." He had the same accent as Baly. "Call" sounded like "coal."

"Everybody's here, yeh," Baly reported and sounded none too happy about it.

Will jabbed a finger at his boys, then jabbed himself in the chest. "With me." He went first.

Two men and one woman stepped forward as he hit the ground, stepped back as the wolves did. They didn't seem scared or surprised—probably they'd been warned that there'd be three wild animals tagging along—but they weren't taking any chances. Like Baly, they were all roughly Will's age.

Maybe they're struggling with their identities too, he thought and almost laughed. *Maybe they're going through one of those quarter-life crises.*

All had caramel skin and black hair. All carried sheathed machetes hanging from leather belts. The men wore loose hemp pants and nothing on top. The woman, half a head taller than everyone there, wore loose hemp pants and a vest with a single button between her—

Will felt something between his legs that he hadn't in a long time, then shame.

The guy who'd spoken to Baly, dreadlocks, chiseled jaw, and light brown eyes, presented his mind to Kade. "Long time. Tigo, man."

Kade presented his in return. "Tigo, Fo. We're grateful to be here."

Fo introduced the other man as Ton and the woman as Jovi. Will stayed at the edge of the torch halos and avoided eye contact with the Nimar and that button.

"Dawlis, yeh?" Fo asked.

"I prefer Will," he answered, eyes on the grass.

"Will, yeh. Tigo. Welcome."

Will scratched his beard. "Thanks."

"You're here to see Peis, yeh. We don't know why, and as far as we can tell, neither does he. It's been a long time, and we haven't spent it wondering about you. But you should know that many of us believe in prophecy."

"This is a mistake, yeh," Baly said.

Will curled his hands into fists and looked up at the Nimar from under his brow. Fo hesitated. He was sweating this. They all were. Because they believed in prophecy. "No, we voted," he said to Baly. "We owe it to Peis, yeh." To Will he said, "It's proven true so far, so? You have some darkness. We all do. I hope you confront it. Our home is open to you now. Steep yourself in it, yeh. Take time to know our history. Take nothing with you when you leave but your memories, which stay between you and the Mind."

"I promise," Will said, and hoped that was enough for them to leave him the fuck alone. They did, for now. They yielded to the path unfolding beneath them, to the cosmic wind shoving them along. They turned and walked into the jungle.

They passed through a tunnel of thick, ten-foot-high stalks with broad, waxy leaves to the bank of a narrow river. It was lined with trunkless trees, a thick tangle of splicing, wavy tentacle branches reaching up and out over the water and seeming to drink of it through bamboo-like tubes hanging down. Three canoes were pulled up on a muddy bank at a gap in the branches and the *drinking straws*, as Will thought of them. Kade and Ton stepped up to the longest canoe.

"We take the groos," Kade said.

"Not a chance," Will replied.

"Tha's the way it has to be."

He was hiding something, but Will conceded. It wasn't worth pissing off the Nimar and maybe having to talk to them again. He lifted his boys up and dropped them into the canoe.

Man, they're getting heavy, he thought. *Goddam, I love them.*

They launched. Fo and Baly took another of the canoes and shoved off next. That left Will and Jovi, who pointed to the front seat of the last once and placed her torch in a ring on the outside of it. Will sat. She pushed them into the current and hopped in. Clear, royal-blue water flowed through the flame's corona.

Color of the sky after sunset, Will thought and figured there were worse places to die.

"It's not a free ride," Jovi said from behind him.

He turned and picked up a paddle. He did not look at that button. The river split. Fo and Baly, arguing in hushed voices, took the lead and led them down the left fork. Kade and Ton followed in silence. Jackson stood in the middle of their canoe staring back at Will. Fred and Orly were lying on the floor.

The river split again, this time into four streams. They took the center-right one, which widened and snaked and split again. Will, whose sense of direction was so bad he had trouble navigating the grid of Manhattan, was already lost. The sound of rushing water grew in the foreground.

"Hard row now," Jovi said. "Directly across."

"Directly?" Will asked as they were fed into a rushing river a quarter-mile wide.

"Come on, yeh. I heard you have some fight in you."

Will didn't feel like fighting, but he wasn't going to slow them down, and Jovi's shouts of "Pull! Pull! Pull!" into the back of his head got some adrenaline going. Fo and Ton called the pace for their respective boats, and the voices echoed as the three torch-lit canoes cut across the royal-blue water beneath the stars.

They reached the far shore and slipped through the straws into a creek barely wide or deep enough for the canoes. Here beyond the drinking trees were ones with great wide trunks and arms nearly as thick that started ten or twenty feet off the ground and spread out over it. Will named them the *Nima trees* and was fantasizing about sleeping in one when a roar up ahead snapped him out of it.

"White water, yeh," Jovi said. "Just do exactly what I tell you."

"Okay," he said, then yelled, "Jackson, sit!"

Fo and Ton's canoes reached the end of the creek and were sucked away to the right. Will and Jovi turned the corner and fell into the rush. Will touched the water with his paddle, and it nearly flew from his hands.

"Dig, man. Right!" Jovi called.

He dug. His wrists almost snapped. The canoe slammed into a boulder.

"Left now, left! Left! Right!"

The torch went out. Will listened for Jovi and tried to feel the river beneath him. He dipped his paddle in time with her calls, felt it catch. They picked up speed. They were in control, then out of control, in tune with the frantic rhythm of the river, then tossed around like a piece of driftwood. Will loved it, the chaos, the thrill. He hated it. He knew he wouldn't die on this river, but somehow death felt closer. He lost track of time.

The river slowed. The blood pumped in his temples. The other canoes slid smooth and straight through the darkness up ahead. "Kade?" he called.

"They're fine," Kade answered.

Will needed to be with them. "Let's go. Let's catch up."

"Easy," Jovi said. "Not far now, yeh."

Will laid the paddle across his legs and scratched his beard.

Not far now.

The canoe lurched, and he was thrown. He surfaced in time to see Jovi rounding a bend.

"Sorry, man," she said. "Just on the left. Nice ride."

He swam ashore to a sinuous stream flowing through a stalk tunnel.

This is it.

The last leg of his path.

He walked along the water's edge and came to a lake. Drinking trees lined the shores. A constellation of torches floated inside the trunk-thick branches of the Nima trees to his right. A rope bridge crossed a narrow river on his left. Beyond the bridge was the triangle mountain, black and far away. In the center of the lake was an island.

A whistle pierced the silence. Will snapped his head around. The lake rippled onto a patch of muddy beach where a torch and a bent stick were sticking out of the mud. The stick was pointing at the island. Will swallowed, stepped into the water, and pushed through the drinking straws toward the beach. He stood in the mud and looked out, terrified and knowing he had no choice. His fears, like the demons from his dream of the frozen lake, were scratching and pounding on the weakened walls in his mind. He shook his head and tried to fling them out. Another whistle invoked his lucid terror, which rose from the depths of his unconscious. Before it could breach, he dove into the lake.

He'd never swam so hard and so well. His legs were propellers, his hands were webbed. He didn't breathe for a long time. It almost felt good, the cool water.

But halfway to the island, his lungs and muscles demanded rest. He stopped and tread, and something moved beneath him, something large and fast. Tears welled in his eyes, and he started forward again, gentle as a black swan. His hammering heart betrayed him. The creatures could hear it! One brushed his foot, and he took off in a blind panic, slapping at the water. Another swam beside him, pulled away. Another crushed his left hand. Bitten! His darkest dream come true, the sharks from his lucid terror. He shrieked and flailed, smashed his head, clawed at a boulder, and pulled himself up.

He looked at his inflicted hand. It was cut and bruised and shaking, but there were no fingers missing and no teeth marks. Blood trickled into his left eyebrow. Across the lake a village of torch-lit huts rested like tea lanterns in the sprawling Nima trees. People were gathered in small groups at openings in the drinking straws and looking in Will's direction. He turned away.

He was at the edge of a field of boulders. He stumbled across them toward the island. The black water jumped and snatched at his ankles. He made it ashore and climbed a grass-covered slope that might have been in Marin County and might have been on some other world. He took a path into a forest, where the imps and devils from his nightmares grinned at him from the trees, swirled and moaned, blew in his ears, and swiped at him with skeleton claws. And Will teetered on the edge of insanity, not for the first time since waking up in Cave Hill.

A floating flame. The wraiths screeched and wailed with hatred and hunger. Will uttered a single word through trembling lips: "Mother?"

"Not your mother, my long-lost brother," said a man. "Come with me. It's time to see."

The rhyming. It was the prophet. He draped Will's arm over his shoulder and led him up the island through the trees. The ether seethed outside of the torch's halo.

"Keep them away," Will begged. "They'll kill me."

"Look them in the eye," Peis said, "and they'll die."

"I'm not ready."

"No one ever is."

They walked into a cave, through a large chamber, and into a small room. A candle burned beside a mat of reeds. Will lay down and held his knees. Peis lifted his head and put a bowl to his lips. He drank a thick, bitter fluid.

A breath. Darkness. Peis's voice: "The way to day is through the night." The door closed and locked.

A warmth dripped down Will's throat and into his chest. His head and limbs tingled. A matrix of energy flowed before him, and for a moment he felt serene.

But in the next, a pair of snake eyes bloomed from the pixels, searching for him. Demons circled in the living darkness. He held his breath. They couldn't see him.

Nothing. Silence. Then the Goon's face cracked open and splattered him with blood and brain chunks.

He screamed. The snake struck, and the demons closed.

KADE SAT IN A HIGH HUT watching and listening to the deliberation below, the groos asleep at his feet. The entire village was down there, men, women, and children, two or three hundred Nimar crowded inside a semi-circle of torches open to the lake, where the Tiralee waded in equal numbers. They whispered, murmured, speculated. They'd been told there would be visitors, and all above a certain age knew the prophecy, pieces of it at least, variations. But a great deal of time had passed since Peis had wandered into their land spewing visions, and some needed to refresh their memories.

"Here to see Peis, yeh?" a young woman at the edge of the crowd asked whomever.

"That's it," replied an elderly male.

Baly spoke up then, reciting the prophecy word for word and sharpening his voice for the last line. This was the boy, he said, there was no doubt. One had only to look into his haunted eyes to see the darkness preying on him. Jovi countered with what she knew of him, that he was an orphan and a true survivor who'd crossed the Shole on foot. Someone asked where he'd been all this time, but no one knew, and this gaping hole in the history did not sit well. The number of voices and their volume grew until Isulu, standing in the water, raised a bony finger, and silenced them with a shrill whistle that Dawlis would have recognized. She knew the whole truth, she rasped, and she would tell them if they would keep their mouths shut and their minds open. The Nimar took seats in the dirt, the Tiralee waded closer to the shore, and everyone got quiet.

She began with how the prophet earned his place in Nima, a story they all knew some version of; but it had mutated over time, and Isulu meant to dispel any myths. Peis had crossed into Nima without permission, yes. He'd been hiking the hu when they caught him and dragged him away. He resisted, but not in protest of his capture. He begged them to leave their homes on the slope. The hu, he said, dormant for an eon, would blow and soon.

"We sensed nothing," old Isulu said, scanning the crowd, daring any to contradict her. "The hu gave no warning. Any who say otherwise are lying. And he seemed mad to some, yeh, but I saw it in his eyes. You all know what happened. Many of you were there. It happened fast, but we were already on our way. Not a soul was lost."

Still, they'd been rattled by how close they'd come, she explained. Rattled too by Peis's prescience. Many sought to put as much distance as possible between themselves and the hu and this seer. Some traveled farther than others, and they formed new villages throughout Nima.

Isulu led one group south. Peis went with them. They came to this lake and found it home to a tribe of Tiralee, whose ancestors—and this never ceased to inspire wonder at the workings of the Mind—had come to Nima around the same time as their own, roughly three hundred turns past. The Tiralee had seen, heard, and felt the eruption. They welcomed the Nimar without hesitation. Neither people had a need for the island. Peis took a liking to it and was given it in thanks.

Isulu paused in her telling, having come, Kade knew, to the part of the story most concerning to the Nimar and Tiralee presently: to why Peis had come to Nima in the first place. He hadn't intended to, he'd insisted. He'd simply left his home, traveled in a direction, seen the hu rising from the horizon, and thought it seemed as good a place as any to wait for a boy who'd died but wasn't dead. Then the hu growled to him in a dream.

"What now?" bellowed a Tiralee from the water.

"The hu vision proved true," cried a Nimar. "And now this one, yeh. What if the boy brings real darkness? Why should we bear it?"

Yes, send them all away.

No, we owe it to Peis. He told us who he waited for, and we let him stay.

Maybe he's stayed long enough.

Maybe the boy only needs to confront his shadow. We all do. He might be as important to us as Peis has been. Consider how long Peis waited just to see him again.

Yes, consider, Kade thought. Eighteen turns, and for what? Who was Dawlis? What would he be to any of them?

Sent by the Mind to know this far place.

There was some purpose. There had to be.

Maybe we killed so that others won't have to.

That was what he'd told Dawlis after the ridge. But he didn't believe it himself. It was nothing but hope. It was wishful thinking. It was a desperate need to believe that they'd snuffed something out before it even started.

Kade sat down then, crossed his legs, closed his eyes, and dove head-long into the brutal work of reliving his killings. He stared them down one by one, the first in the Fenti port, eighteen turns past, the next on the Shole after the long, long wait, the three on the ridge. The furious, guttural screams. The flayed flesh and spraying blood. The dying inside with every death he dealt. He played each scene over in his mind several times and then sealed his sickness in stone, stone that he knew would someday crack open. But he judged himself and Dawlis justified.

Dawlis, who was now likely in the throes of his own confrontation with what they'd been forced to do. Kade had been through the same in Peis's cave after his first.

He stood as the Nimar and Tiralee called the vote. In the end, they tied their fate to the man who came to their land at the perfect time. The stars were aligned after all. Who were they to deny the stars and the Mind that dreamt them?

WILL LAY WRITHING on the floor of the cave, clawing at his eyes and swatting at the air. But these defenses were useless against his tormen-tors, for they came from his mind, or *through* it.

Every one of his insecurities broke from their unconscious dungeon and dragged him down. Every painful childhood memory. Every lonely moment. Every regret. Images of Elle bludgeoned him with what he had and what he lost. Stinking, hot, coppery blood poured from the snake's eyes and into his mouth. The moon flew away and left him for dead.

He felt reprieve. He was coming up for air.

Then the sound of rock on skull split his mind like a rip in time and sent him spiraling back down into the abyss.

Into his lucid terror:

He lays horror-stricken in his childhood bed. The shadow scrapes his spine with an icy claw. Hellions from dark dimensions, realms underlying the universe of stars and life, crash through the windows of the orphanage, which are the windows of his mind, rip him apart, and feed on his soul until there is nothing left.

He is an empty mind floating in space. He's as small as an atom and as big as a galaxy. A star pulses, rushes toward him, and grows into a circle of light. Inside it is the goddess from his other recurring dream. The circle is the mouth of a cave. This is not a dream. It never was. It is a memory, his first. The woman is Lorel. The cave is where she hid him as a child of two turns before rushing out to fight their unknown enemy.

She kisses him on the forehead and leaves. Something tugs on his mind, some gravity. It draws him farther into the cave, to a crevice in the floor. Far down is a faint orange glow. He jumps.

24

Will opened his eyes. Inches away from his face was a perfect teardrop candle flame. A soft orange universe. A hot womb.

He sat up and rubbed his eyes. He interlaced his fingers behind his head, arched his back, and opened his chest and shoulders in the best and most painful stretch of his life. He stood. The blood rushed to his head. He put a hand against a wall, steadied himself, looked around. His pack in a shadowed corner. The mat, the candle, a wooden door with a wooden knob. He flexed the fingers of his left hand, scraped and sore but fine; fingered the cut on his head, tender but clean. He reached down and touched his toes, stood upright again, kicked a foot into each hand, and pulled. He did his groin, his calves, every stretch orgasmic torture. He did them all again. He took his time. Every inch of him hurt, his mind was spent, but he knew where he was and who.

He opened the door and walked out through the chamber and the mouth of the cave into the harsh light of day. Shielding his eyes, he sat on a log beside a fire and waited for them to adjust. Beneath the canopy of his hand, he saw the hemp pants and brown, black-haired feet and ankles of another man sitting on another log. The man was stirring a pot. It was the prophet, Will knew.

Peis Ota dipped a wooden ladle into the pot, scooped steaming stew into a bowl, and handed the bowl to Will. Will, famished, didn't hesitate but didn't rush. He savored the rich, spicy steam, the peppered gravy, the tender fish and vegetables. After a few bites, he lifted his head and took in his surroundings.

They were in a small clearing outside of the cave. The clearing was encircled by low trees with narrow trunks, peeling bark, and lime-green, maple-shaped leaves, rustling in the warm morning breeze. Will named them the *birchmaples*. The prophet was a small man, very tan and very lean. His hair was thick and disheveled and jet black with pinches of salt. His eyes were small and dark and close together. Will leaned forward over the flames and the pot, met those eyes, and said, "I killed two men, so I killed part of myself."

Peis nodded solemnly.

"They would have killed me. I had no choice, but it's hard. I feel like I've severed some connection." He paused. "I lost my girlfriend, I know that now. I want to call to her if I can. I'd like your help."

A line formed between Peis's thick, black eyebrows.

"I'll never meet my father. My mother I saw only twice that I remember, but I'm grateful for that." Will stood up and bathed in Nurin's warmth. He felt wiped out but clear, like a field after a storm. He was not happy or sad or angry. He looked down at Peis. "You can see the future?"

"Two times I've seen across space and time," Peis replied in English. He had no accent. Or it was a blend of too many planet Qol tongues to discern.

"Do you know mine?" Will asked. He himself did.

Peis shook his head. "I saw you in the past. I feel the future, but it's vague. I don't know what happens from here."

"I'll die soon, but it's okay. I'll do what I can."

"Why do you think that?"

"I know it. I dreamt it."

Peis looked into the fire. "It's never felt that way to me, but we'll see. Seems strange that you would come all this way and not stay."

"'Trailed by a great shadow.' Your words."

"But I don't know what they mean. I only sense the shadow like you do. And you've fought those that cast it already."

"It's my shadow."

"You're sure? Sent by the Mind to know this far place. That's been your purpose."

"And what is my purpose now?"

"What did you see while you were there?"

"I only lived my life."

"But no, the enemy was there too."

The Bird Man, Will thought. The race through the city. It seemed like a lifetime ago. It seemed like a meaningless, gratuitous act of violence. But maybe Peis was right. Maybe there were people Will met or things he saw in San Francisco or earlier in his life that could shed light on the ruthless riddle he was living. But how could he remember? How could he know now what was important then? "The worlds are connected," he said.

"Yes, and you discovered that."

"Why are they connected?"

"Yes, why."

Will thrummed with something less than knowledge and more than a hunch. "The Chief's symbol. He placed it in my path. I've believed that since I saw it."

Peis closed his eyes, lowered his head, and held it in the tips of his right fingers and thumb. He breathed deeply once, twice. "Yes," he said. "Kade described it. I've seen it before, in some old book, I'm sure, but I can't remember more."

"Find it."

Peis opened his eyes. "I will."

A bell tolled in the distance in Will's mind. It evoked Needle Pond, revealed to him by a flash of Nurin's light; the rain that saved him; the Pymm hanging Trimus directly above the cave in the pink, purple, and blue aftermath of the sun comet; the symbol of orange gems burning for that brief window of time the next morning. None of this coincidence but *synchronicity*, meaning, purpose in him finding the symbol and carrying it like a torch to the prophet's island. And maybe before the end he'd remember something else important, something in support of that unresolved implication of the prophecy, that the Mind had sent him to Earth for a reason.

But that was it, and that was everything. It was not a specific thing he saw but the fact that he saw anything at all, that he *traveled*. It was the absurd truth that there existed another world of humans and that these two worlds were connected, through passages and through a few finely tuned minds. Will was just a lonely messenger.

He gripped the totems hanging around his neck, the two fangs and the karma stone, and looked down at his shadow. "What now?"

"We hope, and we assume the worst," Peis said, a dark twinkle in his dark eyes. "We begin a regiment, physical and otherwise."

"Let's start. I've stretched already."

"Stretch again, my friend. Far and hard you've traveled, it's true, but I'll work muscles you never knew."

The prophet then proceeded to guide Will through myriad, deliciously painful yogic bends. Fifteen minutes later, Will had never felt more limber in his life. He jumped up and down and ran in place as though testing new legs. "Ready," he said.

"Keep up and ask what you want. I have questions too."

"Peis, wait," Will said and presented his mind to the prophet. "It's very strange to meet you."

Peis smiled like a wily old fox. "I knew I'd see you again. But to actually *see* you."

"Tell me about your vision."

"Follow me."

Peis led at a jog down the island through a path in the birchmaples, light on his feet, spry as a grasshopper. "I had forty-one turns," he said. "Never had a vision before then and only one since. But I always had a sense for certain things. I know when a storm is coming." He leapt and snatched a birchmaple leaf off of a high branch and landed in stride without a sound. "The force was tremendous when you went through. The hill collapsed."

"Collapsed," Will repeated. That unfortunate side effect of passing between worlds. He pictured Nob Hill a rubble-filled sinkhole with a single bloody, dusty leg sticking out of it. Elle's. But no, she would have been at work still. And the owner of the building, a woman who called herself Mana, according to Lorel's letter, a senile former scientist, had built a machine in the basement meant to contain the gravity and keep the hill from sinking.

Will could only hope, knowing he would never forgive himself. He could only wonder, had he felt it all along, the gravity? 'Mind, Dawlis, you'd been living beside it for three turns! Did you feel it? Were you drawn? How did you end up there?' And who the hell was this Mana? All compelling questions, none of which he expected to find answers to in this life.

"This energy," Peis intoned, cutting left onto another path near the bottom of the island and starting back up. "My mind was struck, emptied. I went insane. I wandered the woods for three spins. On the third ninarc, I came to a black lake and saw you in it. I knew it was you immediately, you in the future, standing by a window. An insect clung to the other side. You walked out of a red door in a blue building. You rode in a vehicle across a red bridge, and I saw the city built on hills."

Will stopped. "You saw the bee."

Peis Ota turned. "Bee?"

"The insect. I had a dream about a bee that killed a boy. I woke up and found that one on the window. That was the day after I first noticed

Lorel. Jesus, Peis, that was the day you saw me. And the bee on Earth is an archetype of death and rebirth."

"An archetype?"

"A symbol from the unconscious."

"Deeper Mind."

"We're talking about the same thing."

Peis lowered his head to his fingertips and peered inward. The fox smile grew. "One Mind dreamt both worlds."

Will's subtle body purred. "The minds of people on both worlds have access to the same collective unconscious."

"One Mind."

Peis had seen Will across time and space. Will had seen and heard Elle. How was that possible without some substrate of energy common to both worlds? It didn't matter what they called it. The Mind, the collective unconscious, God, Allah.

It's where our dreams come from, Will thought. *It's been there all along.*

They stood outside of time for a holy moment.

Then time returned. The birchmaples, close on either side, fluttered and sighed. They looked at each other and started down.

They came out of the trees on the western shore. Before them was the field of boulders that Will had crashed into and stumbled over in his delirium the night before when Nima Lake was a phantom-shark-infested black abyss. Now it was a shimmering, bottomless, royal-blue revelation. A school of silver fish deep down cut toward the island as one, cut away, and flashed their scales. Nimar children played outside of the drinking trees along the far shore beneath the treehouse village; their splashing and laughter echoed across the water. Will and Peis walked north along the rocky shoreline to the base of a broad grassy slope, the one where Peis had rescued Will from the wraiths. It was steeper and taller than Will had been able to appreciate when those things were trying to eat him. He appreciated it now as the prophet turned and casually started running up it. Will, expecting to have difficulty speaking before long, asked a few questions at once. "What happened after, where did my parents go, and why did you come here?"

"They dug," Peis said. "For three spins, the time I was missing. Lorel, Ayn, Shaw, Kade, many others from Trill. My vision came, and I ran to them. Kade and Shaw threatened me—they thought I might have had something to do with your disappearance. Lorel let them, but she watched me closely. There was hope in her eyes. She knew I was telling the truth because she felt it too. A mother's intuition. And for all their digging they should have been able to find your body."

They reached a grassy flat beneath a dull ridge of rock that breached the island's mossy top like the back of a whale in a green river. Will clasped his hands behind his head and tried to breath. Peis turned on his heels and started back down. Will, dejected but not wanting to be out of earshot, hustled to catch up.

"Eighteen turns," Peis continued, skipping down. "They wouldn't wait, couldn't. Lorel, Shaw, and Kade went to Fentum to find who came after you. They weren't there long before they were chased out and nearly killed. Kade killed a Fenti, and it nearly destroyed him—he's been through it in my cave too, Dawlis. But they learned of another foreigner who'd come and gone over the previous turn, a bald woman with a limp seen hiking in and out of the hills, some relationship with the villages up there.

She was their only lead, and she led them on. They tracked her across continents but never found her. Kade slipped back into Fentum more than once and learned nothing. Lorel and Shaw went in other directions. They caught the trail again and followed it into a place more isolated than this, the Gontomon, where Shaw got sick and nearly died. He told Lorel to go on, he'd meet her when he was well, but he never heard from her again. No one did. Because she traveled between worlds, we know that now."

They reached the edge of the boulder field. Peis rotated his core once to the left, once to the right, then started up again.

Will lowered his head, dug into the slope, and asked between heavy breaths, "Do you know … where … she went through?"

"No, we thought she was dead. Kade showed me her letter. I know she said that Shaw led her to a passage, but he has no memories of the time he was sick other than begging her to go, to keep searching. He emerged from his illness with nothing but the conviction that she was gone forever. Kade went looking for her but didn't know where to start. We all gave up on her at different points."

"He's … still there?"

"He'll come. I have no doubt he's been watching the Pymm. But it will take time. It's a very remote place, the Gontomon."

A hole in Will's heart dilated: the emptiness of an orphan, the permanent longing to know who created him and why they weren't there. The reunion with his mother had been mercilessly brief, and he hadn't even known it was her. The reunion with his father wouldn't happen in this life.

Yes, I've had misfortune, he thought.

He felt his feelings and performed the alchemy of turning them into fuel, which he channeled into his burning legs. They reached the flat again. "What about … you?" he asked the prophet.

"I also had eighteen turns to wait," Peis said, spinning and dropping back down onto the slope. "And no reason to stay in Trill. I went in no direction. I ended up on the Water of Mind, a large river flowing north to south down the western side of Damarra."

Will remembered it from the map Kade had shown him in the pill, the left half of Damarra's V-shaped smile.

"I saw the hu on the horizon." Peis pointed to the lone mountain. "I thought I'd climb it. For no reason. It was something to do, maybe a place to live and wait. But I've always had a sense for certain things. It roared to me in a dream the first and last ninarc I slept on its slopes."

"A volcano?"

"Humir Nima. Many Nimar used to live on it. They thought it was dead. It blew two spins later."

"Jesus, Peis."

They made it to the shore again. Will's heart was a piston. His legs nearly buckled. "You told ... the Nimar ... about me?"

"Yes, I broke my promise to Lorel, but I knew it would never leave this place. I wanted to stay, so I felt I had to tell them what I was waiting for. It scared them because I'd been right about the hu. But many thought that was luck and still do. And it's been a long time waiting for you."

"Do any know ... where I've been?"

"*That*, only three others."

"I come here ... trailing darkness ... They must ... not be happy."

"Some are worried."

"Kade and I ... should go ... track down the Fent ... or look for a passage." And for a second it seemed that simple. Find another hole in the ground and jump back to San Fran.

"It's up to you," Peis said. "I suggest the regiment first." He hopped onto the nearest boulder and turned back to Will. "Endurance and speed you need, but control is critical when fatigued."

"Not your best," Will said, but he knew that Peis was right, and he was quickly developing an affinity for the street performer and his quirky rhymes.

Peis leapt from boulder to boulder in a mockery of age and gravity. Will took it slow at first but soon found a rhythm and picked up his pace. They stopped at the far end of the field, a quarter of the way out into the lake. Across it and to the north of the village was the patch of muddy beach where Will had found the torch and the bent stick directing him to the island. He thought back on his nightmare swim with a shiver but also with an appreciation for Peis's wisdom in making him do it.

"It was ... the Nimar ... whistling and ... swimming with me?"

"No, the Tiralee."

"Who?"

"You'll meet them," Peis answered, and Will thought that the prophet might be smiling.

They worked their way across the rocks to the northern end of the island and to the face of a brown stone cliff carved with cracks like the rivers through Nima.

"Tired, Dawlis?" Peis asked.

"Yes," Will replied, looking up.

"Good, but only your legs. Now we use the rest of our bodies. Keep your focus, and you'll be fine."

Will knew that he would be, but he still had butterflies. He didn't dare try to keep up with Peis this time. The fractured wall offered plenty of holds, but the rock was sharp in places, and the boulders beneath him were a healthy reminder about the cost of mistakes in survival. He made it to the top eventually and ran after Peis, over the island's backbone. He did a double take down toward the eastern side of the lake, where ten or fifteen large, pale humans were dragging leafless trees through the water.

"Who the hell … are they?" he asked.

"The Tiralee," Peis answered.

"Strong … They can swim."

Peis laughed. "They can swim."

Will's heart dropped when Peis ran straight through the clearing outside of the cave and back onto a path in the birchmaples. But instead of another circuit, Peis cut left at the first fork and led them down to a rocky beach on the southern shore. Floating in the water some fifty feet out was a wooden buoy the size of a small soccer ball.

Peis turned and put his left hand on Will's shoulder, lowered his head to the fingertips of his right, closed his eyes, and said, "At some level of existence we are made of the same. You and I and everyone and everything. We have the ability to realize this, to feel it physically and to sense it in our minds. You have sensed it."

Will got the chills. "Yes."

Peis opened his eyes. "Our thoughts, our consciousness, they're made of *something material.*"

"They have to be."

"The more you feel your connection, the more you are interacting with the universe. But harnessing it is a different thing. It cannot be gained by reaching, only by letting go."

Peis bent down, selected five rocks, and held them in his left hand. "These are rocks, and that is water, and I am human. The buoy is brown, the water is blue. We are different energies, and there are boundaries between us, and that is the truth because we perceive it. But there is an underlying truth as well: *all light is white before it is filtered through our prisms.*"

He took one of the rocks in his right hand, stepped, and threw. He rocked backward, forward, and threw another. The first one hit with a dull pop as the second left his hand. The second hit, then the third, fourth, and fifth. He picked up five more rocks and hit the buoy five more times.

"You try it," he said, and walked away into the trees.

Will sat on his heels and picked over the rocks, selected one, stood, and rolled it over in his hand. "My hand, this rock, the buoy, the same," he said. He believed it. He focused, held his breath, threw, exhaled when the rock splashed not more than a foot to the left.

I can feel it.

He chose another rock, threw, and missed. He picked up five more and threw them in rhythm as Peis had, missing on all. He took a deep breath and reset. "I *will* hit it. My hand, this rock, the buoy, the same." Each of the next five rocks splashed farther away than the one before it.

He stopped. He was trying too hard. He sat down and crossed his legs, closed his eyes, and listened to his breath and the lapping water. Nurin warmed his skin. The soft breeze kissed it. The pixels flowed, and he understood for the first time what they were.

Evidence, he thought.

A sea of energy. Living static where images perpetually materialized, morphed, fizzled out, and reemerged as something new.

Including my dreams.

It was part of his system of perception.

Like light in my head.

A clue to the connection between all things. A clue from his mind. Or his Mind.

He opened his eyes, picked up five rocks, and stood. The sound of the first one hitting broke his meditation, but the second was already on its way. It hit. The next three missed by a good margin. He looked down at his hand, at the rocky beach, and at the water. The pixels, harder to see in daylight than in the dark of night or the dark behind his lids, were there and frothing over everything. He turned and walked up through the birchmaples to the cave.

Candles lined the stone floor of the chamber outside the room where Will had gone through hell and space. Kade was a dark brown shadow sitting cross-legged and straight-backed against a wall beside a door to another room, presumably the prophet's. On the ground next to Kade lay an extra belt and xim, both dark green metal with fire-orange gleam. Kade stood, crossed the candles, and presented his mind. Will did the same, and they hugged.

"You look better," Kade said in the tone of someone who's been there, who knows.

"I feel better," Will said, grateful for this man. "Did you sleep?"

"Some."

Kade lifted the belt and xim and handed them to Will. They were heavy like a ball and chain. Will wrapped the belt around his waist, and it snapped together in front by magnets. He ran his fingers over the smooth disc on his right hip. "We kill so that others won't have to," he said, not without forever-guilt and in full recognition of the fact that life could be horrid and maybe would be again.

"Only those who would kill us," Kade said. "Take it."

Will touched the back of his right hand to the xim. Two small slots opened in it on either side of his hand, and two bands of black metal, smooth and cold, slid out and came together in the center of his palm. He lifted the weapon. "Some good weight," he said.

"It will become weigh'less to you."

"What do I do?"

"Not yet. I wan'ed you to feel it. Now place it."

Will held the xim to his belt. Magnets grabbed it, and the handle retracted.

"You win a fight with your feet, so tha's where we start," Kade said and took off down the line of candles in a smooth, two-step slalom, left-left, right-right, left-left. He reached the end and turned. "Learn the step. Don' make up your own." He came back the same way. "Start slow."

Will completed his first round-trip at a walking pace, the next a bit faster.

"Good. Now with your eyes up."

Will felled a couple of candles but quickly found a beat.

"Now while holding your xim."

It grew lighter with each run.

Kade made a circle with the candles and taught Will a three-step crossover waltz. He made a diamond and did a stutter-step weave up the two right sides, backward down the two left. Will watched each demonstration without blinking and then danced with the devil. He was a vessel. He was an instrument of something, of *two* things, those little flames and the blackness they were warding off. He played and was played. He sweated profusely. He kept going around the diamond until Kade grabbed him by the arm. "Good. Enough for now," he said. "Practice these every spin. You don' need me to do it. Now." He took his xim. "Step as far as it takes to avoid my arc, then back into position. Do not overstep. On your toes at all times."

Will lowered his hand to his weapon.

"No. Leave it for now," Kade said.

"Huh? Oh, I get it. We did this as lacrosse goalies sometimes, took shots without—"

But Kade reminded him with a flash of blue-green and a papercut on his cheek that this wasn't the same thing. Will touched his face, looked at the blood, refocused. When Kade took another shot, he threw his head back and avoided the arc.

"No. Move with your feet. Your head and neck stay still. Same one again. Now." Kade swiped at the same angle, and Will took a short step back, head steady, shoulders turned, then a short step forward. Kade fired down and across his chest, and he turned his hips, then squared up again.

"Now take your xim."

Will did.

"Press with each finger, little to big, then twice with your thumb."

Will pressed the metal bar according to the combination, and a silky, invisible energy glove enveloped his hand.

"It senses you," Kade said.

"Powerful," Will whispered.

"Off is the opposite, thumb first."

Will turned it off, then on again.

"Ready?" Kade asked.

"Yes."

"Is all feel, Dawlis. The more force, the more reach you'll get, out to an arm's length. The more circular your flow, the more arc. Try it."

Will threw a punch, and the xim fired a short, thin slice of arc.

"Flow with force, Dawlis."

Flow with force.

He made a thick, blue-green semi-circle of death.

"Step," Kade said.

He stepped and fired at the floor, slicing the stone. He stepped again and made a full circle with a black hole center. "It senses me?"

"Try it on yourself."

Will didn't balk. He trusted the xim already. It was holding him as much as he was holding it. He cut at his legs. It felt like a sharp blade of air. "Protects us from guns?"

"Three times with your thumb, then hold it."

Will pressed and held, and the xim emitted a concave, blue-green shield that matched his height and width. Kade was a heat signature behind it. Will released his thumb, and the shield disappeared.

"Deadens projectiles up to a certain size and strength," Kade said. "Output from mos' heat weapons is completely absorbed."

"But it's inefficient. Why this when there are guns and heat weapons?" But Will knew the answer the second the words left his lips.

"I did it firs' from a distance," Kade said. "I'll never do it again."

Will reflected on his own suffering. "From a distance would be like trying to separate yourself from the act."

"Which is impossible. We have to respect life even as we to take it, or we have no chance."

Will bent his knees, rolled his neck, and held his xim up beneath his chin.

"Move with your feet," Kade said. "Block and kill with your xim, which is an extension of yourself. Step with every block and every attack. I come high with my xim, you match my step and fire your arc to meet mine. *Never overreach. Never jump.* Ready."

They sparred in the candlelit cave. Will danced the jigs he'd learned minutes ago. Whenever he stumbled, Kade backed off and let him reset. Whenever he felt locked in, Kade put him in his place with a nick on the arm or leg or chest. Every mistake made him better. Every teaching point, he osmosed. He started to anticipate Kade's attacks, to sense his timing and see small spaces in the blur of his arcs. He launched an offensive, which Kade indulged for a few seconds before sending him flying backward with an invisible medicine ball to the chest. He hit the stone floor and coughed up a lung.

Oh, yeah, he thought. *That.*

That singular detail of the scene at the arrowhead that Will had forgotten or suppressed in the misery that followed: Kade tossing a Fenti off the mountain without touching him. Will rubbed his chest and stood.

Kade pulled his arms in as though collecting another ball, then he threw it down at one of the candles, which winked out. "The energy comes from inside us," he said. "But also from around us. There is no empty space. There is a field. You can harness it."

It coursed through Will. "It's the same with our thoughts."

"Different energies, different fields, but all the same at some level."

"Kade."

"Yes."

"I see a field right now. I've been seeing it for a long time." The pixels flowed, swarmed, sibilated. "I think I hear it too, like insects on a summer night."

Kade took a moment. "Tha's good. A rare thing."

"You see it?"

"Yes. Maybe everyone can. Few realize it."

"I think it's light."

"I think so too."

"I saw it on Earth as well."

Kade nodded very slowly.

"One Mind dreamt both worlds," Will said.

They were silent for some time. The peppery smell of stew drifted into the cave. They placed their xims on their belts and walked out into the clearing where Peis was sitting and stirring his pot.

25

Will did not lift his face from his bowl until he'd licked it clean. When he did, he saw that Kade was gone and that Peis was smiling at him from across the fire. "Come on," the prophet said, "I want you to meet someone."

They hiked up through the birchmaples, over the island's shoulder, and down the eastern side, which was a patchwork of exposed brown rock and picnic blanket-sized patches of moss. They stopped at the water's edge on a slab that dropped off into the blue at a sharp angle and seemed to go on forever. Tiralee were dragging logs and leafless trees into the middle of the lake from the far shore. One looked in their direction, disappeared under the water, skimmed beneath the surface, and closed a hundred yards in the span of a handful of heartbeats. He stopped and tread ten feet from them.

Will stepped back. The man's skin was pearl. His head was aquadynamic and imperial, his nose flat. He had shoulders like an ox, python arms, and legs as thick as Will's waist. The man, the waterman, was six-four easily. He had large, glossy, gray eyes and spoke in deep tones. "This is you, then?" he asked. "They call me Vinson." The Tiralee presented his mind to Will with a webbed hand.

Will was speechless. Vinson smiled. His teeth were flat white blades. "No one like us on the other world? I assumed."

So, Vinson was one of the three people, other than Will's parents and their friend trio from Trill (the prophet, the politician, and the world-traveling samurai), who knew where he'd spent the last eighteen turns of his life. It was a relief not having that chasm between them. Will gathered himself and presented his mind. "No. No one like you on the other world." He stepped into the water up to his waist and extended a hand. "This is how we greet there." The waterman walked up the slab on his knees until his shoulders surfaced and mimicked Will with his right mitt. Will grabbed it and lost a breath. The skin was hard and rubbery like shark skin. "The Tiralee were spawned in the water?" he asked.

Vinson let go and looked at Peis, then up at the sky. His eyes seemed to be filled with storms and stories. "We were made," he said in his deep, waterman drawl.

Peis slipped away.

Will's face flushed. "I'm sorry. I shouldn't have asked that. I don't know you."

"No, I'll tell you how we got here. And you tell me."

"Okay, Vinson."

"I can start. You agree?"

"I agree," Will said.

And so, standing in the royal blue water with the prophet's island at his back, fingering his necklaces, Will listened to the story of the Tiralee.

They sailed to the islands to escape oppression and war, close to thirteen thousand turns past. They flourished there, far out in Qol's single ocean, east of its continent cluster, for several hundred turns before an entirely new threat besieged them. The sky turned an impenetrable gray, the rain came, and it did not stop.

The waterlines rose. They rebuilt their cities on higher ground and watched the old ones wash away and churn in debris-chocked tides. A great many died, but the strong adapted to the wet. Nurin became a god that some had faith in but none ever saw. Blue sky was a heaven that all were promised to return to if they endured this life of endless crying.

They sent ships to find the continents, but the ocean, turbulent beneath the swollen, storming sky, swallowed them all. The fifth generation to live in the perpetual rain, their skin a half shade paler and a dozen cells thicker than their forefathers, rebuilt their homes once more, this time on the hill crests. They could only wait as the water crept up. It was something they knew was happening but couldn't really see. It was a slow, torturous apocalypse.

They had no choice but to build ships again and go blind into the open. Three were finished and a fourth was under construction when all were swept away in a final fit of hysterical sadness.

In the aftermath, forty-four souls floating on planks and crates came together where the last tree-covered crest, no more than a tiny islet, still stuck out of the water. They were the first Tiralee in an age to see the stars.

Vinson paused and stared at his hands. "Life is strange," he said in grim baritone. "The next generation, they were strong swimmers."

Will laughed involuntarily, then clapped a hand over his mouth.

Vinson smirked, then turned serious again. "No Tiralee took their own life. Not one. Not in all the time watching their world disappear."

Will understood. This wasn't just a history lesson. It was a story of survival against all odds. And Vinson surely knew the final words of the prophecy.

The survivors recovered rope and tools from floating and sunken crates. They harvested wood from the drowned islands and made a home of rafts tied together around the islet. They made fire with rocks. They boiled water in salvaged pots and ate raw fish. There were twelve women, the Bimali, mothers in the native tongue. From them, the first of a new race were born.

Life, it seemed, had a sense of urgency. By the standards of evolution, the Tiralee's, primed by hundreds of turns of living in the rain, was terribly fast. Genes that had been quivering with readiness and anticipation were triggered. The Tiralee died terribly young in the waterworld, but the sped-up generational turnover only quickened the growth of their lungs, the thickening of their skin, and the encasing of their eyes. A few hundred generations later, roughly twelve thousand turns around Nurin, which had not abandoned them after all, and there were ten thousand evolved humans living on a floating city above the islands.

One spin a man named Mruda was resting on his raft, staring up at a pale-blue sky filled with drifting clouds, when the clouds turned green, the sky turned a darker blue, and Mruda was infused with ancestral knowledge. He swam through the city shouting his vision. There was a continent. The clouds were drifting west. That was the direction he would take. Who would go with him? Who would chase the legends? For they were true.

It was less than a turn after Gideon's discovery and execution. Qol was in a state of political and psychological turmoil. Its very identity was being torn apart. The mystics were meditating on the existence of humans of Gog, the scientists were sleeplessly pouring over the impossibility of getting there, maybe in a few hundred turns, maybe more, when seventy pale, gray-eyed humans emerged from the unknown vastness of Qol's ocean and swam into Damarra's delta.

Vinson stopped there and held out a hand, as though offering to answer any questions. Will had many but decided to hold onto them. He was standing before a different form of human. That was enough for now. It was his turn to share. "Thank you, Vinson."

Vinson nodded his vaulted head. "Now I'd hear how you got here."

So, Will told him.

Nurin dipped behind the island as they parted. Will had forgotten to ask what the Tiralee were doing with the trees in the lake, but it gave him a good reason to go back and talk to the waterman again tomorrow. He walked around the southern end of the island in slanted light, across the rocky beach, and past the bobbing buoy. He skirted the western shore, the lake and village on his left and the grassy slope on his right, and was struck by déjà vu. A bird flapped its wings and took off from the water, turned in a high arc, turned into the pigeon that revealed the door on top of the yellow building, cawed, and was itself again. A gaggle of the same birds, duck-sized and fern-green with crimson heads and sprays of crimson tail feathers, waded at the edge of the boulder field. A boy was sitting out there.

Will walked out onto the rocks. The birds paddled away, and the boy turned, startled. Will held up a hand. "Sorry. Didn't mean to bother you. Or them."

The boy's black eyebrows nearly lifted off his face. "Oh, no, no," he said. "It's fine. Come out. If you want, I mean, yeh."

"Okay," Will said, and took a seat one rock over from the boy. "Scared them off, I guess."

"Cawleys scare easily, yeh," the boy said.

Will pegged him at about ten turns old, twelve or so years. He had a peach fuzz mustache, shaggy black hair, lanky limbs, and a nose he was still growing into. His eyes, rich and dark brown like fertile earth, made him seem older and younger at the same time. He looked at Will in a way that reminded him of how he'd looked at George when they first met, with great, guarded hope.

"You're him, yeh," the boy said, tapping his right fingers on his right thigh as though playing keys, a quiet, nervous tune.

Will smiled. He appreciated the bluntness. "Whoever he is."

"Peis called it out, yeh."

"Sure did."

"Truth, man, truth." The boy's face softened. "Tigo, man. They call me Piper."

They presented their minds to each other. "Tigo, Piper," Will said. "Some call me Dawlis, but I prefer Will."

Piper's eyes lit up. "That's what they call you where you came from. You came a long way, yeh."

And somehow Will wasn't surprised that this kid was one of the other two in Nima who knew. Somehow it seemed right, them sitting there on those rocks talking about other worlds.

"You said it, Piper."

Piper laughed nervously. At the absurdity, it seemed. Will could sympathize. Maybe that was all you could do, laugh at it. Maybe that was the only sane response. Will laughed too, which got Piper going again, this time without the nerves. They fed off of each other, and soon they were howling.

"Stop!" Will pleaded, nearly rolling off his boulder.

"You! I can't!"

They got a hold of themselves, but one glance at each other sent them reeling again. It took a few more false stops before they finally exhausted themselves. They laid back on their rocks, holding their aching stomachs and looking up at the first stars.

"So far away but such a big part of who we are," Piper said. He pointed to the Guide. "Led you true, yeh. Truth."

Will was touched. "You're an interesting dude, Piper. Wise beyond your turns."

Piper frowned and played his fingers on his chest. On cue, a group of teenage Nimar boys and girls swam out from the drinking straws across the lake, hooting and hollering. Piper tried to look like he didn't care, like he didn't want to be there.

"Hungry?" Will asked, changing the subject. "Come eat with us. Peis and me and Kade. You know Kade?"

"I know Kade, yeh. I have to eat at home."

"Tomorrow, then. Show me more of Nima. I need to get off this island."

Piper's smile returned. "I know the best spots, yeh. Let me think … We should have time."

"Time for what?"

"For what?! Game tomorrow!"

"Game of what?"

"Game of what?! Ha! Not from around here! Spiral, yeh." He dove into the lake and swam away beneath the stars toward the torchlit village.

Will walked back up to the clearing outside of the cave. Jackson, Fred, and Orly were there with Kade and Peis. Will hugged his boys, but it was an anticlimactic reunion, for they were more interested in what Peis was cooking.

26

Will awoke in the cave with his wolves in a heap beside him. He lit a candle, meditated, stretched, then walked outside. Nurin had not yet risen, but the sky was paling, and the eastern horizon was flush with anticipation. Peis was still sleeping apparently, so Will started a circuit without him, boys in tow. Barefoot and shirtless in his black Qol pants, he jogged the paths that wound through the birchmaples, sprinted up and down the island's grassy slope three times, and jumped carefully across the field of boulders toward the cliff, where he left the boys behind. He climbed, jogged over the whale back ridge, then down past the cave and through the paths to the rocky beach, where he tried in vain to hit the buoy.

Kade was waiting for him in the cave. They trained. Kade left. Will reset the candles in all of the different patterns and worked on his steps until he had trouble standing, then for a while longer.

At midmorning, he stepped outside again. The wolves were resting around the cold fire pit. The four of them walked down to the lake, where Piper was waiting on a boulder.

"Where to?" Will asked.

"Don't have much time, but I've got a good spot," Piper said, his eyes big and beaming at the wolves.

"This is Jackson, Fred, and Orly. Boys, he's called Piper."

Piper presented his mind with a face-splitting smile. "Let's go," he said, and dove in.

He led them to the southern shore toward a narrow river that trickled out of the lake over a bed of rocks. Tiralee on either side waded inside the drinking straws and worked at wooden shelves hanging between them. They gutted fish, cleaned vegetables, sharpened spears, and mended nets. Some napped in hammocks. Outside of the trees, large, pearly white, dome-headed babies splashed inside a circle of men and women chitchatting in a melodic bass chorus. They took little notice of Piper slipping past. They did of Will and his wolves. He smiled politely and nodded respect. They did not smile or nod back. Half a dozen toddlers popped their smooth heads above the water and giggled. Orly tried to swim over and say hi, but Will shoved him along.

They swam ashore and hiked southwest under the Nima Trees. They crossed several streams and two narrow rivers, climbed a few gentle hills. Their conversation was sparse but meaningful, the silences long and comfortable.

"So, what's the deal, Piper?" Will asked as they started up a sharper rise, taking the boy's example from yesterday of speaking plainly. "You're a bit different than the other kids?"

Piper scowled. "Smarter and more in tune, yeh. I'd rather spend my time with Peis than chasing girls."

"I understand."

"I don't know."

"It's good to be different, man."

Piper stopped, pensive. He looked at Will's necklaces. "Of beast and serpent. Carved them out of their heads, yeh. Why'd you do that?"

Will dipped his hand into his pocket and felt for his knife. "Bloodlust. Extreme anger. But also pride, and so I remember what I've been through." A shadow passed through him then, cold and empty, there and gone. Piper shivered as though he'd felt it too. "My pain is a part of who I am," Will said. "I used to be afraid of it but not anymore."

The last line of Peis's prophecy hung in the air between them.

Piper swallowed. "The other one?"

Will lifted the karma stone off his chest. It felt very heavy and very old, an artifact from a past life. "A friend gave it to me. She got it from a stranger. When he handed it to her, he said, 'Karma stone, boy traveler.'"

Lines formed on Piper's brow, aging him. "You think he knew?"

Will had never considered it. He'd had enough to occupy his mind since waking up in a cave. But everything started the morning after she gave it to him.

One Mind dreamt both worlds.

He was meant to have it. It seemed obvious in hindsight. But one thing didn't tie. That night at the Fillmore, as Elle closed his hand over the stone, she'd said, "Karma means things come around. You're headed back before me, but I'll be there soon." It was strange what the man said, sure. Maybe there was something there. "Or maybe it's just coincidence," Will said aloud to himself.

Piper shook his head. "Coincidence is meaning that people don't recognize. Truth, yeh."

Will started. "Wow, Piper. You're definitely different than any eighth grader I ever met. I love it, man."

Piper didn't know what an eighth grader was, but he smiled from ear to ear like someone seen, someone with a true friend. "Come on, we're close."

They topped a rise, followed a narrow, gurgling river through a tunnel of stalks, and came out at the top of a waterfall twenty or thirty feet high. Piper leapt off without breaking stride and penciled into a royal blue pool. Will peered over the edge.

"Traveled between worlds and scared of a little jump?" Piper goaded.

Will took the bait. He plunged into the cool, foaming water and stayed under, eyes closed, listening to the submarine roar. He rose. Beds of purple flowers lined the shores beneath walls of waxy stalks. Beyond the pool, the river dipped down another small fall. "What a spot," he said.

"I have more to show you … but we have time."

Piper was intentional with those words, Will was sure of it: *we have time.* But the kid didn't seem to believe them. It was the prophecy again, haunting. The future. A storm cloud somewhere over the horizon. Will managed a smile. He was happy in that moment, and he was sad. He was struggling with things unknowable, and he was somehow stronger than he'd ever been.

I won't let anything happen to you, Piper, he thought.

Out loud, he said, "I'm glad I met you."

Wise beyond his turns but still just a kid, Piper blushed and glowed. "Friends?"

"How about brothers?"

"Brothers, then. Truth."

And that's how it was. They were bonded from the start. It was a blessing, but it was also a curse. Because love is a risk, Will knew.

They walked along a ledge, a hundred feet above a rushing river and a boulder-strewn shoreline. "Spiral," Will said. The game Piper mentioned at the end of their conversation yesterday. "What's it like?"

Piper rubbed his hands together. "Oh, you'll see, yeh."

"It's played underwater?" Will asked, remembering the hologram projected from the wall of the pill station.

"Of course!"

"People wearing gear and swimming around in a big tank?"

"What?! Mind, no, not that imitation! Spiral is the Tiralee's game, yeh. Old as the people. Invented in the floating city."

Will thought of the work being done in the lake over the last couple of days, spins. "What do the trees have to do with it?"

Piper stopped dead.

"Piper, what?"

A black centipede crested his right shoulder, paused, and flicked its antennae. Piper looked at it from the corners of wet eyes and mouthed the word *venomous*, as it crawled around the back of his neck.

Will picked up a stick and stepped forward. The centipede rounded Piper's left shoulder, scuttled down his chest, across his stomach, and onto the stick. Will tossed it. "Gone."

Piper, shaken, took off running. The wolves barked and howled, pointing in the direction they'd come from. The ground back there was moving. "Jackson, *come*," Will said, and sprinted along the drop. "Piper, get off the edge!" A stampede of brown, tailless, rat-sized rodents overcame them and snapped at their ankles. Piper lost his footing and went down and over. Will slid, grabbed his arm, and pulled him up. They got to their feet and scampered up the nearest Nima Tree. The wolves stood against the tide, picking off vermin like ducks on a pond.

"What the hell?" Will asked.

Piper shook his head.

A flock of Cawleys squawked overhead, flying in the same direction that the rodents were running and with the same apparent urgency.

"Migrating?" Will asked hopefully, though that didn't feel like the answer.

"They don't," Piper said.

"Chased?" And that was closer to the truth. That was more the vibe Will was picking up. Piper felt it too; it was all over the kid's face. He was thinking what Will was thinking: that Will had just saved his life twice in less than a minute but was also somehow responsible for everything that just happened. Him or his shadow.

Piper tapped a nervous rhythm on his chest, on the path of the centipede. "Let's get out of here," he said. "Game time soon, yeh."

They arrived back at the lake to a scene. A few hundred Nimar were swimming out to the island and running around it to the eastern side as though their lives depended on it, shouting, cheering, laughing, and back-slapping. The smell of barbeque. Offshore, a blurry, white throng of Tiralee swam in a smooth, wide arc beneath an elongated octagon of floating logs. One surfaced and made a sound like a foghorn, causing every Nimar to simultaneously pick up the pace.

Piper grabbed Will's arm and dragged him into the water. "We're late, yeh!" The wolves, caught up in the mayhem, were already on their way. Will swam hard in Piper's wake until they reached the flow of Nimar. Piper charged in, but Will stopped. He had to see. He sucked in a breath and dropped under. In the royal blue distance was a grove of tall, leafless, curly branched trees surrounded by a net. A few scattered Nimar clung to the net, and more were diving in every second, each carrying a pole, some as long as their bodies, some several times longer. The Tiralee circled at inhuman speeds. Will pinched himself and confirmed that yes, this was somehow real.

He surfaced not far from the buoy, swam ashore, and fell into the crowd rounding the island. A few pairs of eyes widened, though most Nimar could not have cared less about their visitor at that moment. He turned the corner and looked up at the island's eastern face. The elderly sat around fires cooking, drinking, smoking, and bouncing babies in their laps. Kids threw balls, played chase, and stalked Jackson, Fred, and Orly as they sniffed around for food. Every other Nimar was gathered in a frenzy around two boats pulled up onto the shore. Three people in each boat were tossing out poles and goggles. Gear in hand, the fans raced out to the octagon.

Will spotted Kade and Fo on the other side of the boats. He thought about calling out to them but then thought better of drawing attention to himself. The crowd squeezed. A teenage girl cut him off. "Ten bits, man! Give me ten!" she shouted up at a middle-aged man working the nearest boat. "Oh, too long!" she growled and snatched a pole out of the air.

Someone said, "Dawlis." He turned. It was Jovi. He avoided her eyes and that button. He opened his mouth to say something, hi, he supposed, when a pair of goggles hit him in the head. She laughed. He looked up in time to catch his pole. When he turned again, she was gone.

Piper appeared. "Where have you been!" he shouted. "Let me see what they gave you, yeh. Oh, you might as well float on the surface! Hold on." He turned and eyed the poles of the Nimar diving past them. A bent-backed old man was doing the same.

"Kiko, here!" Piper said. "I've got what you need, yeh."

The man grinned, baring his few remaining teeth as though he was showing them off. "Tigo, Piper. Short stick for an older? I've got a good trade, yeh."

Piper jumped. "Perfect match, Kiko!" he said, yanking Will's pole out of his hands, swapping it for Kiko's, which was about twenty feet long, and then tossing that one back to Will. It was hard, thin, and hollow like a reed. "Right, Kiko, what do you think for the game? These northern are strong, yeh, but I've got a feeling."

Kiko's eyes flashed. "We start our own cycle today, Piper. Fast Tomit will be too much for them." And off he dove.

"What's a cycle?" Will asked.

Piper waved off the question. "Follow me. Don't stop, yeh. You'll have plenty of time to look."

He led them on a beeline to the northern end of the octagon, then around to the middle of the far side. He stopped, tread, and lifted one end of his pole above the water. There was a small stub sticking out near the bottom, which was plugged. "Breathe through here," he said, pointing to the stub.

"Okay," Will replied.

"Put your yucs on."

"Yes, sir." Will put on his goggles. The lenses were large and curved and not without a few imperfections. The leather around them was thick and soft. It sucked to his eyes and the bridge of his nose as he tied the strap tight behind his head.

"Blow out when you get under. Ready?"

Will smiled. "Why not."

They dropped in.

The field was something like seventy-five yards from end to end, thirty yards deep, and forty wide across the middle, Will estimated. It was enclosed by thick-roped nets hanging from the octagon of logs above and kept taut by rocks tied to the bottom. Brown-barked, thick-trunked, tendril-branched trees, as tall as the field, floated rootless in the middle and at both ends, held in place by the same beautifully rudimentary infrastructure.

Nimar gripped the nets in white-knuckled hands and breathed heavily through their reeds. More fans trickled down on the far side, forming a growing mass at center field. Some gathered in smaller groups or floated alone, high and low, down to the ends. Will and Piper found a two-person gap just left and high of center field on the eastern side, which was less crowded. They blew out their reeds, grabbed hold of the net, and looked at each other. Piper seemed on the verge of exploding. Will did everything in his power just to breathe and soak it in. The school of Tiralee sped around the field trumpeting a rally song that reverberated through the wiggling Nimar. Will watched them come, caught their booming tempo, and swayed in their wake as they flew past.

Alien Davids, he thought, wonderstruck.

He turned back to the field and took stock. Seven trees made a grove in the middle of the field, spanning the width of it and nearly touching the nets with their wavy, coiled branches. On either side of the grove were large spaces of open water, which Will thought of as the *plains*. At the far end of each plain, where the walls of the octagon turned in, stood a pair of trees, which he called the *fences.* Goals were rectangular boxes of wood posts and mesh hanging between the fences and the pinched ends of the field.

Eight or ten Tiralee, men and women, darted through the grove like fish through a reef. Others cut through the plains and whipped grooved, oblong wooden objects back and forth, spirals with rock tips and finned tails that left trails of bubbles, some curved, some straight as arrows. Goalies took shots behind the fences. One made a save, and Will cringed. Rubber balls at ninety miles an hour with a net to catch them in and equipment on was one thing. A spiral at forty-plus would have shattered his hands.

Half of the players wore blue bands around their heads, wrists, and ankles; half wore red. One from either team brandished a pole the length of their bodies and a few inches thick, a drinking tree straw. It was Vinson for the blue, the south. One of his teammates tucked a spiral under her arm, swam at him, and tried to dodge him. He kicked his legs, cocked his pole—it flexed like a tree in the wind—and snapped it over her forearms, freeing the spiral. Another in blue grabbed the spiral, backed up, and zipped forward. He took a fierce whap on his left shoulder but hardly seemed to notice as he juked Vinson. Piper, a look in his eyes like he was seeing victory, shook Will's arm and mouthed, *Tomit, Tomit!*

Tomit was shorter, leaner, and younger, as far as Will could tell, than any other Tiralee on the field. He moved like he did not believe in friction. He carried the spiral in a carefree way as Vinson tried to beat it out of his hands. He had the look of a child who's recently discovered that he can run and so now all he wants to do is run, run, run, no matter how many times he falls and scrapes his knees. And he smiled like it tickled every time Vinson whacked him across the arms with that pole.

The Nimar shook the nets. The Tiralee lapped the field, bellowing their song. A horn bawled. Piper slapped Will on the back, and everyone shot to the surface . . . where they thundered a clarion blend of tenors and baritones.

An old Nimar woman with wiry muscles and wiry gray hair stood on a raft in the middle of the field amidst the logs that held up the grove. She raised a large hourglass over her head, and every last human fell silent.

"Isulu, yeh," Piper whispered. "Presents every game in our water."

All eyes were fixed on Isulu. She rasped: "Game time coming!"

The noise then was louder than Will would have thought possible for half a thousand people. His eyes watered.

Isulu waved her hand, and the roar collapsed into a low, anxious buzz. "Four wins for the north, yeh," she said. "Two to the cycle."

Grumbles and boos filled the octagon, countered by the joyfully defiant cries of a small group of visiting fans gathered at the northwest corner. The northern players, treading above their plain, looked at each other and nodded. The home southern linked arms on their side of the grove and breathed deeply through their flat noses.

"One turn and five phases since the last cycle," Isulu reported.

"Four teams," Piper whispered in quick, sharp puffs into Will's left ear. "East, west, north, south. A cycle is beating the others both in their water and yours, six straight games."

"Got it," Will said.

"Passion for the game above all," Isulu demanded. "Dive!"

A final unified howl. Then the players dove, and the fans followed.

Having heard and felt the ruckus up above, Will could now fully appreciate the muted soundscape below. The loudest cries were the ones in your head. The connection between people was passed in muffled screams and laughter, touches and glances, shared thoughts and mental energy. Everyone waited.

Three players from each team entered the grove. Vinson and a fearfully large man for the north stalked the trees from their respective plains with their poles cocked and two opponents hovering on their flanks. Goalies paced their nets behind the fences. Every player and every fan looked up at the surface.

The spiral hit the water above the grove and caromed through the branches. A southern player reached for it and was bodychecked into a trunk by a northern as another in red snatched it and burst out. The others in the grove and those in the opposite plain followed her through.

Vinson was waiting. He forced a pass, but it was well-thrown straight down to another northern player cutting underneath, who carried the spiral at speed toward the southern fence. Piper pulled Will's arm, and the crowd drifted left. The carrier faked a pass, then cut left and flew through the small gap between the fence and the net. Four more northern players and five for the south threaded through the trees, leaving the big northern poleman and one southern player hanging back in the plain.

No northern player was ever still. They cut left, right, up, down, and diagonal, moving the spiral in a quick rhythm of passes and handoffs, using the entire depth and pinched width of the field in front of and behind the goal (Will got the impression that one could score from either side, and he'd be proven right). Four southern players held to a loose sphere around the goal. Vinson roamed free, watching, hunting, patient.

The north zipped a pass from left to right, then another down, then another under the goal. Vinson and the southern goalie slid around the posts like eels. There was a handoff, a pass up, then another pass right back over the top of the goal. The spiral burned the goalie's fingertips as he and Vinson curled backward over the crossbar. Vinson's pole caught the tail, redirecting it and forcing a tough catch and a rushed shot. The goalie stretched to his left, collected the spiral, and immediately looked upfield in the direction of Fast Tomit. But Tomit was blanketed. The goalie found another outlet, and every player from both sides sped through the fence. The crowd drifted right.

Two northern players smothered Tomit in the plain. Vinson bellowed, and the young hope of the south swam to the surface and subbed out. But his team moved with precision through their plain without him, as though every cut and pass had been drawn up in advance. The north could do little more than drop back through the grove and await them on the other side. A southern player, carrying the spiral by the tail, swam hard through the trees, took a swat on her elbow from the northern poleman, and dropped the spiral to a trailing teammate. This one handed off to another coming across, who sped toward Will and Piper's side, arced around a couple of well-timed blocks, and passed through the fence with ease. The north were half a body length behind her as she charged the goal. They converged on her in their haste, leaving an open man, who caught a sharp pass and finished with a dart to the bottom left corner.

The fans detached from their reeds and screamed into the water. Piper laughed with his head back. Will could only shake his head. They rose and unleashed, leaving the few dozen northern fans yanking on the nets and cursing. The older and the young sang and danced on the island.

"Holy shit," Will said.

Piper slapped his hands on the water. "I'm telling you, yeh! I have a feeling!"

The spiral fell to Fast Tomit on the restart. He took a beating with the pole as he swam out of the grove, but he was smiling as he whipped a one-handed pass to a teammate cutting upward at a diagonal. Double-teamed again, he made a few attempts to get open before swimming up.

The second southern rush was as sharp as the first. The northern communication was harried and uncertain, and they were down two-to-nothing before they knew it.

Will heard only his own gurgling, submarine yell, a personal version of the rapture he saw all around him. The fans kicked to the surface where all became one.

Will had been around the game of spiral for a matter of rus, but it seemed obvious to him that the south had anticipated the northern game plan and executed their own to perfection thus far. He said as much to Piper, who agreed with all his heart but in the next breath scolded Will for saying anything so positive. They had to stay focused. The north would not concede their cycle. Will took this reprimand seriously and swallowed a pit of guilt when, after a hard-fought battle in the southern end, the visitors took advantage of a lucky deflection off of Vinson's pole and put their team on the board.

Barely five rus of sand had spilled through the hourglass, and three goals scored. It was a fast start, according to Piper, though not unheard of. The dearth of scoring that followed, however, was almost without precedent.

There were plenty of shots, and good ones, but the goalies on both teams were unconscious. They seemed to know where the spiral would end up before it left the shooters' hands. The remainder of the first measure and the entire second went by without another goal.

Just as staggering was the torrid pace of scoring that occurred in the third and final measure—and it broke the heart of the southern faithful.

The look on their goalie's face when the spiral hit his net for the second time was one of utter incomprehension. Such a thing simply hadn't seemed possible for so long. He was conscious again. Will could see it in his cloudy gray eyes. And his defense was tired.

Meanwhile, the northern seemed to grow stronger and faster, especially that enormous poleman. He was everywhere at once, knocking down passes and beating the slowing southern players with his big, bendy baton. His teammates, energized and inspired by his play, took advantage of the offensive opportunities he created.

The home fans looked on in misery. So much promise to start the game! They clung to hope, but it was eviscerated. The south did not score for over two measures. The mighty north, down two-to-one to start the third, rattled off five straight goals.

A few rus of sand remained in the hourglass, and there was no longer any doubt that the north would play for the coveted cycle in their home water in twelve spins. Treading above their plain, they could not contain their smiles. A few swam to the northwest corner to embrace the diehard fans who'd made the trip. Everyone knew it was over.

Except Tomit was acting strange. He was treading alone with his eyes just above the water, staring at his satisfied opponents. Will pointed him out to Piper, who spit and said he didn't want to see that face or hear that name spoken ever again. But Will watched Tomit as he swam to Vinson, and watched Vinson as he listened to his young star and then gathered his team in a tight huddle.

Tomit's first goal was meaningless. The north didn't let it happen. They simply had very little motivation at this late hour to lean into the hits that Tomit's teammates put on them. The vast majority of fans didn't notice or pretended not to. Will was one of the few still watching.

The south took control off the drop, got the spiral to Tomit (fresh-legged, thanks to the northern strategy of keeping him out for much of the game), then played defense in their offensive end, hounding the north and leaving Tomit one-on-one with the poleman. He took a pounding, laughed, and kicked into another gear. He passed through the fence without slowing, scored easily, then swam up to catch his rest.

The cheering was sparse and half-hearted: a pat on the back for showing some grit at the end of a losing effort. But Piper, whose life had seemed to fall apart in front of him during the northern onslaught, now stared very seriously at the water.

The spiral deflected off a high branch in the grove right into the hands of Fast Tomit. This time four of his teammates double-teamed both the northern poleman and their fastest player, leaving Tomit outnumbered in the plain but by those least capable of staying with him. The fans had enough time to wonder if perhaps the home team was seriously trying to mount a comeback when Tomit made it six-to-four.

Murmurs of cautious optimism spread over the water like a thin film of nervous energy. Here and there spiked an isolated cry or whistle.

Piper dug his nails into Will's arm and looked on silently as they waited for the restart.

Will figured the game would have been over if the spiral had fallen to the north just once in those final rus. But luck played a role, and he'd never seen a great comeback where that wasn't the case.

The spiral caromed. A southern player grabbed it from the outstretched hands of a northern and backhanded it to Tomit. The north retreated through their plain, through their fence, and into their defensive end, taking away his advantage. He hit the fence at reckless speed, scraping his arms and legs on the branches, and drove a shoulder into the poleman's chest on the far side.

Fans' eyes filled their yucs.

Where's the spiral?! Where's the spiral?!

A southern player drew the panicked north with a fake shot, and another stuck the spiral in the upper right corner.

No one breathed. Tomit and the poleman were laid out and sinking. Their teammates grabbed them and pulled them up.

Silence on the surface. Until Piper, trembling, could no longer stand it. "No cycle for the north, yeh! Call it out for Fast Tomit!"

The fans released their resurgent, manic hope. When Tomit raised a hand, they nearly lost their minds.

Isulu held up the hourglass. A dollop of sand remained.

The spiral fell to Tomit, and it was no surprise. Just as everyone knew a few rus earlier that the north would win, now all were united in their belief that Tomit would tie the game. But the rally was cut off at the knees when he charged into the fence and pulled up, clutching his face. Ribbons of blood spilled through his fingers. His right eye, stuck on a broken branch, rose slowly to the surface.

Will sat alone on a patch of moss on the eastern side of the island staring down into the darkening royal blue water. The field had been broken down, the trees dragged away and tied up along the far shore. No fans lingered; they'd all gone straight home. No cawleys gathered; they'd all flown away. A fish-shaped cloud with a toothy, open mouth and a hole for an eye drifted across the sky. A school of silver fish swam past the island and left one dead in their wake. Will stood up and left.

Kade, Peis, and the wolves were gathered around the fire. Peis had news. He'd been digging through his library (somewhere behind the second door inside the cavern, Will presumed) and found an image of the symbol of orange gems buried in a yellow-paged, leatherbound Kyut text. The Kyut were native Damarrans, ancestors to the Nimar. The Chief was called Eamon. His march across the Shole, an event largely lost to history—for what had it accomplished but the death of many of his followers and the creation of that ornament?—had coincided roughly with far more notable happenings, like the Nimar migration into the river delta, the reemergence of the Tiralee, and the death of Gideon. A busy time for the Mind, it seemed. The symbol was called Nuvium, which translated into *Light Path* or *Light Map*. The text was silent on what it was a path *to* or a map *of*.

That Peis learned about Nuvium, the core of which was an eye, on the day that Tomit lost his did not seem like a coincidence to any of the three men. Nor did the eyeless fish cloud, which Will described in a quiet voice, lest he summon it back. Nor did the dead silver fish left in front of him as though by a funeral procession. Because on Earth the fish was an archetype often associated with dark unconscious contents, and on Qol too it betrayed a troubled Mind.

Will told them again about his dream of three and the coincidences he'd experienced leading up to his fall through the roof, all of which had occurred in threes. As his three wolves lay at his feet. He told them about the centipede, the rodents, and the cawleys. Loose connections to the close-minded. But Will, the man who found him out on the Shole, and the man who saw him coming, were all quite sure, as Will had been sure before his hurried exit from San Francisco, that the universe was trying to get their attention. The only question was when the fish would manifest for the third time.

There was more. The book contained a handful of entries written in English, dating back to the Nimar migration. One referenced, not by name but by a bird symbol, the man who'd taught them the language. Peis drew it in the dirt, and Will confirmed that it was the same he'd seen in Eamon's cave.

What Will did not reveal, what he still kept locked in a box behind his ribs, for reasons he knew he could never explain to anyone but the one who'd signed that bird signature, the other who'd walked the path, was that he was in possession of that other's journal. Here was yet another connection between him and the traveler, strengthening their bond across time. The traveler had taught English to the Kyut. He, like Will, was a link between worlds. Had he been to Earth? Was he from there? If he knew English, why did he write his journal in Korial?

Perhaps it was time to find out, time to hear the traveler's thoughts. But Will, having taken a single step toward the cave to retrieve the journal, was stopped in his tracks by a mournful chorus carried across the water from the Nimar tree-house village. Kade and Peis looked at each other.

"What is it?" Will asked.

"The song for Little Avri," Kade said. "They gather for a meal after every game. They sing this firs'."

"Who is Little Avri?"

"A Tiralee girl. Killed by a vramen, a large fish, eighteen turns pas'."

The year I fell through a hole in this world, Will thought.

"The vramen live in the Nima rivers?"

"In the larges' waters, north and eas', far from here. They never came near the villages. Jus' the one time. Now there are gates to keep them away."

Peis walked into the cave.

Will looked into Kade's dead-still, deep brown eyes. "I'll be up early," he said. "Circuits and sparring first thing."

Kade nodded.

There followed ten days of quiet. Then Will's dreams came true.

27

"Ruve, I'll take it straight tonight."

Ayn had never asked Ruve for anything but a Bell. Not once over four turns. But when Ruve told her about a dream she'd had about dying, as the boy slept on a couch on a high floor of Stilter fresh off his march across the Shole to the city of seven, with every word of the prophecy fulfilled except for that final line—well, Ayn decided, or it was somehow decided for her, that she needed something to drown her thoughts, not stimulate them. So, Ruve drank her own Bell and the one meant for Ayn and later died alone on the floor behind the bar in Alden Lu.

It was still dark when Mays came to Ayn's terub and told her. He'd been crawling around in the local guard network and seen the internal alert. A cleaning bot had found her. Ayn couldn't process it. Her head pounded. She sweated fin. Her mouth was a desert. She didn't remember coming home or if she'd seen the girls. But it was true, she knew it. She didn't need to see the report. She knew it like she'd known that something had been there in that restaurant with them, some presence, some disease. She closed her eyes and rubbed her temples. "We have work to do," she said in Korial.

"What kind of work?" he asked doubtfully. What was she going to drag him into now?

"For Ruve and her family. For the three girls sleeping over our heads. Maybe for all the girls and boys."

"Ayn, you need to tell me what's going on."

She opened her eyes and leaned into him. She smelled liquor on his breath for the first time since they met three turns past. "You got into something, Mays."

"That's both of us."

"I know why you did it. I did it for the same reason."

"Ayn, enough."

She took his hand. "You know why I came to Mon Teles originally."

"Of course. Your friend and her son."

"They're not dead."

He pulled his hand away.

"I'm going to tell you everything," she said. "I've lied to you for as long as we've known each other. Just about the one thing, but it's the most important thing. Now I'm going to tell you."

He was familiar with the first part, the disappearance. Many people were. But like many people he was decidedly unfamiliar with the part about a street performer's vision and its recent realization. And the part about another world. She didn't expect him to believe any of it; she herself still struggled to. Indeed, he looked at her as at someone he only thought he knew, and knew to be sane. But he listened. It was clear that *something* was going on and that she was deeply involved. She needed help, and he loved her. He'd never said it, but she'd known it for a long time.

She put a hand on his leg. "I'm sorry I got you involved in this."

He eyed the hand. "Sure, Ayn. What do you want to do?"

"I want eyes on Fentum, Nima, and everything inside and outside of this city."

"Sorry to inform you, but Fentum and Nima—"

"I know, Mays." Both societies were non-parties to the Cooperative. It meant, among other things, that they didn't allow satellites in their air space or anything else that compromised their privacy and independence. Which meant that Mays would have to redirect the gaze of or even nudge a couple of birds, not just tap into them.

"We'll get caught," he said.

"We can't get caught."

He shook his head.

"One more thing," she said.

"You're serious?"

"I am. Maybe it doesn't exist and there's some other explanation. Maybe it does."

"I need more information. There's a lot of space."

"I'll get access to the guard's research on exoplanets. I'm owed a couple of favors." She paused and dipped her thoughts into the rich, dreamy murk of the mystery. "It's possible Dawlis's father can help too. Something he saw in the stars led Ayn to the second hole."

"Holes," Mays said to himself. "Black holes?"

"Is it possible?"

"Maybe, but extremely small and very deep. And it's just a theory."

"Find everything ever written about it."

He stood up. "None of this will be quick. They're watching."

"Quick as you can."

He opened his mouth. Closed it. Swallowed.

She shuddered. She knew his next question.

"The street performer, what he said. What's this shadow?" he asked.

"Just that. It's what caused us both to drink last night."

He walked out into the cold.

As far and wide as Mays would eventually allow them to see, he first spied the enemy with his naked eyes and within rus of leaving Ayn's terub. She answered a holo call from him and found herself looking through his glasses.

"See that?" he whispered.

She saw only the dark outlines of trees and terubs. "What?"

"There."

A shadow passed between trunks, a spindly man in a round-brimmed hat creeping through the forest in the dark.

"Do you recognize him?" she asked.

"No."

"Please follow him."

The man stepped up to a terub, stood in front of a dark window, and raised a long-fingered hand. The door slid open. He walked around to it, paused on the threshold, tipped his hat, and said something in a language that Ayn didn't recognize.

A muted, guttural, androgynous voice replied from inside in what sounded like Korial.

"This tongue, fine," the man replied in an amused, throaty hum. "Safe, safe." He stepped inside. Mays crept closer to the terub, turned up the volume on his glasses, brightened the night vision, and zoomed in through the window. Sitting at a small table set against the trunk was a person in a white mask with glowing green eyes.

"Ayn?" Mays said.

"I see," she replied, heart pounding.

A mane of dark hair poured out of the mask and down over his or her shoulders. Hands rested on a blanket in his or her lap.

"So," said the man.

The green eyes flicked off, then on again. "You failed. She lives."

The man shrugged. "I know." He crossed his legs. His suit was polished green. "Also, I saw him. I wish you told me. Very exciting."

Lips parted beneath the lipless, plastic mouth.

"Almost hard to believe," the man said. "Our beloved, tongueless seer exactly right so far. Three white beasts and all. I'm sure they'll want to know."

"They *do*," said the person in the mask.

The spindly man scratched his thin nose. "I'll take care of them both."

"Stay quiet for now."

"She was lucky. And who else sitting here failed, twice now? Your goons spooked them in the mountains. You should have told me. I would have handled him. Blunt work, yours."

The green eyes turned off, and the blurry afterimages lingered on Ayn's retinas, hovered in the dark sockets of the mask. They beamed again, and she jumped.

"We'll both answer," said the person. "Dondante comes."

The man gripped the arms of his chair. "There's time."

"Not as much as you think."

The man ran a hand over his mouth, slid the other toward his belt. "I'll handle them. Where did the boy go?"

"Stay quiet."

"What else don't I know? And why this costume? It always disgusts me. You'll shed it when Dondante arrives. You'll beg."

"Dondante will forgive."

"Sure, he'll forgive." The man pulled a heat blade and lunged.

The person caught his wrist and grabbed him by the throat with his or her other hand. The green eyes flicked off and on, off and on.

The man tore himself away and ran from the terub.

"Come," said the person to no one. "Some rest."

28

Mays had eyes on Nima and Fentum in less than two spins. The low-orbit satellites he'd used to track Kade's flight out of Mon Teles toward the Shole had been relatively easy to hack but also easy to defend once the guard figured out there was someone inside. Maybe they didn't expect whoever it was to be one of their own and to be good enough and reckless enough to try and break into the Rings. Maybe the corruption didn't reach that high. Whatever the case, Mays wormed his way into a terrestrial-facing camera on the outside of a rock buster and was able to take control of it for brief windows. He varied his entry and exit times to give the impression of a nagging glitch. Ayn slept in her office and didn't miss an opportunity to watch.

The Fenti port city was a maze of alleys and pitch-roofed, snow-covered, gray-stone buildings, bustling during the day and dead at night, there being no electric light in Fentum. The pale-blue bay was sprinkled with gray sailboats, most of which never moved. Ayn didn't know what she was looking for, but she explored obsessively, watching people go about their lives from about the height of Stilter. She had Mays turn the eye on the mountain villages where Kade had gone looking for signs of that other foreigner all those turns past. Like him, she found nothing but the crater.

Looking down on Nima was solely for peace of mind, a risky indulgence but one Ayn required for her sanity. Dawlis was there and safe and working hard. Kade spent his time in the village or in the cave with Dawlis or carving up the delta in a propeller boat just to be moving. Twice she'd risked sending him short messages. Twice he'd sent short replies. Neither of them had anything meaningful to report, but it was good to be in touch, to share the burden of waiting for they knew not what. Peis had gone into the cave the first time Ayn had a view of Nima and had yet to come out, as far as she knew.

She canceled every one of her appointments not related to the investigation into Ruve's death. During those meetings with the guard, she watched and listened carefully, answered questions intentionally, and omitted for the time being any mention of a person in a mask or another in a round-brimmed hat. She made calls to a select few disreputable characters who she'd done favors for over the turns and asked if they knew anything about those two, but no one did, or they weren't talking. She called a guard researcher whose wife she'd gotten accepted into a medical trial that saved her life and cashed in in the form of a code to the guard's records on exoplanets, though she had no idea which way was up in that black expanse of information.

Her life was reduced mostly to pacing her office and sleeping with her head on her desk. The time between her viewing sessions dragged. But Mays made a mistake one ninarc that gave her the chance to feed her compulsion without putting them at much risk.

"Sorry," he said in Korial. "Switching over. I have Nima."

"No, no," she said, sitting up in her chair and leaning into her holo. "Is that—"

"The inside of the rock buster."

The satellite whose Qol-directed camera they'd been borrowing.

"The guard keeps watch over the operators?" she asked.

"Of course. It's easy work, but it takes a toll. They watch for signs of fever."

"Not a lot of room in there."

"And a long way from home," Mays confirmed. It was a part of his life he didn't like talking about, and she'd never pried. But now her curiosity was peaked.

An operator sat in one of two chairs facing the slanted windshield. He was hugging his knees and staring into space.

"Let's keep this open," Ayn said.

"No, Ayn."

"Just a while. They won't be looking for us inside an internal monitor. Give me audio, please."

Mays clenched his jaw, did what he was told, and switched off.

The far wall of the close, hexagonal room was covered in switches and small, round lights, most of them still, some blinking the steady thoughts of the system. A low, pulsing drone and a single, regular beep were the sounds of its robot rhythm. To the left were two very small rooms. The second operator swam out of one of them, stopped in front of the wall to stretch and yawn, then swam into the other. He came out a few ticks later holding a tray of food, which he carried to the chairs. He sat down, strapped in, and looked over at his partner. "Hey, Gillin," he said in Korial. "Here, eat something."

"It's going to be us, Jonni," Gillin said, still staring, still holding his knees. "Stay ready, partner."

Jonni called up a holo from the dash, some data Ayn couldn't read from her vantage. "I wouldn't get too excited. I keep telling you. Here, have the vegetables, at least. They're not awful."

Gillin sat up on his knees and leaned forward. "I saw something before. Think I did. Just there." He pointed into the vast, star-speckled dark. "We could get some residual. Gotta be ready, Jonni."

Ayn frowned. The system blinked, droned, and beeped. She called Mays.

He answered with a fake smile. "Yes, Overseer?"

"Take a look. One of them thinks he saw something."

"Not anywhere near us or you'd know. But I'll check if it makes you feel better." His fingers danced. "All normal. Wait, did he have his helmet on?"

"No, why?"

Mays breathed in through his teeth. "Classic sign of the fever. That window is for stargazing, nothing more."

Ayn rubbed her temples. "Mind, this is who we have protecting us?"

"I told you, it's not complicated work. You have objects to track, searches and studies to run, and Gog to watch, but the computers do most of the work and feed everything back to *Mother Bird*. You only need five turns in the guard, including two on the tech side, to be eligible. The psych tests are thorough, but they can't replicate the experience. Being up there is a very different thing."

"But they just leave you?"

"It's expensive to move people up and down. And everyone gets a touch of the fever sometimes."

Everyone gets a touch of the fever, Ayn thought.

She could understand why, and she'd only been watching and listening for a few rus and from the comfort of her office safely fixed to Qol's surface. "Tell me more," she said. She was prying now, unapologetically. And Mays, it seemed, was in a mood to exorcise.

The primary job was to watch over the system and make sure it stayed happy and healthy, he explained. The operators ran searches and studies, ran test hacks and contact scenarios, chaperoned the occasional software upgrade, uploaded data from *Mother Bird*, and downloaded data back. That was it, more or less. It was a mundane existence in tight quarters, and the views got old, no matter who you were. The pay was good, which helped keep people like Mays and Jonni coming back up (Mays got a look at the records, and this was Jonni's third term, Gillin's first; Mays had done two), but the real reason anyone raised their hand to make that trip and endure that isolation, the real hook was the once-in-an-epoch longshot of spotting a stray rock on a risky trajectory and seeing those cannons fire. People went for the chance to be heroes.

Sometimes a camera-can operator, after a phase or two of doing little else but watch their holos, developed ideas about comets headed their way or MaGog launching bombs from their holes in the ground. Enough time in a rock buster and a previously stable man or woman might convince themselves it was going to be them who hit the buttons and saved the world. It was like a celestial-sized carrot hanging on a celestial-sized stick inside their minds, and the hardest thing an operator had to do was keep from believing too much.

"A lot of exercise, and on a schedule," Mays said, chewing a fingernail. "That's critical. Keep busy. But still, there's a lot of time."

"Qol must be beautiful from up there," Ayn said, thinking maybe she could bear the conditions for that view.

"It is. I used to look at it a lot. But you have to be careful. It can haunt you. And if you look the other way, you're looking into an abyss. You watch things through the camera cans, but it's all just hundreds and thousands of little lights and rocks and ice balls. You run studies that put you to sleep. You watch Gog, but nothing ever happens. Really, you're waiting for something to get caught in our gravity well, which is perverse, and the odds are so against you anyway. Still, you know it's possible."

Ayn cringed. Every living human over a few turns in age knew the short, checkered history of the Rings. They were conceived as protection against the every-twenty-thousand-turn event, which at the time was debatably overdue. But the Council wouldn't fund the project based solely on microscopic probabilities. The proponents needed a catalyst, and they got it when one of the Gog hives shot down the two satellites that Qol had orbiting the gray planet. MaGog. That's how this little, angry nation referred to itself.

The guard was well aware of MaGog's ambition and their deeply rooted belief that they were owed another world. It was above this hive that Qol had landed its first expeditionary force, fifty-four turns past. It was MaGog's predecessors who'd swallowed the ship and the crew. It was here that the guard's flawed espionage and diplomatic efforts had since been concentrated, with all attempts to date at cooperating with the feared and worshiped leader having fallen through for reasons unrelentingly debated and overanalyzed by politicians, journalists, and academics, with much blame to throw around and very little to show for it in terms of understanding the MaGog mind. But the guard also knew, and the guard took great comfort in knowing, that their neighbors were a generation or more from having the ability to send weapons, let alone ships across the chasm of space separating the two planets. Nonetheless, taking out the satellites represented technological milestones that had not been accurately predicted, and so the decision was made to start building defenses. The proponents of a satellite system for staving off flying rocks finally had their vessels: two Rings, one around the equator and another around the prime meridian.

Except at that first job the guard failed miserably. It was almost impossibly unlucky that the first meteor came nineteen turns past. The problem was that it hit less than a turn before the cannons were ready to fire, which was slightly more than a turn behind schedule. In came down in the hills of Fentum, far from the port city and far enough from any village. No one was hurt, and the guard wiped its sweaty brow, but it was unsettling.

Sixteen turns later, three turns past, against all cosmological odds, another meteor got caught in the well, and the guard had its chance at redemption. But the cannons never fired. Manual override. The meteor, given its estimated size and mineral makeup, was expected to burn up. It didn't. It hit not more than two hundred and fifty kels northwest of Mon Teles. Again, there were no casualties, and a good deal of energy and money was saved, but the Overseer of the Rings was relieved of her post.

Ayn thought back to the chaos of that second hit, one turn into her term as Overseer of the closest city. A trial by fire in leadership if there ever was one. But she was glad in the end that it had happened to her. It had given her ample opportunity to do favors for the guards as they performed their forensics inside their cocoon of security. She supplied their food and spared no expense. She made introductions to Mon Teles's most reputable astronomers and geologists. She built a handful of solid relationships.

Now, sitting before her holo watching the operators in the rock buster do nothing, she was pondering how to leverage those relationships, when the sirens in the satellite started blaring.

"Ho, Jonni!" Gillin said. "Here we go, partner! I knew it. *I knew it.*" He put on a black-visored helmet. "Coordinates fifteen by thirteen. Coming fast, fast, fast at seven degrees. Here we go!"

Ayn's mouth dried. "Mays, are you still there?"

"Hold on," he said. "It's always just a drill."

"Not always," she replied, heart in her throat.

"Relax. I'll try and get inside their helmets."

Jonni put his on. A few ticks later, Ayn saw what he saw, an image of space beamed in from the nearest telescope-eyed camera can. A red square in the top right corner tracked a tailed ball of blue light ripping through space. The word *DRILL* flashed in the bottom left. Gillin either didn't see it or didn't allow himself to. Ayn sat back, exhaled, and laughed like a loon, like someone with a touch of the fever.

Gillin kept it together long enough for him and Jonni to execute the drill, which required nothing more of them than to confirm their system's readings for *Mother Bird* and then flip some switches and push a few buttons in a particular order before she flipped and pushed hers. Less than two rus after the sirens had sounded the alarm, pretend lasers cut through space and halted the pretend comet in a small blossom of silent fire.

Gillin tore off his helmet and slammed it on the dash. "We did it, partner! I told you! Heroes! We're going home heroes!" He jumped out of his seat and swam tight circles around the room in front of the wall of lights, which blinked and beeped like nothing ever happened. "Never pay for a drink again. And the girls, Jonni!"

Jonni had nothing to say. Gillin slowed his laps, drifted back to his chair, and held his knees. "We did it, Jonni," he whispered. "Heroes. Wake me up when they get here." He closed his eyes.

Ayn shut off her holo and paced her office. She needed a drink and something else. She told Mays to come to her office and bring a bottle.

29

"You know they eat each other, yeh," Han said to Kino in English. They were sitting atop a watchtower in the shadow of the hu in the northeast corner of the delta overlooking a wide, smoothly rushing, royal-blue river. It was late in the arc on the tenth spin since Tomit lost his eye. Kade listened from the trees. He'd taken a propeller boat out after training with Dawlis, found a signal, traded brief messages with Ayn, and then kept going. The waiting was starting to get to him. He craved travel. He'd driven nearly all the way to the hu when he got tired of standing and decided to stretch his legs. He beached the boat, took a walk through the jungle, and came upon the boys.

"What are you talking about?" Kino asked.

"The vramen, yeh," Han replied.

"I'm not stupid."

"I've seen it."

Kino sliced open the belly of a fish. "Now I know you're lying, yeh."

"Okay, I haven't. But Wim did."

"Wim says a lot of things."

"Doesn't mean it's not true."

Kino ripped out the fish's spine and tossed it into the river. "You shouldn't believe everything you hear, yeh. Oh, look!"

A large, mud-green shadow moved through the water against the heavy current. It stopped at the wooden lattice gate that spanned the river, butted its flat snout against it, then turned and swam back down-stream.

"They do that," Han said.

Kino stood up. The watchtower leaned and creaked. "That one's big, yeh. There's more down there."

"I'm telling you. This is the season they used to go west, yeh. They don't have enough food."

Kade thought of Little Avri and felt sick to his stomach. The Nimar and Tiralee had, for many generations, known the migratory patterns of the vramen, the twice-annual trips upriver made by the pregnant females to feed on schools of fattened prey. All villages had been built at safe distances from those well-traveled paths. But eighteen turns past, the turn that Dawlis disappeared, a single expecting mother had gotten lost and was still hungry and strayed to where Avri and her friends were throwing a spiral.

The Tiralee built the gates, the Nimar built the watchtowers, and the vramen mothers were denied their seasonal feasts. The population thinned, the strongest survived, and there were rumors that they fed on their own kind to make up for the lost sustenance. But the people of Nima had little sympathy for the vramen.

The Nimar sent coming-of-age boys and girls to the gates several times each turn to test for breaks from the safety of propeller boats, one of the very few forms of technology allowed in Nima. There were radios as well to call Tiralee in for repairs if needed, but that was rare. There was never much to do, there was virtually no risk, and it was a good experience for the youth to see the hu in all its glory and to camp on their own. The boys were especially quick to volunteer, though they were less interested in the hu than in driving one of the machines and seeing the great green fish.

Han and Kino had their chance now, and they were determined to make the best of it. They tossed little chunks of fish flesh into the water, hoping for a fight. It worked. The rumors were dispelled. A dozen vra-men, as long as the Nimar and as strong as the Tiralee, churned in the water and fought over the meager scraps—until they were overcome with hunger and rage and tore the weakest of them apart.

Kade ran back to his boat and drove off, feeling a greater need to leave this place. Clouds rolled in from the north as the ninarc descended and deepened. He slid through the dark ruminating on what to do next. Their choices were limited and not very good, but they were clear: go back to Fentum and see what might surface, search for a passage to Earth to appease Dawlis (though insist he wait for Lorel and Shaw before doing anything rash), or search for a cave where she might come through. Regardless, get Dawlis moving again, get him more experience. He could train as they traveled. He was soaking everything up so quickly. Keep feeding him.

But Kade was starting to doubt very seriously that any of that would happen. Fragments of intuition plagued him. He grasped at shadows. Something about the Fenti. Something about the bald woman with the limp who moved in and out of the mountains and the timing of when she was first seen. Something about the meteor.

They had to leave. Kade knew it in his bones. He just didn't know why. Then the gray cloud ceiling started to glow, and realization crushed.

AYN IS AT A CONCERT. A thousand bodies around her sway like a school of fish in a gentle tide. The music echoes through the dark water, and Ayn buzzes and flows.

A neon-green marble rolls to her feet. She picks it up and throws it up and over the crowd. It arcs slowly, leaving a trail of light. Other happy fish throw orange marbles, red ones, blue, purple, more and more until the space above is filled with hundreds and thousands of tiny neon comets. Only the Mind could dream a scene so beautiful, and indeed Ayn feels a connection unlike anything she has ever experienced, and she wonders if this is the meaning of life, this connection and this light.

Shouting shatters her reverie. A scrum in the crowd. Her love starts to fade, then blacken. A woman comes barreling through the crowd carrying a limp body over her shoulder and yelling, "Sick man! Out of the way!"

The crowd stampedes. Ayn is shoved to the ground and trampled. She screams.

It stops, and she's alone. The sky crackles, flashes, burns her eyes. Thunder splits her eardrums. A storm cloud blooms on the horizon and morphs into a head rising like an oblong black sun, then shoulders rocking, arms swaying, legs marching over Qol. Ayn gets up and runs, but she knows there's no escape.

The sirens again. Ayn opened her eyes as Jonni swam out of the bunkroom. It was always just a drill, except something was off. Gillin. He should have been going crazy.

"Oh, hey, Jonni," he said in Korial as though they were passing each other on the street. "Looks like we got a live one."

"Mays, get up," Ayn said. He was passed out with his head on the glass table in the corner of her office. "Get up right now."

He stumbled over and squinted at the holo. There was a voice coming from inside Jonni's helmet.

"Get us in there," Ayn said.

Mays tapped in.

". . . *Three.* Respond, *Cawley Three.* This is *Mother Bird.* Let me hear you, *Cawley Three.*"

Inside Jonni's helmet was a zoomed-in view of space piped in from one of the camera cans. Readings scrolled down the left side. The word *DRILL* was missing.

Ayn started to sweat. Mays breathed heavily beside her.

The voice called to Jonni, but Jonni didn't respond, only spoke aloud to himself: "Is this real? This can't be . . ."

"This is very real," *Mother Bird* squawked. "I need you to confirm your readings *now*. This is not a drill."

"Coordinates negative eighteen by fifty-seven," Jonni reported in dumbstruck rote. "Trajectory thirty-seven degrees. Velocity nine-point-seven kels per tick. I can't see anything."

"I do, and you will very soon. Straighten your back, crack your knuckles, and state your name for the record."

"Jonni ra si Manoo."

"Jonni, I'm called Ky. We may have a moment ahead of us. I want to emphasize that this is not a drill. There is a meteor on course. We're tracking fine, so we just need to keep our eyes on the numbers."

"Fine, Ky."

And it should have been.

"Very good. Where's your partner? Let me hear from him."

Jonni cleared his visor. Gillin had both hands over his face and was staring out the windshield through his fingers. He turned to Jonni and said, "This is it, partner. Like I said. Gotta burn it down now."

Jonni turned his visor back on. "I'm all alone up here, Ky. My partner's running a serious fever."

Ky grumbled and spit. "Well, that's why there are two of you. Make sure he stays out of the way."

"No problem."

Except Ayn knew different.

"Good man, Jonni."

Because she had a nightmare.

"Hey, Ky?"

"Yeah, Jonni?"

"Are we shooting this thing down?"

Please shoot it down, Ayn pleaded.

Ky took a deep breath. "To be seen, Jonni. I sure hope so. You and I just might be the two luckiest people alive right now."

Here it was. The one-in-a-billion chance. The celestial-sized carrot headed straight for their mouths.

A red square appeared in the center of Jonni's visor. Inside it was a tiny flame, like a match struck at the bottom of a deep well. "Mind, I see it," he said. "I have visual. Long axis five-point-two bits, shortest is four-three. Mass still unknown. Composition unknown."

"Confirmed, *Cawley Three*. I'm waiting on readings from a few other cans."

Mays worked the keys on Ayn's desk, shaking his head.

"What is it?" she asked.

"Hold on."

"Still nothing, Ky."

"I know, Jonni. Hang tight."

"We can't let it through if we don't know what it is."

"I know that, Jonni."

Gillin put on his helmet and chimed in: "Gotta burn it down now."

The meteor was a fluttering light the size of a pinhead, tearing through the black fabric of space.

"What's the call, Ky?"

"Burn it, Jonni. Gotta burn it down."

"Damn it, Gillin, shut up."

Mays said, "It's slowing down."

Ayn dug her nails into his arm.

"Okay, *Cawley Three*," Ky said. "We are cleared to fire. In range in one ru. Start your sequence. I'm warming the guns!"

Jonni flipped switches and hit buttons on the ceiling and dash with a shaking pointer finger. The rock buster hissed and rotated up and to the left. Cannons reached into space from either side of the windshield. The square of light surrounding the meteor inside Jonni's helmet pulsed, and a new set of readings appeared down the right side.

"Oh no, Jonni. Gotta burn it down. Gotta kill it, Jonni."

"*Listen*, partner. That's exactly what we're going to do, but I need you to keep your mouth shut, got it?"

"Is there a problem up there?" Ky asked.

"No! No problem. How long?"

"Half a ru. Hang tight."

"Stop saying that!" Ayn yelled.

She could see the waves of fire pouring off the meteor. She could feel the heat.

"Oh no, oh no, oh no. Burn it down!" Gillin was bouncing on his knees. "Don't let it through, Jonni!"

"Keep him under control!" Ky yelled. "Ten ticks and we're heroes. Enjoy the show, boys!"

"Burn it downnnn!"

The satellite died. Ayn's chest seized. Jonni smacked the side of his helmet, took it off, and tossed it.

Oh, no, Ayn thought.

Orange auxiliary lights made a path across the floor. The ones on the wall were dead. *Mother Bird* had stopped chirping.

A few ticks. That's all it took. The rock buster hummed back to life, and Mays tapped the camera on the outside in time to see the meteor disappear into the clouds over southern Damarra.

30

Will was meditating on the rocky beach. He held his belt and xim in his lap and a white-petaled flower in his right hand. In his mind he reached for Elle:

I'll die soon, Elle, but for a cause. Don't be sad. I love you forever. I'll die soon, Elle, but for a cause. Don't be sad. I love you forever . . .

He repeated it until it was a substance, a thought corpus, a message in a bottle, which he released onto a sea of energy.

The sea resonated through him and around him. It swirled behind his lids. He *felt* the lightly lapping water, the buzzing insects, the rocks, the buoy. He opened his eyes, picked up five rocks, and stood. The first missed by six inches, the second by one. The third hit, then the fourth. The fifth was off. He picked up five more. The sixth hit, the seventh missed by the width of the buoy, and the last three splashed farther away.

He took a step back and a deep breath, pulled his arms in and made a medicine ball with energy drawn from his subtle body, then threw it at the calm lake. No ripples, but he was close.

He ran his second circuit of the morning, trained with Kade in the cave, then hiked with Piper and the wolves to another of Piper's favorite spots. They ate lunch and talked and laughed. Afterward, Piper went home, and Will ran a third circuit.

This had been his routine for ten days. Each day he felt stronger and quicker. Every move Kade taught him, every strategic or philosophical concept, he assimilated almost immediately. His progress was hopeful and foreboding. There seemed an urgency to it.

He and Kade built fires and ate in the clearing each night. Will always sat facing the cave, waiting for Peis to come out, but he never did, and tonight Will was alone. Kade missed dinner for the first time.

Will stayed up late stoking the fire and fingering his necklaces. He was asleep with his elbows on his knees and his chin in his hands when Jackson started barking. The sky rumbled and glowed.

He stood. A meteor lacerated the clouds, lit up the hu, and crashed into the earth. The earth trembled, and something exploded inside of Will. He ran through the birchmaples to the top of the island. A small pool of fire bloomed in the black jungle far away and spewed a growing mushroom cloud.

He wouldn't be that far out, Will thought.

His mentor and friend. The man who found him and killed for him.

No villages near the hu.

Thanks to Peis's second vision.

I should go. I should look for him.

But he wouldn't. Something was holding him to the island, some gravity. The inevitable. Fate come home. Announced by a meteor? There was nothing to do but wait. He walked back to the clearing.

Peis was there. He reached over the fire and handed Will a folded piece of parchment.

"What is it?" Will asked.

"A poem," Peis said.

"A poem?"

"I saw it again, the . . . other world, or . . . I saw her too."

"Who?"

"Your love."

Will's stomach twisted.

"Beautiful," Peis said. "Her spots . . ."

"What else?"

"Fragments. Dim. It was dark in there. Something obscured my vision."

"Speak straight."

"There's no straight. No path."

"None that you can see?"

"No, none. It's very dark. But it was strange that just before the ground shook, a glowbug wandered into my room. And I saw what I saw, and I wrote that poem."

Will allowed a final glimmer of hope. "Will I see her again?"

"I don't know."

Then snuffed it out. "I do."

Peis lowered his head to the tips of his thumb and fingers. Breathed. His eyes held tiny fires. "Never stop loving, Dawlis, or you'll lose this fight."

"I'm here to fight then?"

"You know it."

"To die."

"Then I'll die first. I promise you that."

"What's coming?"

"Something."

Will threw the parchment at the fire. The fire blew it away. He left with his wolves.

They lay on a moss patch on the eastern side of the island. They had an hour at most before dawn. If Kade was not back by then, Will would go looking for him. He used the time. He knew he had to. He shut his brain and body down. He fell asleep with his boys around him and slept deeply for that short time.

31

Many Nimar and Tiralee slept restlessly that night. Kade would hear their stories and tell his own. That was the best they could do, talk through it, relive it from all angles in an attempt to piece together and comprehend what happened. They dreamt of exploding stars, fire, beasts and serpents, teeming darkness, the number three. They sensed, in their sleep, something wrong. The intuition faded when they awoke in the pre-dawn darkness but left them anxious and uncertain. Then the meteor.

The fires were contained by the waterways, but the dust caught a south wind. The villagers farthest north did not hesitate to leave their homes, with the expectation of returning when the air was safe for their lungs, for their children's lungs. Some to the east and west traveled southeast and southwest. Isulu and Vinson also decided not to take chances. They left forty of each people behind to gather several spins' worth of food and supplies and to store the rest. Everyone else, friends and families, went on ahead.

KADE SPED NORTH by starlight toward the strike until he came under the blanket of ash and was left in pitch blackness. He pulled the boat over, sat on the floor, crossed his legs, and steadied his breath and heartbeat. The ash floated down like toxic snowfall and settled on his head, shoulders, and legs. Maybe he dozed.

The first gray grains of light fizzled. Blinking, green lights in the sky in the distance were the first guard ships approaching the hu from the north. Kade shook off the ash, stood, turned the boat's engine, and gunned it.

The smell of scorched earth singed his nostrils, and soon he came to its burnt edge. He tied the boat and continued on foot through the ash rain and blackened trees smoldering beneath Humir Nima. He stepped to rim of the crater.

Mind.

Deep in the center was a black meteor, glowing red and melting.

The guard did not make another mistake, Kade realized, his blood warming. *The guard is corrupt.* The truth burned him like the red radiation. *MaGog is here. They've done it. They're attacking us.*

Owed another world: their deeply held belief for many hundreds of their slow turns around Nurin, many dozens of generations. It was their religion. It was their right and retribution for the near destruction of their world by the very same medium they'd used here. It was a fire fanned by decades of failed relations between the two planets. And now they were attempting to collect their debt? With meteors as weapons? But no, not that exactly. Three fallen in the last nineteen turns . . .

The stone-metal melted down to reveal scaffolding, bubbling foam, and sparking electronics. There were footprints in the ash leading out of the crater. Kade ran.

SOMEONE HAD HOLD of Kino's ankle and was dragging him through the mud. His head and body ached terribly. He tried to open his eyes and managed only thin, blurry slits through which he saw the rubble of the watchtower. He remembered going to sleep in it with Han. He remembered waking from an explosion and being thrown by the hot wind. But he was grateful. Someone had come to help. Then he opened his eyes further and saw who it was.

A man in black glowing red, tall as a woman, thin and sinewy like a young tree. He wore a fitted suit of black scales, a high, black collar, and large, dark yucs. His head was slender, hairless, and ghost-pale. He left Kino on the bank near a propeller boat, not the one that Han and Kino had ridden out there last spin. Han was curled up in the mud moaning. "Kino, I think I broke my arm."

Kino crawled to his friend and covered his mouth. "Quiet, quiet. We have to go, yeh."

But Han was in pain and unaware. "My arm, Kino," his muffled cry.

"Please," Kino whispered, tears spilling down his cheeks. He got up and helped Han to his feet. The man turned and smiled, colorless lips peeling back over sharpened, triangle teeth. He reached back over his right shoulder and lifted a curved black sword.

Han screamed. Kino wet himself. The man kissed his blade, then ran it through Han. Kino turned and walked away, sobbing. One of his legs came off at the knee, and he passed out from the pain.

He awoke to ropes cutting into his chest and stomach and a sound like a seething, snapping tide. He opened his eyes. The man, the pale man in black scales who glowed red, was tying him to the back of the boat. Han hung dead beside him, blood spilling from the eye-slit wound in his chest. Kino's stump throbbed and flared, dripping his own red tincture into the blue water. A throng of starving vramen writhed and rammed the gate from the other side. The man laughed, an awful, joyful, grating trill. The boat pulled away, the gate exploded, and the vramen were released.

KADE SPED TOWARD THE ISLAND with terrible knowledge. Gog, believed to be a generation or more from human spaceflight, had landed someone on Qol and not for the first time. Two more had come in false meteors: the bald woman with the limp, who landed in the Fenti mountains one turn before Dawlis disappeared; and a second, who landed to the northwest of Mon Teles sixteen turns later, three turns past. The guard, some corrupt faction, had cleared the paths through the Rings. The Fenti had been helping all along. All of this beneath the collective nose and all in preparation for the coming of this individual, for Kade knew in his enraged soul that this was the shadow Peis Ota foresaw.

An explosion cracked the morning silence. It came from the direction of the watchtower where Kade had seen the two boys. He drove toward it, hoping to intercept the enemy, hoping to kill before anyone else had to, knowing that to put an end to this before it started would mean nothing less than halting the forces that spoke in prophecy and lucid dreams: a man throwing waves to reverse the flow of a great river.

His eyes shook. His heart was stone. He would die trying.

CAWLEY THREE WAS ON BACKUP POWER for five short ticks before it started droning and beeping again. For all of Jonni's questions (and Ayn's and Mays's), Ky had few answers. They'd been hit by a new kind of virus, but they got lucky. The meteor burned up. That was everything Ky knew and everything the operators needed to know. The job now was to get the systems scrubbed and the cans talking to each other again. Jonni handled the work for *Cawley Three*. Gillin had gone into the bunkroom and hadn't come out.

Ayn paced her office. Mays hunted for the bug. Half the satellites in both Rings had crashed, and the guard was covering it up. That much was clear. Maybe people were dead, maybe a lot of them. But even that didn't account for the acid in Ayn's gut, the sense that this wasn't over. It didn't account for the dream she'd had just before the meteor of a shadow marching over Qol, a dream that felt more real with every passing ru.

Was that possible? Could beings from subconscious realms cross the divide into waking life? Ayn struggled with that question through the last of the ninarc and into the early arc, right up until the moment when the sirens started blaring again.

KADE FLEW DOWN A NARROW SHOOT, engine screaming, the trees a blur on either side, the ash pouring down. Ahead was an opening to a wide river. Another boat crossed, and a MaGog in black suit and dark yucs, glowing red, whipped his white head around, smiled in violent, delighted surprise, and raised a black sword.

Here was the Harbinger, the Archfiend, the Shadow, these just a few of the names he would come to be known by. He was Radin, the Dondante. The Fenti had called his name as they died on the Shole and on the ridge: *"Morrarru Dondante!"* Dondante comes.

Kade set his feet as he hit the intersection and spun the wheel. The boat splayed and rumbled over—what?—vramen! Dozens! A hundred and more! He cut their backs with his propeller, spilled their purple-black blood. The boys, dead, one missing a leg, were tied like bait to the back of Radin's boat. Their heads bounced with the chop.

Kade turned wide of the swarm and closed from the side. He took his xim and threw a wave—and learned another of the enemy's flawlessly guarded secrets. He could count on two hands the men and women on Qol known to have the ability to channel energy into waves. He now counted one MaGog. Radin threw a wave in defense, and the space between them warbled. The boats collided. Xim met black sword. *Shing!*

Kino jolted awake and looked down in terror at the vramen leaping from the boat's wake and snapping at his half leg. Kade thought to end his suffering. He saw no easier death for the boy and one much harder. But Kino freed an arm, took something out of a pocket, and put it to his trembling lips. He yelled into the radio, "The vramen are coming! The vramen and the Shadow!" It was Radin who put him to rest.

FORTY NIMAR STACKED crates of vegetables, dried meat, and tools onto wooden wagons. Forty Tiralee stacked crates of fish, hammocks, and spears onto wooden floats. They were nearly done. They were only a thin sliver of arc behind their families.

Fo was nearest to the receiver when Kino's cry crackled through. He knew what he heard, though it was a difficult thing to process. The vramen were far away behind gates that had never been breached. The Shadow was not a tangible thing. But a meteor had struck their land, and ash was now spreading over it. And he believed in prophecy. Fo picked up his machete and walked to the lake. He yelled for Vinson, then yelled for the other Nimar to gather their weapons.

RADIN THREW WAVE AFTER WAVE. Kade countered, but the waves collided closer to him until he was hit in the chest and thrown backward. The boats crossed. Kade spat blood, jumped to his feet, and drove directly into Radin's thrashing wake, intent on thinning the number of vramen as much as he could.

Radin pointed his sword and bared his sharpened teeth. Kade flashed his xim in response. His heart was dark with murder. "You shouldn't have come, Harbinger," he yelled over the engines and the rushing wind. "So far only to die."

Perhaps Radin knew a bit of Korial. Perhaps he only picked up on the sentiment. He threw his head back and laughed. "Garraruve! Morrarru Dondante!"

Kade charged and fired arced lightning. Radin defended with ease and sliced Kade's arm. Kade jerked his wheel, feigned another attack, then pulled away and sped up a stream.

———————

HALF A DOZEN SQUARES of light tracked half a dozen invisible objects inside Jonni's helmet. "What do you see, Ky?"

"I see what you see, *Cawley Three*. I'm waiting on readings from the camera cans. Could be another malfunction caused by the virus."

"Something's out there, Ky. We need to warm this thing up *now*."

"Hey, partner," Gillin said. "See what I mean?"

Jonni cleared his visor and turned. Gillin floated shirtless behind the chairs, wrists ripped open and pouring blood.

"*Cawley Three!*" Ky yelled. "We have enemies in range!"

Gillin's head slumped. Jonni turned back and called up the image. The number of tracking squares in his visor doubled, then tripled. Inside each square was a flying shadow with a purple tail of exhaust.

"It's not possible," Ayn whispered.

Cawley Three lurched and fired thick blue lasers. *Cawley One* fired from the right, fifteen hundred kels around the circumference of Qol. *Cawley Five* fired from the left, then others from above and below, up and down the vertical ring. A few small flames budded inside the tracking squares. The purple tails lengthened and diverged. A cone-shaped black ship flitted past *Cawley Three* on the left, then another over the windshield. *Cawley Five* exploded.

KADE WOULD COME TO THINK of it and experience it as a violent psycho-spiritual rebirth, an awakening, for himself and for Qol. He would collect stories and share his own, suffer through every bit of the senseless pain, and marvel at the sheer grit and determination, the simple genius.

Qol and Gog were at the closest point in their orbits, a positioning in the celestial cycle that occurred every twenty turns for Qol, every twelve for Gog. They'd been aligned for Gideon. They were last aligned the turn that both Will and Radin were born. MaGog had guarded its secrets obsessively, waited patiently, then executed.

Their fleet of thirty-six was cut in half but took out five satellites and otherwise played its role perfectly, so perfectly that the guard would require even more severe shocks to its system before truly understanding what happened. Radin was sent in advance, through the safety of the briefly disabled Rings, to ensure execution of the task that the first two MaGog explorers and the hired Fenti had failed to complete. For Gog too had its seer and its prophecy, which warned of a man who traveled with three white beasts and threatened their manifest destiny.

NURIN WAS A SMOKEY ORANGE DISC hanging over the horizon behind the screen of ash. Forty Nimar strung stingers, dipped arrows in poison, and sharpened machetes. Forty Tiralee came together in the royal-blue water between the village and the island, carrying spears as long as their bodies.

Piper watched from behind a woodpile, shaking with fear. He wished he hadn't snuck away. If he ran hard, he could still catch up to the others. But he couldn't bear not knowing if Dawlis had been warned about whatever was coming. He dove into the lake and swam for the island.

Dawlis was not in the clearing, or in the chamber where he trained with Kade, or in the room where he slept. A dying candle beside his mat cast a weak nimbus on a small leather book. Piper picked it up. This was not the one that Dawlis wrote his dreams in. That one Dawlis had described as a little blue book held together by a metal spiral. Yes, that one was there too, in a corner beside his pack. This one Dawlis had never mentioned. Maybe it was from Peis's library. Piper opened it and started reading.

ROCK BUSTERS exchanged fire with the black, purple-tailed ships of
Gog. Kade and Radin raced to the island on separate winding paths.
Piper stood reading the traveler's journal. As Will lay dreaming on a
mossy rock.

*Elle and I are in a sea of people, in a field outside of a city, awaiting
some historic event. The air is thick with sweat. The tension is difficult
to bear. We wait with the world to take part in something great.*

*A towering mass lowers out of the sky, a mountain of living tissue,
brown-and-yellow marbled flesh with pulsing red veins. It slides forward and consumes half of the crowd before anyone can react. I grab
Elle's hand, and we run. Everyone is screaming.*

*We run through dark alleys and hallways, deeper and deeper into
the city. The mass is seconds behind us, swallowing buildings. The
destruction is deafening. There is someone else there, above us, in the
ceiling or in the sky. He lowers a hand and yells to us, "Reach!" But
the floor collapses, and we choke on the dust as we fall.*

*I'm standing on the lawn outside of the orphanage dorm. The boy
is standing on the stoop, the boy who killed himself with the bee, the
dead boy from my dream of three. I walk toward him, but he steps
inside and locks the door. The bee lies dead on the bottom stair.*

*I hike through the woods where I was found as a child. The smell
of the loblolly pines breaks my heart. I come to a gaping hole in the
earth where one has been uprooted. I climb down and crawl through
the roots. They wrap around my wrists and ankles, gently at first, comforting almost, then tighter as I try to pull away. I give up, lay down,
and try to fall asleep, but the earth and sky begin to shake.*

THE TIRALEE HUNG suspended in the lake in two spheres, one nested
inside the other. They stared north in the direction of the rope bridge,
which spanned the slow, narrow river that fed the lake. The Nimar

waded in gaps in the drinking straws, stingers loaded, machetes cocked. The blanket of ash cut the sky in half above them, pale blue on one side, gray on the other. They waited.

Kade sped into the lake from the river that trickled out into the south, crossed the lake, cut his engine, and ran the boat aground on the island.

Peis walked out of the cave.

A flake of ash landed on the head of one Nimar, who looked up and scowled. A soft roar in the sky. Another engine to the north getting louder and louder.

The Harbinger came whipping around the corner in his boat and severed the rope bridge with a swipe of his sword. The vramen broke from their tether and poured into the lake. Black ships tore through the half-blue, half-gray sky and crashed into the forest beyond the village.

WILL AWOKE at the first explosion. The wolves barked madly and foamed at the mouth. They ran to the top of the island and stood on the rocky spine. Black, cone-shaped, purple-tailed ships dove out of the sky, smashed into Nima, and threw up towering fountains of dirt and water. A mud-green horde of man-sized fish spread through the water and advanced on a dense ball of Tiralee. A boat crashed into the field of boulders, and a gangly, white-headed man dressed in all black and glowing red jumped out and leapt across them.

Will wiped a tear, took his xim, and walked with his wolves down to the island's plateau to confront his fate.

IT STARTED AS a small green mass in the distance through the blue. It grew larger and broke into several large pieces, then dozens, then a hundred, then more, whipping tails and white teeth, bearing down, the vramen swarm.

Vinson raised his spear. Forty white domes breached the surface. Forty mouths opened and sucked in the Nima air, some for the last time.

"For Little Avri," Vinson bellowed, and the Tiralee dropped under.

They drove forward as one, thrusting spears into snapping mouths and writhing bodies. Skulls were cracked, gills were punctured, and purple-black blood stained the water. The Tiralee were driven backward but allowed themselves to give, as the vramen surrounded them.

One Tiralee, a mother, a sister, and a daughter, was snatched by a leg and dragged off, drawing a dozen hungry vramen. An uncle and brother moved forward from the inside sphere to plug the hole in the outside one. The Tiralee were a single, spiked organism. Their arm-spears were rage-fueled pistons. More flat heads were broken, more green flesh and black eyes were gored, but the vramen were many, and the Tiralee formation began to break.

THE NIMAR RAN toward something, some otherworldly nightmare that they didn't understand but that they knew in the deepest parts of themselves threatened more than their lives. Still, they went to confront it, led by Fo, Baly, and Jovi. They told themselves that they would see their families again. But in their scared, angry hearts, they knew they were only giving their loved ones as much time as possible.

They raced across a glade, jumped over a stream, and passed into a cloud of dust and smoke. The forest burned across a shallow river. An inverted black cone, as tall as the Nima trees it had pulverized, stuck out of a crater at an angle. It was melting and glowing red.

The Nimar said their prayers, paid their homage, sent their final wishes out onto the airwaves, their love and kisses. Then they slipped into the drinking straws.

MaGog appeared on the far shore framed by the blaze, gangly men with pale, narrow heads, dark yucs, black suits, and hand-held black cannons. One tested the water, and they all stepped in.

Half of the Nimar lined up stingers inside of the drinking straws. Half gripped machetes in white-knuckled hands. All tried to breathe. Fo whistled, and the poison arrows flew.

A dozen MaGog dropped dead in the river. A dozen more lifted their cannons and fired glowing red rocks. Mud and dirt exploded, trees were splintered, Nimar were maimed. A new round of arrows flew, then another. Many MaGog fell. More came from the trees.

Fo grabbed Jovi by the arm. "Go! Find them!"

She watched a friend's chest explode. She heard it and smelled it. She felt all of existence falling apart. "I won't run!"

He pushed her away. "Tell them what happened. Tell our families."

She lowered her head, squeezed her eyes shut, screamed through clenched teeth, turned, and ran.

Fo charged out of the straws with twenty or so machete-wielding Nimar. Most reached the enemies and engaged them in the water. Arrows were fired in support, MaGog were culled, but the Nimar were always too few.

IN THE VERSION OF Will's lucid nightmare that he'd experienced out on the Shole, sharks circled him, and then he watched in horror from the top of a hill as a man, his killer, marched up it. Eamon, the Chief, also saw this coming and drew it on the wall of his cave.

Will stood with Peis and his wolves on the island's plateau. The two men took their xims and stared into the churning cauldron of death that was Nima Lake. Radin walked up the grassy slope on tree-branch legs, a curved black sword hanging casually from one thin, bone-white hand. Will locked eyes with him through his goggles and felt a sense of familiarity pass between them, as though they'd met once in a dream.

Kade appeared at Will's side and put an arm across his chest. "Go now," he said. "There's a boat on the eas'ern shore."

Will took a few steps back with his boys but shook his head. "I'll be here, Kade."

The Gog ship thunder ceased. Fires crackled in the distance, white noise pierced by the deep screams of Tiralee who had come up for air only to be pulled back under. The ash snowed.

Peis and Kade threw simultaneous waves. Radin countered without breaking stride. They traded throws then, trying speed instead of force, but nothing would alter the Harbinger's steady, upward path. He cast his own wicked tide. Kade spun, gripping his xim wrist. Peis was tossed.

Radin walked onto the plateau, looked over at the wolves, three howling white beasts, and bore his sharpened teeth in a wide smile.

Kade rolled his wrist and snorted like a bull, eyeballs shaking. Peis lifted himself up off the ground and laughed. Finally, a face for the name, a form for the last dark words of his prophecy! He went low, and Kade went high. Radin crouched and blocked Peis's xim as Kade's sliced the air above his head. He swept Kade's leg, rose, and rained wicked blows down upon the prophet.

Will pulled his arms in and gathered his fear, his fury, and the energy all around him. It pitched in his mind, surged through his heart and core, and he threw a wave for the first time.

Radin stumbled and laughed. *"Garraruve!"* But his expression hardened when Peis and Kade attacked again. He'd run out of patience. He let fly a flurry of wave and black blade. Peis dropped his xim and gripped his stomach as though trying to hold it together. Kade fell to his knees, face in his hands.

Radin turned on Will, and Will unleashed his torment, his loss, his fight, his life, all of himself, upon the Shadow. He made bleary blue-green arcs that chipped away at a bleary black wall. He was repelled and driven backward. He dug his heels and slashed with everything he ever had. Radin opened up—he was *pushed.* Will took the space and shattered the black collar, as the black sword split his collarbone.

He fell. Piper was standing with the wolves, hands thrust out in front of him, eyes wide and traumatized. Kade lifted Will up and draped him over a shoulder. Peis stood between them and Radin, now getting to his feet.

"I'll see you there, my friend!" Kade yelled.

Peis raised his xim in a bloody hand, then attacked.

OUTRO

Will lay on the floor of the boat. The pain in his shoulder faded slowly. The pixels swirled over blue sky and streaming Nima trees, and he thought, *What a beautiful place.* And then, *I loved her.*

He rose and floated above the boat. Below, the wolves licked his wound, Kade pumped his heart, and Piper drove. He tried to reach, to say something, but what?

He stood at the back of the boat, alone now but for a warm presence behind him. Angel Island, divine in its churning, watery cradle, receded. The city built on hills rolled away to his right, and the red bridge passed overhead. The green mountains of Marin loomed large, then grew small, as the boat slid out into the great Pacific.

Will flew through dark space. He was formless energy. Mind or soul or … He slowed and floated, quiet, as big as space, all-encompassing, all-seeing: the eyes of the world. He resonated with profound emotion that seemed the sum of all, building up inside of him.

Inside.

A star exploded light years away, piercing rays fired from a tiny core growing bigger and brighter, and the ringing of a thousand tiny bells growing louder and louder. Will vibrated with this energy, every cell and particle trembling with joy, until all was blown apart and became white light.

The white was all. There was nothing. Will was nothing.

I am something.

He was everything. He was a consciousness spread across all of existence. The white was a sea of infinitesimally small pixels.

I have always been swimming in this sea.

Thin lines of brilliant, sparkling light traced an outline of land and life: jagged mountain tops; a coruscating fall spouting from a cave for the first time and spilling into a river that ran for the first time—*run, river, run!*—through the sketch of a canyon; effervescent meadows stretching to eternity; everything thrumming with legato timbres—*inside*—as though all of existence was singing one song.

Color infused the pixels and spread through the landscape. The yawning canyon walls turned brown and red, the river a foaming dark blue, the flowing meadows green with patches of yellow, red, and purple flowers beneath a virgin blue sky.

There is no sun.

The light came from within.

The world was made.

Will was a ball of light floating in a crevice near the top of the canyon.

I have no hands.

Hands formed out of the energy that was him. He touched his face and body. They felt real. His wound was gone. The scars on his leg and stomach were gone. He wore his boots, brown corduroys, green shell, green quarter-zip, and green T-shirt, the outfit he'd chosen for Saint Paddy's Day.

Another ball of light hovered in a cave across the canyon. It was Peis Ota, he knew. He wondered if there were tears in this world, and tears dripped down his cheeks.

I brought this on you. I'm sorry.

Peis took human form and looked around. His jaw dropped.

How can you be sorry in a place like this?

He changed into a ball of light again and floated away, bumbling through the canyon like a kid riding a bike without training wheels for the first time, and laughing in bright musical tones that echoed off the rock walls. Will presented his mind to the prophet.

A warmth on his back. He turned. Another light floated before him. It pulsed and spoke in a girl's voice: "Welcome, Will. Come." She drifted down a dark tunnel. Will crouched and followed, drawn into the earth.

It was a version of Needle Cave. "Why am I back here?" he asked the girl light.

"You made it so," she said.

"What does that mean?"

"This is a mindworld."

Mind.

A world made of his thoughts. His thoughts were the mountains, the river, the canyon, the meadows, all crystallized on a swirling universe of pixels, of light.

The girl was not his creation. She was Little Avri, and she was experiencing her own world. So was Peis. Worlds as they perceived them, as they *wanted them to be.* This was a substrate, this mindworld, a field of pure energy.

Pure creativity.

Red for Will might be green for Peis, or blue or purple. A field to Will, a lake to Avri. A tree to one, a tower to another.

Interpretations of the underlying.

Will suddenly knew a great many things. He spoke Italian for the first time. He was an expert on the French Revolution, the Ming Dynasty, the Ohlone, the Kyut. Organic chemistry, quantum mechanics, global economics. Facts and intuition in massive doses. But it didn't feel like he was learning. It felt like he was remembering.

I can play the piano.

He keyed the air and played the opening notes to "You Enjoy Myself" on an invisible organ. He laughed out loud and followed Avri deeper into the dark.

She brightened. They were inside a large cavern. The stone rippled like water.

Did I do that? Will wondered.

"Your life," she said.

The cavern went black. Will held his breath. His mouth tingled. He exhaled and spewed swirling color all over the walls and high ceiling: his entire being cast in one master stroke.

My life.

The color coalesced into a thousand motion pictures in planetarium panorama. Will saw it all at once, heard every voice, felt every emotion. Bare to the entirety of his past, his heart filled with love and regret:

He is lying in his bed in the orphanage. The Ladies are tucking him in. They whistle and hum. They tell stories to him and the other kids. They tell them that they are loved, that they are worthy. And Will believes every word, despite it all. *It was a fine childhood,* he thinks. *Hard, but fine.*

George is standing at the bottom of a snowy hill. Will flies down on a sled, stomach rising into his throat. They collide, tumble, and laugh. *George, you were a true father to me!*

He jumps off the high dive with his grade school friends all in a row, dangerously close. They plunge into the cool water. They rise and high five. *Oh, the endless days. If only I stayed in touch.*

He's holding hands with a girlfriend at a movie, desperate to kiss her, staring at the screen in anguish. *The agony of adolescence. What a strange development.*

Losing his virginity. How badly he wanted it. *I thought I knew love. The chains of instinct.*

Winning the state championship, running up the field with his teammates after the final whistle, George jumping up and down on the sidelines. *Such pride. Such hard work. I got lazy and drank too much.*

Hundreds of times he made fun of others, hurt others, turned away, knew he should have done something and didn't, let himself down, let George down.

I have regret. I have failed.

Hundreds of times he made others laugh, helped others, smiled at a stranger, sacrificed and felt good, set a goal and reached it. *I have loved. I have potential.*

Sitting in the common room in college, contemplating life with his roommates, ruing the world's pain, determined to do something about it somehow, someday, sad and angry and hopeful, breaking from their shells together, discovering themselves in those very moments, knowing there was more to life, knowing they were touching it, knowing they would have hold of it forever. *If only others saw what we saw.*

San Francisco. The hills. The Fillmore and the music that changed his life. The beats and flashing lights. The crew together navigating quarter-life. The love. The confusion. The great unknown. The highs and lows. *Thank you for everything. I love you all.*

The pigeon launching from the roof of 1449, arcing high around the door. Being watched in the grocery store at Stinson. The conversation with Lorel, the mother he never knew. *Just ten more minutes!*

Gunshots. Racing through the city. Waking in the cave. The beast, the serpent, the Gray, the wolves, Kade. The city of seven. The island, the prophet, Piper. The battle and his death.

All of his life relived and its meaning revealed.

Will is an orb of light, a conscious energy, present and all-knowing. This he has always been. He forgives himself all past failures. He is flooded with overwhelming bliss, which manifests in images of Elle, the final scenes of his life review, his last look before moving on. The entire planetarium is devoted to her, and he watches without pain or longing, only love, which he transmits through the worlds: thought fingers to brush her face as she sleeps.

Sprinting up the lacrosse field, always the anxious and fierce performer, she stops on a dime, forgets the game, and looks over at him for a holy moment. *Oh, thank you!* The whistle blows, and she's off.

Sitting next to him in Russian lit, she puts her foot on top of his. *Mind!* They pass notes like children. They *are* children. Always were, always will be.

Standing in the far corner of a bar in a cone of light, talking to shadowy friends. She sips a beer. *Look up. Look up.* She does. *I love you!*

Waiting tables, moving through the restaurant. She stops, lifts an eyebrow, and puts a finger to pursed lips as she tries to remember an order. *Ha! A favorite for all time! Save a copy!*

Walking on the beach at Crissy Field. She throws a tennis ball, and Raider flies across the sand, ears back, tongue hanging out. *Go, Raider, go!*

Napping together on the futon, his two loves, on the third floor of 1449 Washington, blue building with a red door.

And a final image. The best saved for last. Will's review is coming to an end, but he is not sad, only grateful to have lived, to have been with her for any time at all, to have seen her in that moment:

> At an '80s party in the infancy of their love. She's standing on a red-carpeted staircase, red cup in her hand, back to a dark wood wall, surrounded by a blurry, buzzing crowd of friends. He gazes at her from across the room; she gazes back, and it dawns inside of them—*inside*—a revelation, a new plane of existence, a world within the world, a heaven.
>
> Her side ponytail. The collar of her neon shirt pulled down over one shoulder. *Have mercy! Elle! Forever, I swear it! Live and love, and I'll see you again when your time comes.*
>
> The music softens. Darkness grows from the edges of the image toward the center.
>
> The stairs disappear, the sea of friends.
>
> Her legs, her bare shoulder, her freckled face.
>
> At last, her gray-green eyes.

The cavern was dark but for Will pulsating gently, dead but eternal, moved on from the world of five separate senses.

The symbol of orange gems flashed in the space before him, and a feeling distinctly human returned, a sense of anticipation, of knowing something but not knowing it. "Do you understand the purpose of your review?" Little Avri asked.

"What? I—"

He tried to play the piano and couldn't. The world was harsh and dissonant again.

Two doors appeared in the stone wall. Will-orb walked-floated toward them. The first opened up to the mountains, canyon, and river that he created, here in the mindworld. He thought of Elle, and a yellow butterfly appeared, fluttered over the grass, and landed on a purple flower. A wave of happiness washed over him, and he recited the opening lines to A *Tale of Two Cities* in Japanese just for fun.

Behind the second door was a black squid floating in dark water, its rubbery tentacles wrapped around a mangled, human carcass. One released, oozed, and reached for him.

He looked from door to door. The afterglow of the symbol floated on a butterfly wing and in the large, dull eye of the squid. He was an orb. He was his human self. An orb. Human. An orb...

With a great gasp of life, his back arched, his eyes flew open, and Will awoke in the boat in the soiled land of Nima.

EPILOGUE

Radin sat against a tree, fingering the gash on his neck and watching the guard ships circle the island in the distance. Naked of his collar, he wallowed in guilt. Uncertain of his execution of phase one, he burned with anger. Still, there were moments when he wondered, and not for the first time, what the tongueless seer's vision really meant to him, what future he was supposed to destroy or create. He looked around at this world and asked himself why it should be hers. He rolled his neck and indulged in shameful thoughts of betrayal and freedom.

One of his Dondarra and a guard came out of the bush. "Dondante, no sign," the Dondarra trilled in their native Vrrgrrul. No sign of Dawlis.

Radin put a vial to his nose and took a fat pull of dust. His eyes grew cold. His lust and adrenaline surged. He stood and looked at the guard. "Time?"

"Yes, Dondante, it's waiting, the flyer, follow me," she babbled in hideous, trill-less Vrrgrrul. Her eyes were there and not there. She had the look of someone listening to a voice in her head. Radin knew that soon, at long last, he would meet the owner of that voice.

"Though, Dondante," his Dondarra said, "something else. Someone to see you."

"Quickly," Radin said.

The Dondarra stepped back into the bush and returned leading a tall male with a bent neck, large nose, and beady eyes. The male stared at Radin through strands of greasy black hair and smiled.

Radin spoke, and the guard translated into English: "Say who you are and why you're here."

The male shook his head in disbelief. He pointed to the sky. "You came from another planet?"

Radin reached down and picked up his sword. "You should answer. I have a message for your people. You can deliver it. You can live."

"My people? Nooo, friend. Tell me. You came here for someone?"

"You should answer."

"I know why you came. I'm also here for him."

Radin smiled. This male was intriguing, at least. "I killed him," Radin said.

"You're sure?"

Radin shrugged.

"Do you know where he comes from?" the male asked, tilting his head.

"It doesn't matter to me."

"You think he is from here, from this planet?"

Radin froze. "Not from Gog."

The male's small eyes glimmered. "Not from here."

"Impossible."

"Not impossible. I've traveled the worlds."

"Another system?"

"Yes."

Radin wanted so badly to believe it. "And you're from there?"

"Nooo, friend. Not from there."

ACKNOWLEDGMENTS

Thank you, readers, people I know and people I don't. I had you all in mind. I wanted to reach out in this way. Thank you for listening.

I owe a debt of gratitude to my editor, Matthew Patin, founder of Full Measure Editorial. When I first sent him a draft, I was a hack with a vision who thought he was almost done. After many years of implementing his feedback, I think I became something resembling a writer, which was my goal in life.

Thanks also to Laura Duffy of Laura Duffy Design for politely scrapping my cover idea and coming up with one that I will love forever and ever.

Thanks to Karen Minster of Karen Minster Design for the interior design and composition, which until seeing her work, I didn't realize was an artform itself.

C.G. MATTEINI played sports, which taught him a lot. He became a psychology major in college, simply because he heard it was relatively easy. It was one of the best accidents of his life. At some point, he developed a sense for the ineffable. Not long after that, he was introduced to the writings of C.G. Jung and a layperson's book on quantum physics. These works shaped his worldview a great deal. The two best things to ever happen to him were the births of his two sons. He finds it mind-blowing that one day he crossed paths with the woman who would become his wife and the mother of his children, when the day before they had no knowledge of the other's existence. He is forever grateful to the musicians, writers, actors, and filmmakers who have inspired him over the years and continue to inspire him.

Please consider leaving a review of Lucid on Amazon.
It takes a few clicks, and, if you want, a few words.

Thank you.

- C.G.